**TOM CONRAD**—the brain, the farmer's son who loved learning as much as he loved the land. Though the land taught harsh lessons, Tom remained dependable, kind—and ultimately unknowable.

**BEN WILLIAMS**—the brawn, the town doctor's son whose ambition went far beyond Allendale. An aura of action and excitement surrounded handsome, good-hearted Ben—and exerted a heady allure on a small-town girl.

**SHELLY DILLON**—the "mouth," as she labeled herself. But the most important things in her life were hard to talk about, and the things she needed were hardest of all to ask for....

# ABOUT THE AUTHOR

Before turning to writing full-time six years ago,
Stella Cameron edited medical texts. Her dream
then, and even as a child, was to become a writer.
Stella and her family live in Washington state.

## Books by Stella Cameron

### HARLEQUIN AMERICAN ROMANCE

### HARLEQUIN SUPERROMANCE

### HARLEQUIN INTRIGUE

Don't miss any of our special offers. Write to us at the
following address for information on our newest releases.

Harlequin Reader Service
901 Fuhrmann Blvd., P.O. Box 1397, Buffalo, NY 14240
Canadian address: P.O. Box 603,
Fort Erie, Ont. L2A 5X3

# FRIENDS

### STELLA CAMERON

# *Harlequin Books*

TORONTO • NEW YORK • LONDON
AMSTERDAM • PARIS • SYDNEY • HAMBURG
STOCKHOLM • ATHENS • TOKYO • MILAN

For Angela Butterworth,
a dear and courageous friend

Published August 1989

First printing June 1989

ISBN 0-373-16306-1

# Prologue

*Shelly*

A sound came from nearby. Shelly stood still and listened. There it was again, a clear "Sshh."

The afternoon sun glared and she squinted. Stickery bushes lined the lane from the school yard to the main street in Allenville. Behind the bushes was a blistery old wooden fence. And the whispers had come from there, along with the scuffle of feet on dry grit.

Her tummy felt all tight and sick. She set off again, slower, shading her eyes to see the end of the lane. Her book bag dragged because Mrs. Osborne, her fourth grade teacher, had given her a pile of old magazines.

"*Shelleee.*" The kids. They were waiting for her. She wasn't liked but she didn't know why. "*Shelleee Dillon.*"

Another sound came. Mrs. Osborne pulled her old red Chevy far to the right of the lane as she passed and waved. Shelly waved back. Now there was no one around—but her and the kids and the lonely walk along the deserted road to the center of town.

Anne Billings was the first to step out from behind the bushes. She hopped on one foot, then planted her feet, doing imaginary hopscotch to the middle of the path, her fat brown pigtails flip-flopping. Then she faced Shelly.

Shelly's insides shook. They wouldn't hurt her, would they? She made herself walk on, getting closer and closer to Anne, who was so much taller, so much bigger.

"Here she is," Anne said in a high sing-song voice. "Here's teacher's pet. Come and talk to teacher's pet."

Jimmy Thomas moved in behind her. His folks were seed potato farmers. Many people were around here, and his clothes weren't new like Shelly's, whose folks ran the town's only general store. Beattie Smith and her brother Walt sidled out. He was younger and still in third grade, but he was brawny and not very smart and he did whatever Beattie told him to do. Renny Carrol joined the rest and little Cathy O'Leary walked in his shadow.

"Helpin' Mrs. Osborne again, were you?" Anne said. She was always the leader. Mrs. Osborne had said it wasn't bad to be a leader if you led people to good things.

Shelly kept her head down and walked beside the fence.

Jimmy Thomas stepped in front of her. "We wanta be friends," he said. "We want you to join our gang."

"I've got to get home." Her voice sounded funny and her throat hurt.

"I've got to get home," Anne mimicked. "I've been a good girl and helped Mrs. Osborne and now I've got to be good and go home."

Jimmy grabbed Shelly's hand and she couldn't pull away. He swung her around and she dropped the book bag. Magazines shot over the ground, their shiny covers brilliant against the June dust. Her mom said Idaho summer dust was the worst thing in the world—until it turned to Idaho winter mud.

The rest of the kids linked arms to make a circle. And in the middle Jimmy twirled Shelly until her eyes hurt. Then he let her go.

"Don't!" But it was too late. She slid on the slick magazines and fell against Renny. He waited until she'd hit the ground and scrambled up before he shoved her back at Jimmy.

"Shelly Dillon is a teacher's pet," Jimmy sang out. Again he swung her around, and again he let her go to sprawl on the gritty dirt that stung her hands and knees.

This time she didn't jump up. Sitting on her heels she looked at the palms of her hands where little spots of blood showed. She wouldn't cry. She wouldn't.

"Come on, Shelly, ya scared or somethin'?" Anne yelled.

"Why don't you leave her alone?"

Shelly raised her face. Tom Conrad hovered outside the circle. He was ten the same as she was and so quiet she'd never heard him say more than a word or two before.

"Go on home, Tom Conrad," Anne said. "This ain't nothin' to you."

Tom ducked into the center of the circle and started picking up magazines.

"Yeah," Jimmy said. "Nobody asked you to join in. You better get home before your mommy gets mad. You ain't supposed to hang around after school. You got your daddy's work to do."

"I got time," Tom said, continuing until he held all the magazines in his big hands. He was a tall thin boy with straight hair, all streaky from the sun, and his pants were too short. Shelly remembered that his pa was sick a lot of the time and the Conrad farm didn't do so well because they were short of help.

The circle tightened around them. The kids all grinned. Shelly stood up beside Tom, stood close so their arms touched. She checked his face and he didn't look scared.

"You better cut this out," Tom said.

"You gonna make us?" Jimmy said and made a space for himself between Anne and Walt. "You sweet on her or somethin'? Hey, guys, dirt-poor Tom Conrad's got a crush on the teacher's pet. Kiss her, Tom. Kiss her."

Shelly's face throbbed with heat. She couldn't look at Tom, but he didn't move away, only started shoving the magazines back in her bag.

Suddenly Jimmy fell, his knees buckling, breaking the circle. He pitched forward and howled when his face hit the rocky ground. Behind him slouched the new boy, Ben Williams. His father had taken over as the town's doctor a few months before and Ben was in the same class with Shelly and Tom, but he didn't talk much.

"Watcha do that for?" Jimmy sat up.

"Do what?" Ben said and crossed his arms. He was the biggest boy in fourth grade. Not fat, just strong.

This time Jimmy was the one who decided to stay where he was. "You saw what he did." He pointed while he looked at Anne and the others. "He kicked my legs. Get him."

Instead of advancing on Ben, the kids stepped back, parted.

"Get him!" Tears drizzled through the grime on Jimmy's face and his arm shook.

Ben went down on his haunches beside him. "You want to fight me?" He looked at the other kids who were almost to the fence now. "Then any of the rest of you can have a turn on the ground."

Cathy was the first to run, and in seconds the rest were on her heels. Jimmy got up and went more slowly, sniffing, wiping his nose with the back of his hand. When several yards separated him from Ben he turned to walk backward. "I'm gonna get you, Ben Williams. I'm gonna tell my dad about you."

Ben took a step toward Jimmy, and he took off, still yelling, but not anything Shelly could make out.

"Thank you," she said. An only child, she'd never made friends easily and wasn't good at knowing what to say to other kids.

"Yeah," Ben said. "Sure."

"You've got a hole in your skirt," Tom Conrad said. He had a very quiet voice. "And your socks are all dirty. Will your mom and dad be mad?"

She shook her head and took her bag from him.

"Why'd they pick on you?" Ben kicked at a rock with the toe of a new Keds sneaker. He had nice things. Shelly knew he also didn't have any brothers or sisters.

Shelly shrugged. "They don't like me. Never have."

"Me, neither," Tom said. "They say we're dirt poor—" He closed his mouth and turned bright red.

"They say I'm stuck up and a teacher's pet," Shelly said hurriedly. Tom was nice, and her parents said his folks were good people who'd had bad luck.

"Guess we've got something the same," Ben said. "I'm the new kid and they don't want me, either. I wish we'd never moved here. I had lots of friends in Chicago."

"Chicago?" Shelly was impressed.

"Allenville's okay," Tom said. "My folks have lived here just about forever. And I want to live here forever, too. It's just this school stuff that's bad. The kids, I mean. I don't mind math and all that."

"Me, either," Shelly said.

"I hate everything," Ben said. "'Cept sports and we don't do much of that here."

They stopped talking. Shelly held her bag in both hands. She should get home before her mom and dad got worried.

"Look," Tom said. "You don't have to or anything, but we could kind of do things together—in school at recess. Stick around, that kind of thing."

Ben nodded. His brown hair curled and didn't look as if he combed it too often. "Sounds okay to me."

Both boys stared at Shelly. She hunched her shoulders. Maybe Tom meant he wanted to be friends with Ben. He wouldn't want her.

"How about you, Shelly?" Tom said and the red shot out behind his freckles again. "You're skinny but you're tough and we could have our own gang."

Boys didn't usually ask girls to be in their gangs. She smiled a bit, feeling warm. "Okay."

Tom wiped his hands on his worn jeans and held them out, crossed at the wrist. "Shake on it. Friends, right?"

Ben promptly did the same, holding one of Tom's hands.

Shelly dropped the bag, crossed her forearms and put one hand in Ben's, the other in Tom's, and they shook hard. "Friends," she said.

## Ben

THIS WAS COOL. Dad's convertible was the neatest set of wheels in Allenville and getting it for senior prom night made Ben feel like a million. Shelly sat beside him, Tom in back. Tom's sister, Mary, had been going to make up a foursome but had come down with the flu.

"Where to?" Ben said, raising his voice over the hot wind that tore his words away.

"River," Tom shouted. "Our place."

"River," Shelly agreed and sank lower in her seat.

"Prom was okay, huh?" Tom asked.

"Yeah." Shelly rested her head back. Early in the evening, when she'd come to her door in the strapless white dress, she'd made Ben forget for a minute that she was his old buddy. Now she'd pulled the ribbon and band from her ponytail and her long blond hair blew free.

Ben pushed against the wheel, locking his elbows. "If the prom had been that okay we'd still be there," he said, smiling to himself. "What we need is a little quiet time." Damn he felt great. High school had been a gas but college would be better, particularly with the football scholarship he had in the bag. He was going to play, really play.

He found their usual parking place on a high dirt track a few miles out of town and pulled in.

Shelly was the first out of the car. By the time he and Tom caught up she was swishing her taffeta skirts through the tall Camas, their blue blossoms a luminous waving sea in the moonlight.

"Ouch! These darn shoes." She stumbled and Tom caught her around the waist.

Without ceremony, he hiked her onto his back and jogged on. Ben laughed. Tom, sporting his rented black tux with the elegance of a man who wore black tie daily, took on the shape of a long night creature with billowing white wings.

What they called the river was no more than a creek, which probably had its origins in the Snake River.

"You weigh a bit more than you used to, Shelly Dillon," Tom said, puffing as he set her down on the bank. Their spot was among pine trees ten or so feet above the creek.

Ben dropped to the grass beside Shelly. Tom remained standing, leaning against a tree.

"Less than two weeks to graduation," Shelly said. She pulled off her high-heeled sandals and dangled them. "Then a lovely long summer."

"Then college," Ben said and silently cursed himself. He and Shelly had agreed not to mention college, not in front of Tom.

She was silent.

"You two have got to be excited," Tom said, but there was a stillness about him, and Ben kept his eyes on the water below.

"You're the one who should be going," Shelly said quietly. "You're the one with the brain. You're valedictorian."

Ben felt his throat tighten. The muscles in his jaw ached from clenching his teeth.

"A man's got to do what he's got to do," Tom said, dropping his voice theatrically. In his normal tone he added, "I'll make it there when Dad's better. I couldn't leave the family now."

Tom would always be like that. Responsible. Ben glanced sideways at Shelly and met her eyes. In the moonlight they turned from gray to silver and they glistened. Tears; he didn't blame her. The thought of going to the University of Idaho in Moscow without Tom was upsetting them both, taking part of the shine off the triumph. Tom could go on a full academic scholarship, but without him his family's farm would probably fail and Tom, the oldest of three kids, the other two being girls, refused to take the risk.

"You'll come for weekends, won't you?" Shelly sounded miserable. "You promised and it isn't so much of a drive."

"My mom says you can borrow her car anytime," Ben said. Tom's old pickup didn't always want to leave the farm.

"Thanks," Tom said.

Ben swallowed. Tom wouldn't borrow the car and his "I'm okay" act didn't cut it. They all knew one another too well.

"You will come?" Shelly repeated the question, twisting around to look up at Tom. "Remember the old pact? Us against the world? That means all three of us."

Tom didn't answer but he knelt between Shelly and Ben and clapped a big hand on each of their necks.

They stayed like that for a long time, touching, staring out at the place where they'd played, and talked for hours and felt their bond grow stronger and stronger.

"We thought it would never end, didn't we?" Tom said at last. "Kids can be pretty stupid sometimes."

"No, Tom—"

"Shh." Tom pulled them close in a fierce hug. "We're maudlin because it's that sort of night. I'll come to see you at college. And nothing's going to let us forget what we mean to one another. We'll never lose touch."

"We'll be back for good one day," Shelly said.

"Sure you will."

"Yeah," Ben said and breathed against the uneasiness in his belly. He couldn't play in the pros and live in Allenville. Geez, why did he have to feel so mixed up?

Tom stood up, bowed and offered Shelly a hand. "Time to get you home, Cinderella. Time to get me home. Five in the morning comes earlier every day."

Five, Ben thought, when Tom started the two hours' work he did before school every day. Ben fell in behind his friend but only went a few steps before reaching for his arm. Tom looked back and this time Ben saw a sheen in his bright blue eyes.

"Nice act," he said, keeping his voice down. "But we're going to find a way to get you into college. There's no damn justice in this world if you don't go and we do."

Shelly came to stand with them. She slipped an arm around Tom's waist and the other around Ben's and they linked arms behind her.

"I'm telling Tom we've got to get him to college with us," Ben told her. "There's got to be a way."

"Not now," Tom said. "But one day. I'm sending you two ahead to scout out the territory. You've got to find us a river and a few private trees, maybe a pizza parlor and a beer joint—for future reference of course."

They laughed but there was no joy in it. Tom was right. They had no choice but to accept things the way they were.

"We'll call you once a week," Shelly said.

"That'll cost too much."

"Between us we can manage," Ben said. Something was slipping away from them, something they'd never get another shot at.

"What are good friends for?" Shelly looked at Tom, smiled, and Ben felt her tremble.

"Friends are for keeps," Tom said, smiling down into her face.

"Yeah," Ben heard himself say. "For keeps."

## Tom

THE APPLAUSE ROARED around him and Tom clapped and rose to stand with the rest of the audience at the University of Idaho.

He strained to see Shelly and Ben. He'd arrived late and had to sit at the back of the auditorium. And he'd missed everything except the closing speech but he knew they were there somewhere, holding their college diplomas. Shelly would become a teacher. That made Tom feel good. Allenville grade school had a vacancy—he'd already checked—and teaching jobs didn't come up very often there. Ben was the problem. He had been drafted by a pro football team and would go to Cleveland.

Tom shrugged his shoulders inside the unfamiliar dress shirt and sports coat. The tie bugged him. He stood on tiptoe, not that his height didn't give him a pretty clear view over most heads.

They were coming now, the streams of gowned figures, tassels swinging on mortarboards. He hadn't seen Shelly and Ben since they'd been home for Christmas. Leaving the farm had been impossible since last fall when Doc Williams had warned Tom and his mother that Jack Conrad didn't have long. The fight with Hodgkin's had been well fought but in vain. Dad made it through Thanksgiving, and now Tom was the man of the house.

"Hey, Ben!"

A voice nearby startled Tom. Doc and Mrs. Williams stood three rows in front of him with Shelly's father and mother.

Then Tom saw Ben...and Shelly. Arm in arm they came, laughing, waving at their parents. Mrs. Williams had called Tom at the farm and offered him a ride, but they'd been leaving a day early and he couldn't afford the time.

The din rose and rose, and the throng flowed out through great doors and a stone archway onto green lawns.

Minutes later Tom climbed onto the brick rim of a circular flower bed to locate the Williams's and Dillons who had been swept from sight.

It was Shelly who found him. "Tom. Get over here now. I thought you hadn't bothered to come."

And she was in his arms, her huge gray eyes smiling, her wide mouth parted in that grin he saw in his mind anytime, anywhere, even when they were apart.

"Would I miss this?" He picked her up and swung her around.

"Tom, there's so much to tell you." She was breathless. The mortarboard had disappeared and her pale soft hair blew around her face and slipped over the hand he spread between her shoulder blades. She was beautiful. He felt his own smile fade.

"Hey up." Ben reached them, looked down on Tom from his six-foot-four-inch vantage point. "What a day, Tom. Can you believe this?"

The brown eyes Tom knew so well shone with an almost glassy brilliance. Ben, big and handsome was overpowering, and Tom was so proud of him.

Mrs. Williams approached and kissed Tom's cheek. "Glad you made it. You three will want some time alone," she said. "Us old folks will go back to the hotel. Ben, you and Shelly should bring Tom along when you're ready. We've made reservations for dinner at seven."

"Okay," they agreed in unison.

"Come on," Shelly said. "There's a place over by Plant Sciences where we can talk."

He let them lead him, laughed when they looked at him, hurried when they urged him on. Plant Sciences. They'd forgotten he would have spent most of his college time there. What was wrong with him? He'd made his own choices, and if some of the chances had been lost never to be regained, he could live with that. The farm was important. His mother and sisters were important. And he had these special friends. He was glad for them that they'd done so well.

The place Ben and Shelly showed him was an old bench by a shadowed wall, and they sat there, suddenly very quiet.

"You look great, Tom," Ben said finally. "Those seed spuds must agree with you."

"Yeah. We're having a good year, thank God."

Shelly put an arm around his shoulders and rested her face on his arm. "We've missed you. It's been hard waiting for you to come."

"I wanted to, but you know how it is." He stroked her hair and frowned. She felt... He glanced at Ben who smiled guilelessly. Shelly felt so good, and the sensation wasn't new, only new with her. He was a fool. Of course they couldn't go on thinking and feeling like kids....

"Tom, we've got something to tell you," Ben said, leaning forward, the black gown stretching over his immense shoulders. "We want you to be the first to know."

Shelly sat up and watched him intently, too. A coldness crept into his body.

"It's all happening," she said, folding her hands around his wrist. "Ben got picked for the pros and I did well in school. I'm not going to have any trouble finding a job."

"I asked—"

"And we're getting married," Ben said, interrupting Tom. "We're getting married, and Shelly's coming to Cleveland with me. It's going to be great."

Tom swallowed, narrowed his eyes. He had to keep smiling. He had no right to be anything but glad for them. He felt old.

"Tom?" Shelly shook his arm. "We've surprised you. But you're glad?"

"You bet I am." His damned voice better not sound the way it felt. He turned to Ben and slapped his back. "So now I have to trek all the way to Cleveland to see the two of you. You'll make a world traveler of me yet." Only he'd never go to Cleveland. He might be slow but he'd finally figured out that he wasn't a saint. Was it so wrong to be jealous?

"We'll marry in Allenville," Shelly said. "We plan to tell the folks at dinner...not that I think they haven't guessed."

"Look." Ben fumbled beneath his gown and produced a small blue velvet box. He flipped open the lid to display a diamond solitaire. "Shelly and I picked it out together. She'll put it on tonight."

"Great," Tom said. Great and expensive. Maybe as much as the new truck he'd needed for years but couldn't imagine being able to buy.

Tom stood up and sank his hands in his pockets. He needed time to take it all in. He turned to face them, apologetic grin in place. "I'm going to have to pass on dinner," he said. "I've got to get back home."

# Chapter One

Gladys Dillon definitely moved more slowly around her store these days. Tom stopped her from trying to lift a sack of flour to the counter. "Leave it be, Mrs. Dillon," he told her. "I'll take it straight out to the pickup." He'd called her Mrs. Dillon when he was ten and at thirty-three he still called her that. Wouldn't seem right to do otherwise.

"I won't argue." She straightened.

"Mr. Dillon feeling better?" Tom asked.

"Fair," Mrs. Dillon said, returning her attention to the list Tom had given her. "February and March are always hard on his arthritis. April, too, most years. He seems to pick up with the thaw."

"Don't we all?" Tom said and rubbed his hands out of habit. He nodded at the ring of old-timers crowding the black pot-bellied stove in the middle of the wooden floor. They kept up a drone of conversation, mostly reminiscences of long ago, while they drank the strong coffee always available. "'Course, I suppose there's some who miss the excuse to sit around and chew the fat when summer comes." He laughed. Mrs. Dillon didn't.

She seemed different today. Was that why he'd noticed how deep the lines on her face had become . . . the preoccupied manner?

A case of canned tuna joined the growing stack of provisions on the counter.

Something was wrong. Mrs. Dillon had been part of his life long enough for him to sense a big change in her.

"How's your mother?" She startled him.

He stared for seconds before saying, "Fine."

"Mary?"

"Great." Mary and her husband and their two sons lived in their own house on the farm. They were all involved in the Conrad holding.

"Betty still happy at college?"

Tom frowned. The questions were mechanical. Mrs. Dillon trudged back and forth getting supplies, never meeting his eye.

"Betty's doing very well." He couldn't think of his youngest sister without a flash of pride. Recent years had been good to them and she was at the University of Washington getting the education she deserved. Betty would be a lawyer one day. "What do you hear from Ben and Shelly?"

Mrs. Dillon dropped several spools of thread into a box. "Cleveland's no place to bring up a family," she said, her voice sharp.

He hadn't seen them and their boy for two years. Maybe that was it. The Dillons were hurting because they hadn't had a visit from their daughter for so long. Tom took a deep breath and looked through the steamed-up window at the blurred white land outside. How long was it since he'd heard from Ben and Shelly? More than a year. Here, surrounded by the familiar smells of pickling brine and grain and warm oil, it was easy to visualize his old friends with whom he'd sat around the stove so often. He missed them, but the sense of loss had dulled with the years.

The door from the store to the house opened and a slender blond boy came into the big room, a skateboard under one arm.

"Gram, can I skate in here?" The boy wore a heavy yellow parka and jeans and his face was flushed. "Mom says I can't."

Tom narrowed his eyes. "Philip?" Of course it was Philip Williams. Two years older and taller than when he'd last been in Allenville, and so much like Shelly at...the boy must be eleven now.

"Uncle Tom." Philip hesitated only long enough to drop the skateboard before launching himself at Tom. "I wanted Mom to bring me out to see you this morning but she's too busy." Two years didn't seem to have made Philip more self-conscious. He'd always responded to Tom like family.

Tom hugged the boy and met Mrs. Dillon's eyes over his head. She glanced away quickly. "When did you get here?" he asked.

"Yesterday. We flew into Idaho Falls and Mom rented a Jeep to drive up here. Geez there's a ton of snow."

"Always is this time of year," Tom told him. "But I guess you were never here in March before." The last time Shelly and Ben came to Allenville had been in summer.

"Philip, Tom doesn't have time to waste with you now. He's got work to do." Mrs. Dillon came from behind the counter that ran along three sides of the store. "I think that does it. Tell your mother the yardage she ordered isn't in. Should be next week. I'll call you." She wanted him to leave.

"Can I come out to the farm, Uncle Tom?"

"Hush now, Philip. You don't invite yourself to go places."

Tom looked from grandmother to grandson. The boy's eyes pleaded, but interfering was out of the question. "Give me a hand to load up," Tom said. "I'm sure you'll be able to come over soon." Why hadn't Mrs. Dillon said Shelly was here? Why hadn't Shelly written to say they were coming?

He shouldered the bag of flour and picked up a box. Philip rolled a hefty wheel of cheese into his arms and followed Tom outside. They crunched through hard-packed snow piled beside the road, their breath making milky clouds, and retraced their steps several times until Tom had stashed all his provisions in the pickup.

He closed the back doors of the canopy. "So," he said. "How long are you here for?"

Philip shrugged. "Dunno. Guess I'm going to school here... for a while, anyway."

That must mean Ben and Shelly were off on a trip and needed to leave Philip, although it had never happened before. He leaned against the truck, tipped his hat lower over his eyes and crossed his arms. "Will you be happy here, Phil? You're pretty much a city boy."

Again the shoulders came up. "I guess it'll be okay. As long as I can find a place to use my board. Anyway, I don't like Cleveland anymore."

Tom studied the toes of his boots. Ben had taken a while to get used to Allenville but eventually he'd stopped talking about Chicago.

"You'll have to go a bit easy on your grandparents. They aren't so young anymore." Maybe the boy wasn't mature enough for this kind of talk.

"Yeah. That's what Mom says."

"Is your dad coming up?"

Philip bowed his head. "Nah. His schedule's too busy."

Tom hadn't read much about Ben last season but there had been mention of trouble with an old knee injury back in November. "What's your dad busy with these days?" The off-season should give enough time for a trip home to see his family.

"Stuff."

There could be times when Tom missed a nuance, but not when it smacked him between the eyes. Something was going on here and he intended to find out what it was. "Is your dad okay? He isn't sick or anything?"

"No."

"He and your mom on a trip for a while?"

"No." Philip looked at him and for a moment Tom thought he saw misery.

Tom hitched himself away from the pickup. He might be a childless bachelor, but he was used to Mary's kids and he could tell an attempted evasion when he encountered one. The direct approach would work best. "Why are your mom and dad leaving you with your grandparents?"

"They aren't. Mom heard about a job up here."

Grasping what the boy said took a moment. Why would she do a thing like that?

"Some teacher at the school's retiring and Mom's going to take her place."

This made less and less sense. "Is your dad quitting football."

"Maybe."

"So they're moving back here?" The feelings that thought evoked were chaotic.

"I don't know what's gonna happen for sure."

The store door opened and Gladys poked her head out. "Philip, get in here. Your lunch is ready."

He scuffed at a clump of ice. "When can we come to see you, Uncle Tom?" Too serious for eleven. Too desperate under the surface.

"You'd better go in for lunch." He mustn't promise the boy anything until he knew the deal. What he should do was speak to Shelly.

"Philip!"

The boy raised his face, and brown eyes like his father's glittered. "My mom needs you, Uncle Tom. She said so."

Tom's jaw clenched. There were enough tense cross currents here to throw any man off course. "Tell your mom I'll be at the farm if she wants to contact me."

Philip walked slowly inside and closed the door. The kind of ties Tom had to Shelly and Ben didn't just go away. Sometimes they got pretty thin with neglect but the thread remained. His question now had to be whether he could cope with being drawn into their lives again without the old feelings coming back. Resentment was a destructive thing.

He walked slowly around the pickup, absentmindedly checking the tires. Then he scraped snow from the windshield before climbing into the cab.

The engine started on the first try, and he wiped the glass in front of him, waiting for a little warmth to come through.

He let the clutch out and eased forward. *Mom needs you, Uncle Tom. She said so.* What did that mean?

SHELLY LET HERSELF into the store and saw Philip coming in from the front. She crossed to peer through the windows. When she rubbed a pane with the backs of her fingers, cold struck back. Her mother came to her side.

"Tom's here," Shelly said and made a move toward the door. "Why didn't you tell me he was here?"

"Wait." Her mother held her wrist. "It's too soon."

"What do you mean?" Shelly watched Tom who circled a dark blue pickup, looking at the tires. "He must have come into town expecting to see me."

"No he didn't," Gladys Dillon said. She waved Philip away. "And keep your voice down. We don't want our business all over town."

Tom stood and leaned across the hood to scrape the windshield. Shelly smiled. He was still a slim man but not skinny the way he'd been at ten, or even as raw-boned as he was at twenty. He wore a Stetson, its wide brim pulled down so that all she could see was his angular jaw, the end of his straight, narrow-bridged nose, and his wonderful wide mouth that was so great when he laughed.

What her mother had said sank in. "You did tell him everything, like I asked you? I told you I couldn't face doing it myself."

"I decided we'd best wait until you were here and ready to listen to some sense. Spread a load of gossip around and the damage is done. Keep your own council and it's easy to undo something that was never meant to happen."

Shelly looked at her sharply and back at Tom. He didn't know. For an instant she'd been afraid he did and that he was angry with her... avoiding her. That might have been better because at least she'd know where she stood.

"We're not going over this again," she said. Tom opened the cab door, hitched his sheepskin jacket more comfortably over his broad shoulders and yanked the zipper all the way to the neck before swinging his long legs inside.

"Mom, Uncle Tom said—"

"Enough." Gladys interrupted Philip. Her face was unusually pink and her hair looked mussed. "Out to the house with you and wash up."

Shelly pursed her lips, irritated at her mother's interference. "I'll be right there, Philip. See if your grandpa needs anything." She glanced back outside in time to see the pickup move away. Her throat tightened. Whether she had a right to turn to Tom now didn't matter. She had to talk to him. He would help her see things straight. He was the oldest friend she had.

As had been done as long as Shelly remembered, the customers in the store were left in charge while she and Gladys went through the back door and across the snow-packed yard that separated the store from the house.

Suffocating warmth hit as they went inside. Shelly's father would already be at the big table in the kitchen. He moved slowly these days and made a point of situating himself early so no one had to wait.

Gladys stopped Shelly from going into the kitchen. Instead she led the way into the small, stuffy parlor that was seldom used, and shut the door.

"I wanted to talk to you last night but you were too tired, and this morning you weren't awake."

Shelly raised her brows. Her mother sounded censorious.

"Your father and I, and the Williams, had hoped you and Ben would get this sorted out yourselves."

"Oh, Mom." Shelly dropped into a lumpy blue sofa. "When are you going to give up."

"We're not. Nothing that's happened can't be overcome. We're all in agreement on that."

"*You're* all in agreement? It isn't you that's involved—" She hesitated. "I don't mean that. Of course you are because you care. But you don't understand. You've never wanted to listen to the truth—"

"Don't." Gladys covered her ears. "I won't listen. What I want you to do is take some advice from people older and wiser than you. Keep your own council about the problems you and Ben are having—"

"Mom—"

"No, don't interrupt me. Don't tell Tom or anyone else. Sort out your differences without outside interference."

"Tom isn't an outsider."

"You know what I mean."

Shelly rested her head back and closed her eyes. "I don't think I even want to try. I've got a job here. How do you propose we explain that I'm taking Mrs. Osborne's place and putting Philip in school. You don't do that kind of thing unless you're planning on sticking around for a while.''

"I've thought about that."

Shelly sighed. "I bet you have."

"We say you and Ben are getting tired of Cleveland and decided to start settling in here again. He's still with the team but you had to take the job when it came vacant. That'll buy you time."

"You don't understand—"

"I do. And while you're under my roof you'll give me the respect of crediting me with some intelligence."

Shelly opened her eyes. She hated being sharp with her mother but there would be no returning to the role of dependent offspring. "I'm grateful to you and Pops for taking us in for a while but it'll only be until we can find a place of our own."

"I didn't mean that," Gladys said in a rush. "We wouldn't hear of you living anywhere but with us until you and Ben can sort things out."

She was so weary. "Let's drop this for now. Lunch will be getting cold and you know how Pops hates that." She got up and straightened the lace antimacassar on the back of the couch.

"But you will remember my advice," Gladys said. "You won't talk about your business outside."

Philip, pushing open the door, made it unnecessary for Shelly to respond. "Gramps is waiting," he said.

Gladys gave Shelly a hard, meaningful look and hurried past toward the kitchen.

"Mom." Philip, his hands shoved deep in his jeans pockets, stood his ground in the parlor. "I talked to Uncle Tom."

"Yes." What had he told him? Had he poured out more than even Shelly cared to share yet?

"Gram doesn't want us to talk to him, does she?"

This made her uncomfortable. She didn't want distance to form between Philip and his grandparents. "They want what's best for us."

"Gram said I shouldn't talk about family stuff to anyone."

Already she had gotten to Philip. "I'm the one who makes decisions for you and me." She ruffled his straight blond hair. Sometimes he reminded her of Tom as a boy, except for the eyes, which were uncannily Ben's.

"Yeah, that's what I thought. And you said you needed to talk to Uncle Tom."

"I know."

"I told him."

She wished he hadn't but that wasn't his fault. "What did he say?"

"He said why didn't we come by this afternoon because he'd be at the farm."

Shelly frowned. If Tom had that definite a plan in mind, why hadn't he stuck around and driven them himself. "This afternoon? You're sure?"

Philip was already walking into the hall. "He said you could find him at the farm."

TOM HEARD THE SOUND of an engine and the chatter of tire studs on ice. Probably Cully, his hired hand, coming back from lunch. One of the few nice things about winter was that they could take things a little easier. At least, everyone else around here could. He seemed constantly nailed to his desk . . . when he wasn't making his rounds of the storage cellars. Not that he minded any of it. Conrads' had become a name among those who bought Russet Burbank seed spuds. His father wouldn't recognize the old place.

The engine noise came back in the direction of the shop, which doubled as his office. Not like Cully to drive much once he was out here. Tom got up and opened the door of the old wooden building that had once been a storage unit for spuds . . . until the new metal cellars had taken over.

A black Jeep approached and crunched to a stop. Tom knew who it was even before Shelly hopped to the ground.

He opened the door wide and stepped outside. Instead of running to him as she usually did, she stood by the car in a puffy blue parka, her arms tightly crossed. He could see she'd grown thinner. Always slim, the hollows beneath her high cheekbones were more marked. Her fine gray eyes didn't hold their usual sparkle, and her full mouth was set.

For the first time Tom felt awkward with her, standing there, a few feet apart, as if they were two suspicious strangers.

A gust of wind whipped a spray of snow off the bank and tossed it into Shelly's face. She wiped it away, pulled off her knitted hat and pushed back blond hair that was longer than Tom had ever seen it and worn slightly curly.

"Shel." He cleared his throat. This was crazy. He walked toward her, arms outstretched. "Come here, you. Why didn't you say you were coming home?"

The beautiful familiar smile broke out and she ran to him. A second later she threw her arms around him and kissed his cheek. And the old feelings started. The damned old feelings he'd told himself over and over again were dead.

"Oh, Tom. Am I ever glad to see you." She rested her face on his chest.

"Let's go inside. I'm freezing my . . . I'm freezing."

Shelly laughed. "You don't have to clean up your act for me. We're old friends, remember?"

"Yeah." He held the door open for her. Sure they were old friends. To her that had always been clear-cut and he never intended her to find out the arrangement hadn't been so easy on his side.

He stuffed a few more pieces of wood into the stove and when he stood up she had shed the parka. In an oversized sweater of some fluffy gray wool with her hair loose about her shoulders, she didn't look so much different from the Shelly of ten years ago. To him she was still the loveliest woman in the world. Again he cursed behind the smile he gave her. Now he was sure. He couldn't go through it all again.

She came close and put her hands on his shoulders while she looked him over closely. "You look fantastic. Thirty-three suits you."

"It suits you, too."

"Bend your head."

"Why?"

She tutted. "Just do it. You always had to argue about everything."

He did as she asked and she made a satisfied noise. "Good. You've still got that fantastic thatch in place. Not a hint of a bald spot."

"Hey, enough of the inspection. How do you think that makes a man feel?"

He tried to edge away but she held fast with long thin fingers. "This isn't an inspection. I'm just checking you out for your own good. Your face looks great, too, handsomer than ever. And the body's the same knockout it always was, more so with all the muscle."

"Shelly! Will you cut it out?"

She let him go and laced her fingers in front of her, trying for a contrite expression. "So I'm still incorrigible. Someone has to look out for you and it's obvious no one else has."

How was it that regardless of the defenses he decided to put up with her, the years slipped away the minute they were together and they were back as sparring buddies. "What do you mean? Look out for me?"

"I'm going to be around for a while so I intend to do something that should have been done a long time ago."

He planted his hands on his hips and waited.

"Mmm. You look particularly sexy like that. All long muscly legs and slim hips...and broad shoulders." She glanced at his middle. "Nice flat belly, too."

"Shelly! Cut it out."

"Well, it's important. I've got to get you married off and the father of a healthy brood to help with the farm. I can't understand why you haven't been caught before now."

Tom had a sensation that a little something more had died inside him. God, while she was in Allenville, let him get through without making a fool of himself. Let her go back to Cleveland quickly...for both of their sakes.

"How about it. Aren't you ready to settle down?"

"I've never been much else but settled down. Raising seed spuds has been a full-time job and in case you hadn't noticed, there aren't many available women around here."

"Don't make excuses. A man like you could have anyone he wanted."

Not quite anyone. And he didn't want to continue with this. Changing the subject was paramount. "How about coffee? Conrad's best doesn't match up to Dillon's but it's fair."

"I'll get it." She moved around quickly, filling two chipped mugs from the blue pot on the warmer and pouring milk into both. To one she added a teaspoon of sugar. She hadn't forgotten what he liked.

When she faced him, holding out his coffee, the playful smile was gone. Sadness was what he saw now, and strain. Little lines fanned out from the corners of her eyes and spanned her brow. The dimples still showed beside her mouth, but so did the faint bracket of more lines.

He motioned her toward an old couch that was close to the stove and covered with a bedspread to hide popped stuffing. She sat and sipped her coffee.

No more tiptoeing around. Whatever was wrong would come out now. He sat beside her and let the silence get uncomfortable. Shelly had never been good at not talking.

"It was nice of you to invite us out this afternoon."

He frowned. "I'm sorry?"

"Philip told me you said we should come. I took him up to the house. He's with your mother. She said Mary's boys would be home soon and he should meet them. Then she sent me down here."

"Ah. Good." Evidently Philip possessed advanced manipulative skills, but Tom found that more amusing than irritating.

"Did Philip tell you we're staying in Allenville?"

"Uh-huh. You're going to substitute teach for Mrs. Osborne."

Shelly slipped her hand into his and threaded their fingers together. Tom returned her grip.

"I'm not substituting. I'm taking her place permanently. She's got an older sister in Pocatello who needs live-in care. I take over in a week."

The news should surprise him, but it didn't. It only made him edgy. If he didn't watch himself he'd start spouting questions. She should tell him what she wanted him to know.

"We had a good childhood here, didn't we, Tom?"

He wasn't thinking too clearly. "Yes. It was mostly good."

"I want that for Philip. Big cities aren't as good for kids as small towns. Here he'll have a chance to put down roots."

"You're moving back here because of Philip?"

Shelly outlined the tendons on the back of his hand. "Some people thrive on big city life. Ben does."

"I know. You do, too, don't you?" She'd been glad enough to go.

"No. I thought I would. And I put up a good show for years . . . for Ben's sake. But I found out I couldn't stand it any longer."

There was a catch in her voice and he held her hand tighter. "A break will set you straight."

"Ben loves all the parties, the adoration, the groupies screaming after him. He never believed that I felt like an outsider. And he hated that I insisted on working. Mrs. Ben Williams didn't need her own identity or interests."

She sounded bitter and Shelly had never been that way.

"Maybe you only thought that's how he felt. I can't imagine Ben not wanting you to be happy."

"He wanted me to be happy as an extension of him. Never as my own person."

Tom shifted uncomfortably. "Ben's a good man, one of the best, and he loves you." The words hurt to say but they were true. "It sounds as if you need a little breathing space away from each other. Everything will be okay, you'll see."

"Maybe I shouldn't have come here." She removed her hand from his. "I'm not sure why I did, except I heard about Mrs. Osborne's job and suddenly all I wanted was to be with the people I trust most."

That's what really puzzled him, the job. She couldn't need money, and it made her visit sound like something permanent, which it surely couldn't be.

"Tom." She put down her mug and took his away. "Hug me. It's like I'm falling into little pieces and you could always make me feel better."

He did as she asked and closed his eyes at the sweet scent of her, her softness, the silky texture of her hair against his face. "Shh," he heard himself say. "I'm here."

"The day we met you were rescuing me. Guess not much has changed, huh?"

"You were always strong, Shelly." And he was good old Tom, the way he'd always been. White knight with no needs of his own. Hell, he hated this jealousy. It ate him up and he'd vowed not to let it rear its ugly head again.

"I need you."

There it was, the familiar theme. Someone else's need. But whose fault was it if he didn't attend to his own wants. He rallied and straightened until he could see Shelly's face. Her lashes were wet about those big gray eyes he . . .

"Listen to me, friend. Everything's going to be fine." He forced himself not to think too deeply. "Remember how it was when we were kids? Ben was the muscle and you were—"

"The mouth," she finished for him. "But you were the brains. I've never gotten over the unfairness of your not becoming all you should have."

"I'm fine and I'm happy," he told her, telling mostly the truth.

"I hope so. I don't know exactly how to put this, but I guess I'll put it the way you did once."

He raised his brows.

"I think it went kind of like this—you don't have to or anything, but we could be good friends, stick around together when we're not working." She crossed her wrists and after a pause he did the same and grasped her hands.

"I've been afraid to write and tell you Ben and I split up."

Now he was definitely very cold.

"He doesn't want it, but it's the only way."

"For now," Tom said. "Until you work things out. And you will."

She shook her head emphatically. "Will you be my friend?"

"I already am. Always have been."

"There are going to be lots of times when I need an ear and a shoulder. Can you handle that?"

Fate hadn't finished with him yet. "What do you think?"

"That you'll be there for me. My folks don't want anyone to know. Neither do Ben's. They still think the rift is repairable."

"It is. It is." He shook her hands hard.

Her brow puckered. "I guess I still haven't made it clear, have I?"

He could only return her gaze, uncomprehending.

"Tom, I should have called a year ago but Ben begged me not to and I listened. He still believes he can get his own way in everything. And I know he's going to start making this hard because he's disappointed and hurt."

"You're not making sense." His nerves leaped and he'd had enough hedging.

"It's over. Completely over with no going back. Ben and I are divorced."

# Chapter Two

"Has Tom called?" Shelly closed the kitchen door and flapped her hands. Outside, the ceaseless wind had forced the temperature to ten degrees below freezing.

"Where have you been?" Her mother said from the table where she sat with Shelly's father. "You dropped Philip off after school and didn't even bother to tell us where you were going."

"Now, Gladys, Shelly isn't a child. She doesn't have to check in."

Shelly gave her father a grateful look. As usual he managed to say the right thing to defuse a potential war between his wife and daughter.

Gladys wasn't about to give up so easily. "Philip said you had an appointment."

"Yes." Shelly slowly unzipped her parka. "I asked if Tom had called." In the week since she'd gone to see him he hadn't contacted her or returned any of her calls. Today she intended to make sure she saw him even if she had to go out to the farm and sit on the doorstep.

"Did you tell him?"

"Tom didn't call," Shelly's father said. "Was he supposed to?"

She went to sit beside him. He was so often in pain but managed to keep a smile on his creased face. "Not really, Pops, but I want him to give me his opinion on something."

"What?" Gladys leaned farther across the table, agitation lighting her eyes. "You haven't involved him, have you?"

"Mom," Shelly said, exasperated. "Let's get this over with please. Tom knows Ben and I have been divorced for almost a year. And he knows I plan to settle here in Allenville—unless you make my life so miserable that I have to find somewhere else to go."

That closed Gladys's mouth for a while. She settled her pale lips in a line and her eyes became suspiciously bright. Shelly was instantly contrite.

"I'm sorry," she said, covering her mother's clenched hands with one of her own. "I shouldn't snap like that. You've been through a lot. But you have to let me make my own decisions. Tom understands me . . . and Ben. He cares about both of us and I trust his judgment. That's why I want him to go look at this house with me."

Gladys pulled her hands away. "What house?"

"The house I went to see after school. It's the one that belongs to the Leonards, the people who owned—"

"I know who the Leonards are. They've left town now their shop closed. What are you thinking of? You can't buy that house in the middle of nowhere. You don't want to buy any house. You've got a husband who wants you . . . he's waiting for you and Philip to go back to him."

"Damn it all." Shelly covered her mouth. "I'm sorry, but you push me too far. When are you going to get it into your head that I divorced Ben a year ago because we were incompatible. And we still are. One day we may manage to be friends. I hope that happens. We will never be husband and wife again.''

Gladys bowed her head, shook it slowly. "I don't know how you can do this to Ben."

This was impossible. "I divorced him. You seem to forget that. What it means is that I had grounds. When will you accept that?''

"Go easy on your mom, Shelly. And don't be so quick to close off a whole section of your life. Ben's Philip's father. Children need their fathers.''

"Yes, they do. But he was never a real parent, which is one of the reasons we aren't together anymore. Ben never had time to do anything with Philip. And if I mentioned it I was nagging. There was always time for parties and—'' She stood up. "I don't want to do this. I promised myself I'd start remembering the good times and try to move on.''

"I still don't think you should have told Tom so quickly," Gladys said, a stubborn set to her chin.

"Quickly? It happened a year ago and it started a long time before that. I've got to go out.''

"Where?" Gladys rose, too. "It's dark and we could get more snow.''

"I've got my own transportation now." She'd bought a Jeep similar to the rented one that had been returned. "And I've driven plenty around here.''

"Why do you have to go now, sweetie?" Pops said, and his knobby hands twitched as they always did when he was anxious.

Shelly didn't want to hurt her parents but being so close to them wasn't working. "I don't want to risk someone else buying the place before I decide if I want it," she said. There wasn't much risk that she'd lose the purchase but she was desperate to end this conversation. "I can only keep the key overnight and if I want to buy I should put in an offer right away."

"Do what you like." Gladys raised her palm. "You will anyway. Never mind that we love you and want the best for you. Just go your own way. Of course we're too old to know anything."

The well-worn tactic that Shelly knew so well only irritated her more. "I'm not going to argue with you. Do you mind if I use the phone."

"Don't be silly," her father said. "You know anything we have is yours. And we do only want what's best for you."

She smiled at him, bent to kiss his papery cheek. His hair was still thick but had turned snow white, giving him a benevolent appearance.

Seconds later she heard Alice Conrad's voice on the line at the farm. "Just a minute, Shelly. I've hardly seen him for days. Let me call out back."

The sound of the receiver clacking down was followed by silence. Shelly hadn't told Alice that she'd tried Tom's line at the barn several times and got no reply. If he was there and simply not answering his phone the one sure way to get at him was through his mother.

"Hello."

His voice, the flatness, sent goosebumps up her arms. "Hi, Tom," she said too brightly. "What happened to you all week?"

"I've been busy."

Too busy to talk to her? "You always have been. I never knew anyone who works as hard as you do."

Silence.

Shelly met first her father's then her mother's eyes as they watched her intently. "Right, well, I need your expert opinion on something."

More silence. He wasn't going to help her one bit. When she'd told him she and Ben were divorced a year ago he'd been incredulous, and now she wondered if he resented both of them for not confiding earlier.

"Do you remember the Leonards' house, the people who had the clothing store for a few years?"

"Yes."

*Damn you, Tom Conrad.* He was sounding as judgmental as her folks. "Well, I may be interested in buying it and I need to make up my mind quickly. I'm going out there now. Any chance you can join me . . . kick the pipes, make sure the roof isn't leaking?"

"If the roof's leaking you'll know it."

"Good. You know where the house is? On the road to your place?"

"Shelly—"

"Great. See you there in half an hour." She hung up. No way would she give her parents the satisfaction of thinking Tom agreed with them about the course she'd taken and no way would she allow him to continue to avoid her. If he had something to say let him say it. And if he didn't show at the Leonard house she'd find him wherever he was hiding out.

She gave her rigid mother a hug, smiled at her father and ran upstairs to say goodbye to Philip. He was stretched on his bed under the sloping roof in the attic room, which had been hers as a child.

He looked up from his *Thrasher* magazine just long enough to wrinkle his nose at her kiss. Anything written about skateboarding was his passion.

The night was bone-cutting cold. Shelly wore layers of clothing, silk liners for her down-filled leather gloves and several pairs of thin socks inside shaggy after-ski boots. The icy air managed to find a way through them all. She shut herself in the new maroon Jeep, started the engine and turned the heater on full, waiting for the windshield to clear before she slipped it into gear. The sky was clear, black, pricked here and there with stars. Snowfall didn't seem likely after all. The Jeep bumped on scattered clumps of hard-packed snow the plows had missed, and dry sand sprayed from beneath the wheels.

Renny Carrol who'd grown from a scrawny boy into a prematurely corpulent man with balding head and glasses too small for his pudgy face, now ran the town's only real estate office. He'd seemed genuinely pleased to see Shelly, considering what a nasty kid he'd been.

Renny had shown her three houses. But the Leonard place was just what she was looking for. Surely Tom would come and check it out.

She clocked the distance from town to the Leonards'. About ten miles. Another eight or ten would take her to the Conrad farm.

A blue pickup stood close to the low fence that ran around the isolated house.

Shelly drew the Jeep up behind the pickup, switched off her engine and sat with her arms wrapped around the steering wheel. Her heart made an uncomfortable revolution. Tom was angry with her, she knew it. They'd had their arguments but she had a hunch this wasn't going to be like anything that had passed between them before.

His tall shape emerged from the pickup and he walked back to open her door. "Hi."

"Hi." She took the hand he offered and jumped to the snow. "Thanks for coming."

"You didn't give me much choice."

"Maybe—" She closed her mouth and checked his eyes. In the dark all she could see was a glitter.

"Maybe what?" He shoved his hands into his jacket pockets.

"Nothing," she said, turning away. She'd almost said that she'd made a mistake thinking he'd back her up. That wasn't fair. "Let's get inside."

He made no comment. She felt him at her side, heard the solid thump of his boots on frozen ground. The cold stung her eyes, and she squinted as she walked up the path. A scent of pine from nearby trees mixed with the sharp subtle odor that snow seemed to have.

She unlocked the front door and reached inside to find a light switch. "It's in pretty good shape," she said as she led the way into a narrow hall with stairs at one side leading to the three bedrooms upstairs. "And it's definitely the right size."

Tom made a noncommittal noise and walked into the living room with its garish flower patch paper. At night, with a yellowish overhead light, the place looked shabby.

"Everything would have to be redecorated, but I kind of enjoy that."

"Ever done any?"

Now he was digging at the easy life she'd lived with Ben. He resented her and the most likely reason that came to mind infuriated her: he was siding with Ben.

"I haven't done any decorating lately," she said, controlling her tone. "What do you think of the place?"

He took off his hat and rolled the brim between his gloved fingers. "Okay so far. Isn't there room for you and Philip at your folks'?"

The messages she was getting were all the same—don't make permanent decisions. But she needed to. "There's room, Tom. But I want a place of my own. You should understand that."

He walked back into the hall and out to the kitchen, a big room with a dining area at one side and a free-standing stove. Slowly he walked from end to end, glancing at every-thing but with no apparent concentration.

Shelly put her hands on her hips. Her cool was definitely slipping. "What is it with you, Tom Conrad?"

He stood still beside the stove and looked at her. Even as a boy he'd had a way of making her uncomfortable when he leveled one of his intensely blue and cool stares in her direction.

"Don't look at me like that."

"Like what?" Skin kept tanned by an outdoor life-style heightened the brilliant color of his eyes.

"Like you're mad at me. You've avoided me all week and I want to know why." Her heart sped. Ridiculously she felt the start of tears. "You are mad, aren't you? You think I should have told you about Ben and me last year."

"You're putting thoughts into my head," he said very quietly.

Tom was always controlled. Just for once she wished he'd lose his temper and say what was on his mind. "It's easy for you to be cool. You haven't had to face up to the fact that you wasted years of your life because of one mistake. You also haven't had to come back to a place you left with high hopes. How do you think I feel? Do you think I like it that I failed in marriage? Do you think it's going to be fun to put up with heckling from my parents and Ben's . . . then the whispering I'm going to get around here for a while?"

Tom worked off a glove, continuing to stare at her. A frown drew his straight brows together.

"Do you?"

"What happened, Shelly?" he said at last. "Ben's a good man, the best, we both know that. He wouldn't do any-thing to hurt you. He's loved you from when we were kids and I don't believe that can have changed." He turned his back abruptly and his coat stretched across wide shoulders as he crossed his arms.

He was closing her out. Choosing not to consider that she must have had reason to want out of her marriage. Shelly took her gloves off and slapped them against a palm. Her hands shook.

"You have been avoiding me all week." The tears were getting tougher to hold back.

"I told you, I've been busy."

She took a step toward him but stopped, afraid to get too close. "We were never too busy for each other. Whatever was going on in our lives we made time if one of us needed it."

"Not when—we aren't kids anymore."

"Does that mean you wish I'd get lost? That I'd gone somewhere else—anywhere but where you are?"

"No!" He faced her and the stress in his face jolted her. "You know damned well how much you—you and Ben mean to me. I'm confused, that's all."

"Confused? I can explain—"

"Yeah, confused." Color flashed along his high cheekbones. "That's exactly it. I'm...I can't figure it all out. Maybe I'm just a dumb country boy, but I thought you and Ben had the world by the tail. There's got to be more to it than what you've told me. Incompatibility sounds like one of those catch-all legalese terms that don't mean anything."

"It means a lot in my case," Shelly said softly. "It means Ben and I should never have married. I'm not sorry we did because of Philip. But he's going to be fine and my staying in a dead relationship wouldn't make him any better. It might even have ruined him eventually."

Tom tossed his hat on a white-tiled countertop and sent his gloves after it. He unzipped his jacket and rested his fists on his hips.

"You don't believe I didn't do anything wrong, do you?" she asked him. "In your mind Ben's perfect and I'm some kind of monster."

"Oh, crap." He spread his arms wide. "I don't know what to think. Can't you see that? But if you believe I'd take sides in this, you're all wet. You and Ben just happen to have been the best friends I ever had and . . ."

"Have been?"

"Stop it." The redness in his cheeks intensified. Tom, losing his temper was a rare spectacle.

"Tom—"

"No. You listen for once. I love you. I love you both. My life may have been a pale shadow of yours and Ben's but I am capable of deep feeling. Good old quiet Tom is supposed to be stoic, right? Isn't that what you think of me?"

"Yes, but—"

"But nothing. I am pretty level, but you can't come riding back into my life, announcing what you've announced and not expect me to react. Sure, I admit I've stayed out of your way all week. But I've done nothing but think about you. What *happened*? Did you get bored, or what?"

Shelly's throat hurt. She swallowed against the pain. "I was right. You've held your own little trial and found me guilty. Damn you." She splayed trembling fingers over her mouth. "Yes, Ben's a good man. I'm so sick of hearing how good he is I could scream. It's also true that he puts himself first, second and always."

"I don't think—"

"Yes he does, and has. He fitted me into his life when it was convenient. Tom, remember how I never liked parties much?"

He leaned against the wall now, half-turned away from her. "Yes. Neither of us did."

"But Ben did."

"I never saw him as too much of a party animal."

"He turned into one. You don't know what it's like to be an appendage to someone who walks in a pool of glitter. You get a lot of shiny dust in your eyes and not much else if you don't enjoy all the noise and the phony back slapping. Everyone loves a star...they tolerate the spouse. How about not knowing whether a person likes you for yourself? There isn't one friend's name I can give you in Cleveland. After I left Ben, not one person called me and asked if I needed anything."

"Did Ben want the divorce?" He looked at her over his shoulder.

"I...no." Why had she thought Tom wouldn't take Ben's side.

"Did he . . . was there someone else?"

Poor Tom. He wasn't used to any of this. "No. There wasn't anyone else."

"Does he have someone now?"

"No."

"Do you talk to him?"

Her control slipped a little more with each question. The lawyers had asked the same questions and her answers felt the same now as they did then, as if they had no substance. "Ben calls. He didn't want the divorce. He doesn't accept that I won't change my mind and go back to him."

With an almost violent shrug, Tom straightened. "You will go back to him, won't you? Isn't that what this is all about? Making him take notice of you? Don't you think a year is long enough to be sure he's suffered enough? Taking a job here and buying a house is going a little far."

Blood rushed into her face. Her legs felt formless. "I'm not ... I'm not trying to get Ben's attention. I want him to leave me alone. Tom, he treated me like a nice pet. I begged for some of his time and I wanted him to be the man I married, not the icon he became. I'm not going to assassinate his character, not to you of all people, but I'm the one who hurt for years, not Ben. He tried to stop me from doing anything that made me feel like a complete individual. And he was jealous, and—" She paused for breath. "That's it. I care too much for Ben to talk about him. We weren't right as husband and wife. Leave it at that. There's no going back. He doesn't see it yet, but we are very bad for each other in marriage. Sooner or later he'll stop fighting the truth and accept it."

"Okay," Tom said. He didn't meet her eyes. "But do you think it's a good idea to go so far as to buy a house here?"

She sighed. "You haven't been listening to me. I need to make a life for Philip and me."

"Sure. I only meant that ... well, sometimes we think we're absolutely certain what we want but then we change our minds. Buying a house is a pretty definite step."

Frustration mingled with disappointment. Shelly went to him, half-expecting that he'd move away. He stood his ground and she gripped his sleeves. "Look at me, Tom Conrad. Don't you dare look anywhere else until I've finished."

He did as she asked and the familiarity of his features struck a sweet-sad chord.

"My folks make me feel unwanted here. I don't think they mean to, but they do."

"Your folks think the world of you. They must be wiped out by this."

"Yes, they are." She'd like him to hug her, the way he used to when she was upset. "And this is where I want to be.

Tom, I don't want to leave, but Mom and Pops make me feel I've got to."

"No." He shook his head and his straight blond hair fell forward. He raked it back. "You're all your parents live for."

She gritted her teeth. "If they can't accept the way things are, I'll have to put some distance between us."

"Don't do that." Always he thought of other people's feelings.

Shelly put her hands on his chest. His heart beat fast beneath her fingers, and she closed her eyes. She was causing him unhappiness and she detested herself for that. "You don't want me here, do you?"

He bowed his head, shook it slowly.

"You're like my folks. If I won't go back to Ben you'd as soon I went somewhere else."

"No. And your parents don't feel that way, either. They don't accept it's over, that's all. I know exactly what they must be feeling."

"Everybody knows how everybody must be feeling, except for me, right? Nobody knows, or cares, how I'm feeling."

"Shelly—"

"Are you afraid I'll be a nuisance? Is that it?" She tried to take her hands away but he trapped them against him.

"Of course it isn't that." Tom pulled her into his arms and held her in a bear hug. "I never could resist you. The day we really met I was putty in your hands. You know how I hate confrontation, but there I was with those little rats, picking up your magazines while my heart jumped out of my chest."

She smiled, lifting her face. "You never told me you were scared. You didn't look it."

He turned her head until her nose pressed into his coarse old sweater that smelled of leather and soap. "Now you know. I'm a chicken. Buddy, I'm not afraid you'll be a nuisance. I'm only afraid you might make a decision or two that you'll regret later and I don't want that."

"So you don't think I should buy this house. I've got to live somewhere and I really don't think it will work out with my folks—for Philip's sake as much as mine. Mom's irritable with him because she's unhappy with me."

"Buy the house. It's great."

She strained to see his eyes. "You mean it?"

"One hundred percent."

He was a good-looking man, handsome despite the way the elements weathered a person's skin. Tom should definitely have a wife and children, and she could try to help him with that.

"You could always make me feel great," she told him. "Honestly, I'm sure I'm doing the right thing for Philip and me."

"So am I." He smiled then pressed his lips together.

Shelly felt a slight tremor pass through him. "You aren't just saying that because I got upset?"

"Absolutely not. This is a good house. It'll be perfect for you. Great investment, too. Is the price affordable?"

"Yes. I've looked at several places and this is definitely the best for the money."

"Go for it."

"There's a lot that needs doing—"

"I'll help. I did my place. Fixing up is one of my hobbies." He smiled broadly now, showing his strong square teeth.

Shelly relaxed and the tears she'd almost conquered sprang free. "Thanks, friend. I'll find ways to pay you back."

"Hey." He tipped up her chin and wiped her cheeks with rough thumbs. "No crying. Remember, we agreed we were too tough for that stuff?"

"I'm relieved, that's all." She rested her brow on his shoulder. "You were the one I wanted to see most this past year. If you knew how I've longed to come running to you."

"Shh. You're here, now. I'll help you get things straightened out." He folded her close again and put his chin on top of her head. "We'll get this place whipped into shape in no time."

"Sometimes you may have to be patient with me. I do this more often than I used to—cry I mean."

"We'll handle it."

"And Philip's a good kid but he's been through a lot and I don't always cope as well as I should."

"Boys need fathers. I . . ."

"I know." She slipped her arms around him. His warmth and solidness gave her more comfort than she remembered feeling in too long. "You would understand that. It was hard on you as a kid, I know that."

"Dad was a terrific guy. He couldn't help being sick." His deeply indrawn breath brought fresh tears to Shelly's eyes.

"I worry about Philip not having a father figure around. He's never . . . I worry about it, that's all."

Tom was silent awhile before he said, "Relax, Shel. I've had practice with Mary and Jimmy's boys. I'll pinch hit with Philip as much as I can."

"Oh, Tom." She threw her hands around his neck and kissed his cheek soundly. "How did I get lucky enough to have a friend like you?"

## Chapter Three

The thaw had set in. Some years it came that way, suddenly—solid packed snow one day, patches of green the
next. Tom reckoned they'd probably plant around mid-May,
three weeks from now. Then the prayers would start that
there wouldn't be a June frost.

He stood by the window in the old storage shed he'd decided to turn over to Philip as a place to skate. Behind him,
the boy attempted to whistle while he scuffed among the
boxes and debris that would have to be cleared.

Tom smiled and ran a finger down the list of supplies he'd
written according to the boy's instructions. He was about to
build a ramp, which Philip assured him would be a cinch.
But there was the planting to think of and a whole lot of
other concerns with the farm.

Then he had Shelly's house on his mind. She'd gone
ahead with the purchase and hoped to move within days.
But the two weeks since she'd bought the place hadn't given
nearly enough time to do what must be done there.

Tom whistled, himself, and flexed his shoulders as he bent
to move heavy tools. This old building hadn't been used in
years. There were holes in the roof and parts of the wooden
walls sagged, but it was safe and fairly dry and big enough
for Philip to skate.

"Mom'll pay for the wood and stuff," he said from the floor where he'd sat down, cross-legged, with a plan spread before him.

Tom stepped back from hefting the circular power saw onto a makeshift workbench and regarded the boy. "I thought we agreed we should keep this ramp a secret from your mother and surprise her when it's finished."

Philip blushed and leaned farther over the plans. "Yeah. But when we do finish she'll pay you back. That's what I meant."

In other words Philip was feeling indebted. "She won't have to. The tools are here and I already had most of the stuff. But how about a deal. Come planting time, you can help out like my nephews do and that'll cover any extra expense plus give you some pocket money." He was steadily getting drawn in tighter with Shelly and her son. Parts of him reveled in the chance; parts of him were scared.

"No lie? I get to work like Kurt and Aaron? In Cleveland they wouldn't believe we get out of school for the planting and harvesting."

"You may not be so thrilled when we get going. It's hard work." The friendship forming between Mary's boys and Philip pleased Tom.

Philip pushed his blond hair back, and yet again Tom found it hard to look into eyes that were a constant reminder of Ben. "I like hard work. Kurt and Aaron said you plant other stuff than potatoes. Barley and peas and things."

"Mmm." Tom dropped to his haunches beside Philip and studied the plan. "You have to rotate crops to keep the soil the best it can be. That's even more important with seed potatoes than other crops." He'd better shut up before he bored the kid to death. "Anyway, do we have a deal?"

"Yeah. I want to do it. Kurt said the peas are for beer."

Tom laughed. "Not quite right, sport. The barley goes mostly to beer companies, although some is sold for feed. The peas are the kind you use for seed. We usually plow them in, though. They're good fertilizer. Now, we don't have very long so we'd better get on with this. When's your mom through her meeting at school?"

"Dunno. Hour or so, I guess."

They'd decided to add a corner to a basic wooden ramp. Tom had already figured out the distance they needed between cross braces for the frame and he took a pole and held it vertically, figuring how high the structure would be.

"Geez." Philip stood up and rolled his eyes. "This is gonna be awesome. I know guys who would kill for it."

The warmth Tom felt was something new. Having a kid around who needed you wasn't all bad, in fact a man could get real used to it. And that was another danger he hadn't forgotten. Getting too attached to Philip and Shelly could spell a lot of pain if and when she decided to move on. He couldn't convince himself that she wouldn't eventually.

"Put these on." He handed Philip a pair of safety goggles and slipped his visor over his head. "I'm going to teach you to use the saw."

The boy's face flushed with pleasure as he followed Tom to the bench. He would be tall like his father, but not as heavily built.

Tom switched on the saw and its high-pitched scream split the quiet afternoon air. He motioned Philip to stand where he could see and started cutting along pencil lines on a piece of plywood to make a template for the corners of the ramp.

A draft hit the back of his neck and blew sawdust from the bench.

"Tom!"

He turned at the muffled yell. Ben's father, big, burly as ever but with gray shot through his black hair, advanced into the shed.

"Hi there," Tom shouted, lifting his safety visor and grinning. Doc Williams was an institution in Allenville and finding someone who didn't admire the man would be hard. "What brings you out this way?"

Doc retraced his steps to close the door and returned to the bench. "You going to shut that infernal racket off or are we going to keep ruining our larynxes?"

"Sorry. Didn't think." Tom switched off and removed his visor. "Good to see you. Did someone call you out?"

"No. Everyone at Conrads' is in fine shape as far as I know. Did anyone tell you I'm opening a clinic?"

Tom wiped his hands on a rag. Doc put an arm around Philip and hugged the boy who smiled up at his grandfather with open adoration.

"I heard some rumor that you might, now the hospital's closing. Good idea. We need something with the number of work-related injuries around here."

"We certainly do. Lucky and I are going full steam ahead with the plans."

Mrs. Williams continued to be her husband's partner in all things. Tom hitched himself to sit on the bench and swung his feet. He was edgy. Irving Williams wasn't likely to drive all the way out here to shoot the breeze about his clinic plans. He might have come to see his grandson, except that Tom doubted he'd expected him to be here.

"Philip," Doc said, massaging the boy's shoulder. "I just came from talking to Mrs. Conrad. She said there's fresh cookies coming out of the oven and you should go up and have some. Why don't you run along."

Tom's apprehension grew.

"Uncle Tom and I are building...building something."

"We'll get to it," Tom said, smiling with an effort. "Go on up to the house and tell my mother I'll be in after a while."

"I'll come see you before I go, Philip." Doc Williams let the boy out and shut the door again before facing Tom. He began to pace, his hands characteristically clasped behind his back. "Thanks for being good to him. He needs a man around, especially now."

"I enjoy him," Tom said, bracing himself while his stomach contracted unpleasantly. "Shelly's done a great job." Diplomacy had never been his strong point.

Doc didn't appear to notice the slip. "Nevertheless, you're a busy man. Do what you can but don't feel you have to be available all the time."

Tom had the sensation the man was working up to the real reason for this visit.

"Shelly hasn't been over to see Lucky and me in the last week or so."

"Oh." What was he supposed to say to that?

"We're beginning to think she's avoiding us."

"She wouldn't do that. Anyway, she knows how important Philip is to you so she wouldn't keep him away. She's been busy, that's all."

Doc cleared his throat. "That's what I wanted to talk to you about. I talked to the Dillons and they're as worried as we are."

"About what?" Tom immediately wished he hadn't asked.

"You know. This nonsense Shelly's insisting on."

Tom hoisted himself farther onto the bench and spread his hands on his thighs.

"She isn't telling her folks the plans she's making. You were always close to her, and to Ben. What does she say about the future? Is she coming to her senses?"

They hadn't accepted that Shelly had made up her mind about what she really wanted. "I think she's being careful what she does, and the reasons why, if that's what you mean."

"Cathy O'Leary at the library, she told me Renny Carrol said Shelly's definitely considering buying the Leonard place. Damn fool thing to do. It'll only be one more thing to deal with when she goes back to Cleveland."

Tom stared, disbelieving. He couldn't grasp that Lucky and Doc didn't know Shelly had definitely bought the house. And he was irritated at the thought of Cathy O'Leary talking about Shelly's affairs.

"Tom, what does Shelly say to you?"

He didn't like being pumped but he couldn't blame Doc for trying. "When did you talk to Cathy?"

"About ten days ago."

"Shelly bought the house. She and Philip will be moving in shortly."

"Damn." Doc shoved at his unruly hair and plunked himself down on a wooden crate. "You're going to have to help us. She trusts you."

The situation was becoming intolerable. Not one of these people considered that Tom might have his own needs. As soon as he thought it he realized that they must never know how his life had been affected by Shelly and Ben.

"You'll help us, won't you?"

He sucked in his lower lip, before he said, "That's going to depend on what you expect me to do. Shelly's a big girl. She'll do what she wants to do, and pushing her one way will only make sure she goes in the opposite direction."

"Stubborn is what you're saying and you're right. But you were the one could persuade her out of these little notions of hers. We want you to help us get her back to Ben.

It's a nuisance she's bought the house, but we can deal with that.''

Tom's gut ached from tension. "She's got a job here, too, remember. That was one of the bones she had with Ben. He got in the way of her job. She was asked to leave her last position six months after the divorce because he constantly showed up at the school—"

"I know that." Doc cut him off. "But it won't happen again. Ben told me about it himself and he knows he was wrong. He'll even pull some strings to get her a job as soon as she goes back."

Tom frowned. Ben would fix things. "I don't think Shelly wants him arranging her life for her anymore. I think that's been one of the problems. She got to feel stifled, as if she didn't get to do anything for herself." What was he doing. He'd promised himself not to get involved in this. And...he was beginning to resent talking about Shelly and Ben as husband and wife. He had to keep a hold on himself.

"That's not the important issue," Doc said. "Choose your time. Don't be obvious and don't let her know you've talked to me or she'll stop listening to you as well. Tell her she should go back to Cleveland and give Ben another chance. He wants that and we all know Shelly does, too, only she won't admit as much."

"That's not what she says." He didn't want her to go. Damn it all, he was definitely losing the distance he'd sworn to keep between his mind and his heart.

Doc got up. "She wouldn't admit it because then she'd be saying this is some sort of silly hoax."

"Hoax?"

"Shelly's lonely and confused. Ben admits he caused her to feel that way and he's sorry, but she won't even talk to him. Why do you think she protests so much? Because she wants to be persuaded, that's why. She wants attention and to be courted. Lucky thinks Ben didn't give her enough attention, and we blame ourselves for that. We probably spoiled him as a kid so he learned to think of himself first. But he's had enough of a shock. Shelly left him to get the attention she wanted and now she has it."

Just like that. Matter-of-fact analysis of the situation and good old Tom shouldn't mind being squarely in the middle.

"I'd better move along," Doc said. "I expect Shelly's coming out to pick up Philip and I don't want to run into her."

"Right," Tom said absently, sliding from the bench and following to the door.

"You will talk to her, won't you?" Doc turned anxious brown eyes on him. "Be subtle but steady. Wear her down without her realizing what you're doing."

Tom gritted his teeth. What could he say? No, I don't want any part of this. I'm enjoying being with Shelly myself.

"Tom?"

"I'll mention the subject to Shelly." Why couldn't he stand up and say he wouldn't do what Doc wanted.

"Good man. I'd better not risk going up to the house. Philip will probably tell Shelly I was here. If he does, make some excuse, will you?"

"Sure."

The door closed. Wind, still bearing the dying winter's cold, grabbed its chance to squeeze in, and Tom narrowed his eyes against the bite.

He'd agreed to work on Shelly to get her to do something she didn't want to do. Or did she? Was Doc right? Did she really want to be wooed back into Ben's arms . . .

Tom picked up his safety visor and switched on the saw. Then he switched it off again. How many times was he going to allow himself to be used?

Rage, the kind he'd only felt a handful of times, shot through his body. He'd do what he'd said he'd do, but he didn't have to like it.

The visor hit the wall with a splintering crack.

"THIS FEELS SO GOOD," Shelly said, stripping a sheet of wallpaper from the living room in the Leonard house. "Why does tearing something down satisfy me like this?"

Tom looked down on her from his vantage point on the step ladder. "Because you're working on something that's yours." He didn't add what he thought, that she probably needed ways to vent some sort of frustration.

"Whew, it's hot work." She wiped the back of a hand across her brow. Her hair was tied in a ponytail and from where he stood she looked to Tom very much as she had at eighteen.

He slathered more water from a bucket onto the paper and worked a ceiling edge loose with a scraper. Shelly had arrived from her staff meeting at school fuming over old-fashioned methods. Coming here to work had been his idea and he didn't mention that his nerves were as much in need of mindless exercise as hers. They'd dropped Philip at the Dillons', grabbed a hamburger in the town's one fast-food place and headed out to the house.

"Are you sure you like the new paper?"

Shelly dropped her scraper and went to unroll the pattern she'd chosen. Tom smiled. She was distractible and if she were truthful she'd admit that the novelty of monotonous manual work was already paling.

He glanced at the white background of the design with its fine gray stripe and what looked like dashes of blue flowers. "I like it fine. I'm not good at those things."

She lifted her face, frowning. He never got tired of looking at her soft gray eyes, or her soft mouth . . .

"What does that mean? You like it fine but you're not good at those things. Is that like saying it's probably awful but you don't care?"

"No." He laughed. "Women. You're all the same."

"And what does *that* mean?" She pointed at him with the roll of paper. "When did you become the great authority on women? I thought you'd led a chaste life."

He kept a smile on his face, forcing down a rush of resentment. She was joking and he wasn't narrow enough to get mad because she probably did think he'd lived pretty much like a monk all these years. "Let's just say that in my limited experience I've found the female of the species to have certain characteristics in common. Like a need to goad every man in sight."

"You don't like the paper."

"Give me a break." He looked heavenward and leaned over the top of the step ladder. "The paper's great. Will you stop procrastinating and strip the wall. We don't have all the time in the world."

"I wasn't procrastinating—"

"Work. That's an order."

"You are one pushy guy." But she attacked the job ferociously while she continued muttering.

Tom watched her awhile. An old sweatshirt, baggy and stretched, showed the pale skin at the back of her neck. That skin was smooth, vulnerable . . . Her full breasts moved with . . . she wasn't wearing a bra. He glanced away, then back. A few weeks at home had put color back in her cheeks and ironed out some of the strain. She tilted her chin up at him and smiled, and his heart did something odd. The Shelly of fifteen years ago was with him, pretty in her distinctive, finely cut way, slim but shapely and curved in all the right places. Her cheekbones were well defined but rounded and her brows arched gently. No, not the Shelly of the past, just that girl made more appealing by maturity.

"Who's wasting time now?" She stood up, hands on hips, and it was with difficulty that he kept himself from looking at her body again. "You're daydreaming and to quote you, we don't have time."

"You're right." With the bucket in one hand, the scraper tucked in the back pocket of his jeans, he climbed down. He had to do as he'd promised Doc. "Shelly, are you sure you're doing the right thing?"

"What?" She swung around.

"Shelly—"

"What are you asking me?"

"Exactly what it sounded like. Are you sure you aren't making a mistake by getting entrenched in Allenville."

Her scraper clattered when she dropped it to wipe her hands on her jeans. "We've been over all this. I thought you were on my side. My folks and Ben's are still nagging, but I didn't expect it from you."

"I'm not nagging. But I wouldn't be doing my duty if I didn't ask one more time. Maybe you want to be with Ben after all. If you do, don't hesitate to follow your instincts. There's no shame attached to changing your mind." Hell, he should have gone on the stage. He even sounded sincere.

"I don't believe this." She advanced on him until he could see black flecks in her eyes. "I've been so happy these past days. And it was because you made me feel wanted here, but I made a fool of myself again, didn't I? You're probably in cahoots with my folks. Are you, Tom? Did they ask you to talk to me?"

He swallowed and ran a hand over his face. "No." Lying went against all he believed in. "But Doc Williams did have a few words with me. Now don't get mad."

She made a grab for her coat on a nearby chair, but he pulled her back. "Shelly, cut it out. There are a lot of people involved in what you're doing and you have to consider them, too."

"I trusted you, Tom. I thought that even if everyone else was on Ben's side, you'd be fair."

He noticed the temperature of his skin rising. "I'm on your side and I'm also on Ben's. I don't know whose fault the divorce was... both, I expect. Isn't that usually the way it goes?"

"I'm not an expert on divorce, and I'm not going to tear Ben down with you to make a point. But I don't want to hear anymore about whether or not I've made the right decision in opting for freedom." She shrugged away. "I wouldn't want to get you in trouble with my folks and Ben's. So why don't you drive me home and I'll tell them you tried to persuade me to go back to Cleveland. I'm sorry if I've put you in a difficult position around here."

"Damn!"

Shelly's eyes opened wider. "Tom—"

"Be quiet and stop behaving like a spiteful kid. What you're saying is that if I don't do what you want, then I'm not what you thought I was. If I don't accept everything you say without question, you'll punish me."

"I—"

"If you wanted to get everyone's attention—congratulations, you've done a great job. I'm a busy man. Believe it or not, even potato farmers take what they do seriously. I want to because it's important and there isn't a whole lot of time left over for feeling sorry for myself. Maybe that's what you need, less time to think about yourself and—" What was he saying? He didn't know everything she might have been through. He was shouting at her out of his own hurt.

She turned away. "I don't want attention . . . not the way you think. All I want is some peace." With that she walked from the room and he heard her go into the kitchen.

He'd lost control, let his own frustrations pour out. "Shelly."

In the kitchen, she stood staring through high windows over the sink into the blackness beyond.

"I'm sorry. You didn't deserve that. It's tough, feeling split into pieces between two people who mean so much to me. And, frankly, Doc Williams pushing me to speak to you didn't help much."

"It's not your fault."

The distance between them was nothing, two strides, but it yawned like a pit to Tom.

"Can we forget we argued and get on with what we have to do?" He saw the sharp outline of her uptilted jaw. "Let's finish stripping that paper."

"No. I don't think so."

"I was wrong. Can't we let it go at that?"

Shelly looked at him over her shoulder. "I'm the one who was wrong," she said. "Why should you be expected to take me on as a charity project just because I decide to walk back into your world. It was selfish of me not to think about what I might be doing to you. You don't have time for someone else's problems—and I'm not being a brat when I say that, just objective for the first time."

"Oh, Shelly. I'll always have time for you. Maybe I'm tired or something. This time of year always sets me on edge. It's exciting and challenging, but there are also a lot of timing variables to gauge and so on."

"Exactly." She bowed her head so that he couldn't see her face anymore. "And I've ignored all that. How could I have been foolish enough to come barging back in here the way I did. All I've done is cause trouble for people who don't need any more."

He wanted to suck back the angry words. The best he could do was turn her into his arms. He held her a moment, then lifted her to sit on the counter. "This is where you belong. Where else would you have gone? When we're in trouble we go home to the people who love us." His throat hurt, and he narrowed his eyes against the ache.

Shelly crossed her wrists behind his neck and rested her brow on his shoulder. He felt her fingers in his hair. Tom closed his eyes and couldn't seem to think clearly, only feel. He stood between her knees, her slight weight braced against his chest.

"I shouldn't have gone off at you like that. It's just that with my folks and Ben's on my case, it hurts to wonder if you don't want me, either."

"Of course I want you." Carefully, he settled his cheek against her soft hair. "We'll get you settled and through this tough time. Then things will calm down for you."

"Thank you." She kept her arms around his neck but lifted her head. "Oh, Tom, you look so hurt. I'm sorry I've done this to you."

Careful, he must be very careful. He'd never been good at hiding his feelings. "Don't worry about me."

"I do," she said. Her hand, stroking the side of his face, felt like the gentle hand of a lover. He blinked. One slip, one wrong move and it would be all over.

"Philip's a great kid," he said, grasping for safe ground while his body felt raw with longing.

Shelly smiled. "Thanks. But don't change the subject. You're disappointed in Ben and me, aren't you?"

"Disappointed?" Thoughts weren't clicking quite right.

"I can see the pain in your eyes. You wish Ben and I were still together. It hurts me, too, because I didn't want us to fail. One day you'll marry, yourself, and you'll make a success of it, I know you will. Don't feel a happy marriage isn't possible just because we shattered your illusions."

"Please, Shelly—"

"Shh." She put a forefinger on his lips. "Stop worrying about us."

Her eyes were close and so gray. Was this punishment for some sin he'd committed? Would his penance be to suffer forever, near her, yet never close enough? How many times could he feel her arms around him, her breath on his face, her body touching his, without giving himself away? He was very sure she had never thought of him as more than a good friend and would never think of him differently.

"You don't have to say anything," she told him, smiling. "I'll convince you that what's happened is for the best. You do believe I can do that, don't you?"

"Do what?" He wanted to kiss her mouth.

"Show you that I've done what had to be done. Then we can enjoy each other just the way we used to."

Tom nodded, drawing away. "You bet." *The way we used to.* God, he wasn't a saint.

# Chapter Four

"You all right, then, Tom?"

He turned his back on the stove at Dillons' store and faced Walt Smith. "Great, thanks. How about you?" A lumpy kid who had walked in his sister Beattie's shadow, Walt had grown into a thickset slow-thinking man. Beattie, married with four children, continued to call the shots with her bachelor brother.

Walt fished a pickle out of a barrel and sucked noisily. "Trouble with the back," he said. "Makes working tough."

"Hmm," Tom said, thinking that work had never been tops with him, any more than it was with Beattie's feckless husband, Chester Green.

"Still working out at Russ Carrol's place?" Russ was Renny Carrol's older brother and he ran the family's potato spread.

"When I can," Walt said, looking pained. "Russ is a hard man."

In other words, Russ expected Walt to do a fair day's work for his pay. "You'll probably be planting out there shortly," Tom said. Carrols' bordered the Conrads' to the east.

"S'pose so. Beattie thinks I may have to take it easy this year, though. She'll be in shortly. Went to park the pickup, but y'know how women are. Probably jawing along the way."

Tom took in Walt's babyish features and greasy tow hair, and swallowed dislike. "Where's Mrs. Dillon?" he said. She hadn't been in the shop when Tom arrived and he'd waited ten minutes already.

"Went over to the house," Walt said, lowering himself into a chair by the stove. "Fred's been pretty bad. This stuff with Shelly can't help much."

Tom felt a chill. Outside the immediate family no comments about Shelly had reached him . . . until now.

The shop door swept open and Beattie Green came in. Tall, dark-haired, still slim and pretty, Tom had always felt she was a woman who could have made something of herself.

Jimmy Thomas, Tom's brother-in-law followed her inside and closed the door.

"Hey up, Tom," Jimmy said, taking off his hat and scrubbing at his wiry gray crewcut. "What's keeping you? We gotta get back." They'd driven in from the farm together. Jimmy's task had been to go to the post office and mail invoices to customers while Tom was to pick up supplies.

"Mrs. Dillon had to go out to the house," Tom said and wandered to look over a row of new rubber boots on a shelf. Mud season, "gumbo," as the shiny black muck was called around here, had arrived, and Dillons would do a fine trade in these.

"Yeah," Walt put in. "I was mentioning to Tom that the Dillons are taking it hard that Shelly's brought all this trouble on them."

Jimmy joined Tom by the boots and looked sideways at him.

"Should think she'd be ashamed to come creeping back here after what she's done," Beattie said, and Tom turned at that. "For better, for worse," she continued while she lined items on the counter. "Mostly better from what what I hear. We know Ben gave her everything. And it isn't every woman can walk out on her husband and end up with her own new house and car and anything else she wants."

Tom knew he was being felt out, tested. Shelly couldn't know the kind of hell he'd started going through for her, and would keep on going through if his instincts were right.

"Ben thought the world of her," Walt said.

"Ben still does think a lot of Shelly," Tom said carefully. "But marriages don't always work out, do they? We all know that."

"Maybe we should come back for what we need," Jimmy said, coming to Tom's side. "Cully wants help going over the equipment."

"You always said Shelly had notions that were too big for her boots, Jimmy," Beattie said. Her blue eyes held a greedy light, greedy for the vicarious excitement gossip brought to so many people.

Jimmy cleared his throat. "That's history," he said. "And I don't think it's right to talk about this, particularly not here." He hitched his jeans up around his slim hips and buttoned his fleece-lined oilskin jacket, making leave-taking motions.

"Beattie knows," Walt said from his chair as if he was only listening to his sister's half of the conversation.

"Not always," Tom said, making no attempt to check the sharpness in his voice. "Talking about other people is a mean pastime. I avoid it and maybe you should, too. You don't know anything about Ben and Shelly Williams, so why pick at them."

"I wasn't picking," Beattie said, but she settled herself against the counter and crossed her arms in an attitude that suggested she had a lot more to say. "You always were soft on her."

The words dropped like cold little pellets into Tom's brain. He didn't know how to respond.

"Yeah," Walt said. "People are talking about that. Beattie's husband's folks mentioned it."

"The Greens?" Tom turned on him. The family ran the town's uninviting café. "What do they know about anything?" Losing his temper could only suggest he had something he wanted to cover up. He deliberately poured coffee into a tin mug from a pot kept on top of the stove. "Enough said. We'd better all mind our own business." But his heart was thudding slowly, distinctly.

"It was a shock to all of us to see Shelly back," Beattie said, "But you must have known what was happening a long time ago, Tom. I expect it was your idea for her to come back here."

He met her eyes and read the avid interest there. If this weren't so sick he'd laugh. What Beattie didn't know was that Tom wished Shelly had come to him early in the rift with Ben and that they had made some agreement to move forward together. Dreamer.

"You always were a quiet one, Tom," Beattie said, pretending deep interest in boxes of cereal. "But still waters run deep. Isn't that what they say?"

"That's enough, Beattie," Jimmy said, then to Tom, "We should go."

Tom put a hand on his brother-in-law's shoulder. "Soon enough. What does that mean, Beattie? Still waters run deep?"

"You know as well as I do," she said, averting her face defensively.

"Maybe I don't. Why don't you explain."

Walt lumbered from his chair. "She means there's a lot more to you than meets the eye. Isn't that right?"

"Hush, Walt," she told him, glaring.

Walt wasn't about to be squelched. "Beattie's husband said you and Shelly and her boy are together a lot. Maybe more'n you should be."

Tom looked not at Walt but at Beattie. "What prompted Chester to make assumptions about Shelly and me one way or the other?" Tom didn't like the man who seemed to make a living filching from his parents' meager takings.

"Don't you get all high and mighty with me, Tom Conrad," Beattie said, lifting her chin. "You take note of what's being said, that's all. Chester's mom and dad said you and Shelly and her boy were in for dinner the other night... brazen as you please."

"Brazen?" He choked on the word. "We were having a burger, not making out on one of those dirty red benches the Greens don't clean."

"Tom!" Now Beattie's eyes became round. "Don't you talk to me like that."

Jimmy, shaking his head, grabbed Tom's arm. "This isn't worth getting het up over. Beattie," he glowered at her, "not another word on the subject if you know what's good for you."

Undeterred, she advanced on Tom. "You're the one who'd better think about what's good for you. You and Shelly always did think you were a cut above the rest of us. But there's things we simple people won't tolerate. Think about *that*, Tom Conrad. You two may believe you look innocent as babies, but I'm not fooled and neither is anyone else around here. Don't tell me you've held off from getting married because you're too busy to think about women—"

"That's enough, Beattie," Jimmy said, cutting her off. Her face reddened and she busied herself finding a box to put some of her groceries in.

Tom stood very still, a dull throbbing in his temples. How much did the people in this town talk about him? Regardless of the answer, for Shelly's sake, he might take a trip into Idaho Falls one of these days. There was a nice woman there who was always glad to see him. Yeah, he needed that. And he'd make sure one or two people here knew he was going.

The sensation that he was watched filtered slowly into his mind and he glanced around—in time to see Gladys Dillon inside the door to the backyard. She stood very still and her eyes tacked him to the spot.

"Hello there," he said, while his mouth dried out. How much had she heard? From her expression he'd say plenty, and that the ideas planted in her head were completely new.

"Tom." She nodded at the others and returned her attention to him. "What can I do for you?"

He found inspiration without trying. "I just wanted to ask you to give Shelly a message for me," he said, aware of the tension around him. "Would you tell her that my mother would like her to bring Philip over for dinner on Friday night, tomorrow, if she'd like to come. I'll pick her up around five. We thought Philip would enjoy some time with Kurt and Aaron."

"I'll tell her, Tom," Mrs Dillon said, a smile softening her lined face. "And I'm sure she'll want to go. You and your family are being so good to her in these difficult times." She looked significantly at Walt Smith and Beattie Green. "Which is more than I can say for some people."

"We gotta go," Jimmy said urgently. "Good day to you, Mrs. Dillon." And he tromped outside with Tom in his wake.

Beside the pickup Jimmy paused and leaned his elbows on the hood. The cold made Tom squint to look at him. "What's the matter?"

"You know what's the matter."

Tom stared into the distance where the Tetons were an endless line of jagged white peaks against a blindingly blue sky.

"I can explain not picking up the provisions." He wasn't putting anything over on Jimmy but he could always hope. "I'll say—"

"To hell with the provisions. How long do you think you can pretend?"

Tom leaned against the pickup and crossed his boots at the ankle.

"Shelly isn't interested in me as more than a friend, Jimmy. She never was, so stop worrying."

"Not good enough," Jimmy said. "I didn't hear you say anything about you not being interested in her."

Tom rubbed his face and didn't answer.

"You're walking a tightrope, friend. And I don't mean only with the small-minded cusses in this town. They may make life difficult for a while but they'll get bored eventually. What I'm talking about is you. Do you know what you're getting yourself into?"

"What does that mean?"

"You want Shelly, don't you?"

"I never said that. You're guessing." He walked around to the driver's side, and Jimmy was already in his seat when Tom climbed behind the wheel.

"I'm not guessing. I know and so does Mary and we're worried sick about you."

"Don't be." Tom closed his mouth firmly. "I'm not a kid and I can handle myself."

"Will you handle it if you get in so deep and then Shelly tells you she's ready to go back to Ben?"

"I—" Tom turned the key in the ignition but made no attempt to put in the gears. "Shelly and I are good friends. Nothing more. We'll never be anything more."

"You believe that?"

He swallowed. "Yeah."

"It's what you want?"

"Yeah, dammit."

"Tom Conrad, either you're a liar or a fool. Let's get out of here."

A liar or a fool? Tom gritted his teeth until his jaw ached. He was both, and there was nothing he could do to change that . . . not unless Shelly made a move first.

THE SMELL OF BAKING BREAD met Tom when he came in from the barn to the mud room behind the kitchen. He had to let his mother know he'd invited Shelly and Philip to dinner the following night.

"He'll listen to you, Alice."

Jimmy had beaten Tom into the house and was talking to his mother in an urgent hurried tone.

"He knows his own mind," she said.

"In some ways," Jimmy said, sounding truculent. "But he hasn't had a whole lot of experience with women and he's falling hard, I tell you."

Tom gave a grim smile. He didn't like what he was hearing, but the thought of Jimmy talking like a man of the world was humorous. Mary had been his first and only love.

"Tom won't do anything to embarrass Shelly," Alice said, opening up the oven door. "And it would embarrass her if she thought he was interested in her in a way she couldn't return. So let it drop."

"You weren't at Dillons' this afternoon," Jimmy said "If you had been you wouldn't be so calm."

"What happened at Dillons'?"

"Walt and Beattie were there. Mrs. Dillon had gone ou back and you should have heard Beattie take off on Tom'₅ case."

Alice laughed and made no reply.

"Take this seriously," Jimmy said sounding irritable "This is a family matter and in a small place we can't af ford to be a laughing stock."

Tom made a move to walk into the kitchen but changec his mind. No point in wading in while he was mad.

"Why would we be a laughing stock?" Alice asked "We've had tough times but this family has always walkec tall and we always will." Tom thought he heard an unusua hint of exasperation in his mother's voice.

"I know all that," Jimmy said. "But we're the main talk of the town, I tell you. They're saying Tom and Shelly are involved as more than old friends, and there's a lot of sly snickering going on. Talk to him, tell him to back off for a while—at least until things settle down. Next thing we know the boys will be getting flack from the other kids at school and I won't have that."

Tom pushed open the inner door so hard it banged against the wall. His mother stood at the stove stirring something that sent billows of steam into the air and turned, her plump face red. She eyed him speculatively before she smiled. Tom was surprised to see that Mary sat quietly at the table.

"Hello, son," Alice said and Tom noted her significant glance at Jimmy.

"Hi," Tom said. "Bringing shame on the family, am I?" He seethed at the injustice of it all.

Jimmy spread his hands while his broad face turned red. 'Not always a good idea to listen behind doors. You can hear things you're better off not hearing."

"If I'm going to be the main topic of conversation around here I'd like to know. Doesn't a man have the right to defend himself—and his friends?"

"Not if he isn't objective he doesn't." Jimmy, regaining confidence with each word, advanced on Tom until he looked up into his face. "Beattie remembered how you always hung around Shelly. Don't you think everyone else will? They'll say you were just waiting for a chance to step into Ben's shoes."

Tom's blood heated. Too many times lately he'd felt this burst of anger. "All I ever wanted was for Ben and Shelly to have a good life together. Anyone who says otherwise is a lousy gossip."

"And that's the point." Jimmy's chin came too close for comfort. "There are a bunch of gossips around here. That doesn't bother me normally, but it does if it affects my family."

"Jimmy," Mary said in a soft voice, "Tom wouldn't do anything he shouldn't."

Jimmy rounded on her. "Says who? You mentioned yourself that you were worried about it."

"Only because I don't want my brother hurt," Mary said, sounding miserable.

"I think enough's been said." Alice dragged an iron skillet from a back burner and stirred pungent onions. "What Tom does is his affair as far as I'm concerned."

"Damn it all," Tom said, ramming a hand into his hair. "Have you all finished deciding what I should or shouldn't do with my life. Shelly and I are friends, nothing more. She asked for my help while she gets settled and there's no way I'd do anything but give her what she needs."

"You should have heard Beattie," Jimmy said, on a rol now. "She was warning in a way; shape up or else. I won dered if there was a threat there."

"I'm sick of this." Mary stood up. "Some things nevei change. Beattie always was a big mouth. I remember tha from school."

"Oh, she's not so bad," Alice said mildly. "She doesn' have an easy time with that husband of hers."

"She's the one who wanted to marry him," Mary said and then looked uncomfortable. "Not that I wish her any harm."

Tom continued to simmer. "I thought you liked Shelly," he said to Jimmy. "You've certainly been pleasant enough to her in recent years. Or was that just because Ben's a football star."

"Tom! You two have known each other all your lives," Alice said. The steam had made her fine white hair cur! tightly and she patted it into place. "There's nothing to ar gue about. Just think how that silly Beattie and Walt would like it if they thought they'd managed to upset us."

Jimmy crossed his arms and scrubbed a hand over his eyes.

"Everything will be fine," Mary said, her thin face, sc like Tom's, unusually pinched. "I don't know what all the fuss is about. We've never bothered about talk before."

"Of course not." Alice took flatware and napkins to the table. "Now stop all this. Kurt and Aaron will be in shortly. This is supposed to be a family meal, and I won't have everyone's digestion upset."

"That's right," Jimmy said with a forced grin. "If I overstepped the mark I'm sorry, Tom. Believe me, I do want what's best for you."

"Right," Tom said. He wasn't hungry anymore. "Is it all right with you if Shelly and Philip have dinner with us tomorrow, Mom?"

She glanced up, frowning slightly. "You know it is. Shelly's welcome anytime. She always was."

Tom gave her a grateful smile. His mother had suffered but she also loved and accepted more than most. He kissed her cheek. A pleased smile creased her face.

"Want a beer, Tom?"

He glanced at Jimmy's anxious face and at the can in his hand. "Not for me, thanks. I only came in to say I'm going into Idaho Falls."

That got everyone's attention. "Now?" Alice peered outside. "It's dark, and the roads still ice over in places at night."

"Yeah, now. I made this date weeks ago."

Silence followed him as he walked out. He might not be a fool but at this moment he was definitely a liar.

SHELLY TOOK A PLATE from Alice Conrad's soapy hands and wiped it carefully. The thick, willow pattern china felt familiar, comfortable. Tom's home had always been a place she loved to visit. Even as a teenager, when his dad had been very sick, she'd been made welcome and treated as one of the family.

Mary lifted a stack of saucers and put them into a cupboard. "Like old times," she said, smiling over her shoulder at Shelly. Mary's light brown hair was short and softly curly and suited her better than the longer style she used to wear.

"Mmm." Satisfaction stole over Shelly, a sense of rightness. Tom and Jimmy had taken the three boys out to a storage shed where they were working on a secret project. Philip's face, as they left, had glowed, and she held the memory of it in her heart. Her son needed the kind of family closeness that existed here.

"How are your folks?" Alice asked. There had been little chance for adult conversation over dinner while the boys had dominated with their loud enthusiasm.

"Mom's about the same," Shelly said. "Dad's not so good, I'm afraid. He doesn't complain, but arthritis is a painful disease."

Alice made a sympathetic noise.

"He doesn't lose his sense of humor though," Mary said. "The other day I was in the store, and he wanted to know if we might need a hand planting this year. Said he could make furrows pretty fast with his sticks."

Shelly laughed. "That's what keeps him going. That and Philip."

"And you," Alice added, looking at her squarely and with no trace of a smile. She didn't add what they were all thinking, that the breakup of Shelly's marriage couldn't have helped him.

An hour went by, then another. Mary lighted a fire in the parlor, and they sat close on tufted chintz furniture that had also been in the house as long as Shelly could remember. Alice crocheted, Mary worked methodically through a pile of mending, and Shelly, never good at sitting idle, persuaded Alice to let her start a sweater intended for Tom.

Clumping and laughter heralded the arrival of the men and boys. Jimmy stuck his head around the parlor door. "We've got some tired customers here. They say they're ready for pie and hot chocolate."

Immediately Mary and Alice got up. Shelly took the knitting with her, unwilling to stop until she'd at least finished ribbing the bottom of the back.

"Wait till you see it, Mom, its—"

"Philip." Tom cut the boy off and smiled at Shelly. "A secret, remember. We want to surprise you." She caught a look that passed between Tom and Jimmy and wondered if she was going to like this surprise.

Hot chocolate was set in mugs on the table, and beer for the men. Alice produced a bottle of sherry, and Shelly was too polite to say she didn't care for it.

"What's been going on here?" Jimmy asked, planting a kiss on his wife's mouth as she turned her face up to him.

"Mending," Mary said, ruffling Kurt's tow-colored hair as he slurped froth from the top of his mug. His younger brother leaned on his mother's shoulder watching her swift needle at work on a button.

Shelly looked into Tom's blue eyes. He wasn't smiling. Quickly she returned her attention to the navy wool in her fingers. She'd always enjoyed knitting. Maybe she'd ask Alice if she could work on this for a while.

"What's that?" Tom asked, and she met his unwavering stare again. He was moving away from the harmony here, taking her with him whether she wanted to go or not. The sensation confused her.

"A sweater," she said, unwilling to say it was one his mother intended for him or how much she liked feeling she was doing something for him.

A little jolt passed through her. She did like doing things for Tom and the sense that she was a part of his life. She took a deep breath. That was as it should be between friends.

Laughter and talk continued to rush in and sweep away, gusting about the room in cheerful, comfortable eddies. But Tom wasn't with them and with every click of her needles Shelly felt his eyes upon her.

Again she glanced up. And he gave her his somber regard, the old, cool assessment that had always unnerved her.

He couldn't relax with her here, and the pleasure of the moment seeped away. She was an intruder after all. Her fingers stilled. By the time she wound up the wool and speared the needles into the ball, he'd left, walking quietly through the door that led out to his barn.

Tears prickled in her eyes but she blinked them away. Philip must not see her like this. She got up and returned to the parlor, murmuring that she'd forgotten something.

Mary was on her heels and closed the door behind her. "What's wrong?" she asked Shelly.

Shelly set down the knitting and warmed her hands over the fire.

"Shelly? You're upset."

"No, I'm not." She shoved her hands into her jeans pockets. "Yes I am. Who am I fooling? It's Tom. I thought I knew all there was to know about him but he keeps surprising me."

Mary sat on the edge of a chair where she could see Shelly's face. "Why don't you explain what you mean?"

"It's my fault, not his. I expect too much of him because... he's all I have, really." She glanced at Mary and blushed. "That must sound weird but I mean that I've always been able to trust Tom and that hasn't changed, or I don't want it to. Only I think he doesn't want the responsibility of worrying about me anymore. I should probably stay out of his way and let him get on with his life. I'm being selfish putting extra burdens on him."

Mary got up and put an arm around Shelly's shoulders. "Tom's always been one to go off on his own. We're used to it. It upset you when he left just now, didn't it?"

She had no claim on him. Talking as if she did wouldn't be right. "I thought I'd driven him out because he's used to being alone with his family. I don't want to cause difficulty for him. He works so hard."

"You hit it," Mary said. "Tom's a bit of a recluse and I think he needs to be, with the pressure he's under. He's always had so many responsibilities. At twenty-two he became the official man of the house, and he had the job long before that." A distant expression entered her eyes, a sadness. "Tom adored Dad, and as long as he was alive things were kept as if he was in charge. But it was really my brother who made most of the decisions from when he was about eighteen. That's a tough load for a kid."

"I know," Shelly said, feeling small and mean for worrying about her own concerns. "Tom always put other people first. It didn't seem to worry him when he didn't get to go to college—even though he was such a good student."

"It bothered him," Mary said, dropping her arm. "He never said so is all. But I could see how he pined to go and I was the only one who saw him cry out there in the fields when he was trying to work off the frustration. I mentioned it once and he said he had sweat in his eyes. I knew better."

Shelly made no attempt to hide the tears that sprang into her own eyes, and Mary put her arms around her again. "The thing with Tom is that so much depends on him and he doesn't take time for himself. Maybe you can help him change that by pointing out that he needs to live a little. He's lonely, Shelly. Go on out and talk to him. This time of year is the worst when he's edgy about timing the planting."

"And I'm adding to his burden," Shelly said hearing the bitter note in her voice. But she did as Mary asked and made her way out into a clear, star-encrusted night.

Tom's barn lay fifty yards from the house, a tall weathered building with a sloping roof, the only lights came from a row of high windows at loft level.

She knocked on the small door to the left of the main entrance, which was sealed now. There was no reply and she knocked again.

"Tom!"

No response, though he couldn't be sleeping yet. She turned the handle, and the door opened easily but with a muffled creak, and she stepped inside.

She'd never been here before. Tom wasn't in sight and she stood on the threshold looking around.

He'd turned the main floor into one big, comfortable room. Cedar plank walls had been left exposed but oiled and the floor had been given the same treatment. She breathed in the wonderful scent of the wood. A freestanding black stove was vented through a long pipe that ran past the open loft that was obviously his bedroom. From up there she heard running water and assumed he was showering.

Slowly she made a circuit of the room. The furnishings were inexpensive but comfortable. Bentwood with boldly striped cushions in shades of black and brown gave a warm effect, so did a scatter of braided rugs. Shelly picked up the top issue from one of several piles of magazines. *Idaho Potato Grower*. She smiled.

Her gaze shifted to the walls. Bookshelves covered one side of the big room. She wandered to check titles. The classics, well-used encyclopedia, textbooks covering subjects from law to seed propagation. A tightness formed in the region of her heart. Why should she be surprised? That Tom was extremely intelligent was something she'd always known. Naturally he was the type who would continue his education by whatever means was open to him.

Water stopped running, to be replaced by the sound of him singing, slightly off-key. Shelly smiled again. She looked around. The room held no television but the bank of audio equipment was impressive. Tom must love music.

If he came down in the buff they'd both be embarrassed. "Tom," she called. "It's Shelly."

The singing ceased. Seconds later she started at the sound of his voice from above. He leaned over the balcony built along the loft, his wet hair on end, naked to the waist of his unzipped jeans. One bare foot poked between two balusters.

"Hi."

"Hi," she said, attempting a cheerful grin. "I decided it was time I got to see your domain."

He lifted an arm and taut muscles moved in his chest and shoulders. "This is it. Not much, I'm afraid." Light played on skin that was slightly damp and shining. Dark hair spread wide over his chest and narrowed to disappear at the waist of his jeans.

Shelly crossed her arms and smiled, a genuine one this time. "Tom Conrad, you grew into one spectacular man."

She thought he colored, and that turned her smile into a satisfied grin. "That's something I came to talk to you about. Get down here."

He came slowly, watching her narrowly. "What did you come to talk about?" His voice was gruff and he cleared his throat.

"You."

He passed very close and she smelled soap and some musky scent. Not an ounce of fat had accumulated on his tall frame. He went to put wood into the stove, and as he stooped, the broadness of his shoulders and back, the slimness of his waist, was marked. Shelly was used to men in great shape but there was something...she breathed through her mouth. Drooling over male bodies had never been one of her failings, and starting with Tom would be bizarre. But he was...she glanced away.

"Why did you clam up in the house?" she asked.

"Did I clam up?"

"You know you did."

He turned to look at her and she was aware of the rise and fall of his chest, his flat belly, the little gap where his jeans parted at the navel. Tom would be shocked if he got an inkling that she was responding to him in... Good grief she must be losing her mind.

"I'm sorry if I seemed antisocial. Creature of habit is all. I like time on my own and that's hard to come by around here."

It was her turn to blush. "And you wish I'd get lost right now?"

"I didn't say that."

She stepped backward. "Mary said she thinks you should spend more time living. I guess I'll leave you with that thought. I'm sorry if I've intruded."

"Garbage." He reached for her wrist and pulled her near. "I'm the one who's sorry. It's just that sometimes I look at Jimmy and Mary and their boys and I feel—" His heightened color turned crimson for an instant before it ebbed away and he looked at the ground.

Without thinking, Shelly took him in her arms. She slipped her hands around him and held his hard body close. "That's what I'm worried about," she said. "You're a man who should be married with children of his own. It's a waste for you to go on living like a hermit."

His flesh was warm and firm against her and she closed her eyes realizing for the first time in months how much she'd missed the touch of a strong man. The thought that this man must be destined for another woman brought a sweet sadness. Maybe one day she would be ready to start over with someone else, and she hoped she'd find a man half as wonderful as Tom Conrad.

His silence began to make her uneasy. Her face was against his shoulder, held there by one of his firm hands. She thought she felt him tremble. He wasn't happy, and she wished she could wave a wand and erase the burdens, replace them with the happiness he deserved.

"Tom," she said quietly, "maybe it would be better if Philip and I stayed out of your way for a while, at least until the planting's done. We're fine. I've been selfish asking you for so much time."

He straightened so abruptly she stumbled. Tom caught her shoulders. She couldn't read his eyes. Anger, hurt—he was so complex.

"You aren't in my way. Accept me as I am, that's all I ask. If I'm quiet, understand that I've been that way all my life. It doesn't mean anything. I need...I want you around, do you understand?"

"Yes." She felt wobbly. His emotion was intense. It seeped into her. "Tom, are you all right? You aren't ill or anything?"

His white teeth pulled at his bottom lip. "I'm as healthy as a horse. A bit tired today."

"The boys and their secret project may be something you should put aside for a while." She was intensely in tune with the aura around him, the tensing and untensing in his body. A small muscle twitched beside his eye and the left corner of his mouth turned down. Why hadn't she noticed the way he did that? It made him look . . . vulnerable.

He moved away from her to sit on a stool and she felt bereft at the loss of his warmth.

"The boys are good for me. I'm tired, that's all. Guess I was out too late last night."

She studied him curiously. "What happened last night?"

He shrugged dismissively but turned a clock on a pine table so that he could see the face. "Nothing much. Long-standing commitment in Idaho Falls."

The dropping of her stomach was overwhelming. "Hot date?" Her smile had better not look as weak as it felt.

"Something like that." This time he picked the clock up.

Shelly pushed at her hair. He was signaling that he wanted her to leave as politely as he could without saying as much.

"Well, I'd better pick up Philip and get home." Then she remembered that he had driven them out to the farm. "Maybe Jimmy will run me into town so you don't have to come out."

Tom leaped up. "No such thing. The guy who brings you takes you home." The upturn of his lips brought no warmth to his eyes. "Go on over and get Philip ready. I'll throw on the rest of my clothes and join you."

"Are you sure it's no trouble?"

"No, I want to." He paused, turning his head away. "It's on my way."

Shelly waited for him to continue.

"I promised a friend I'd run back into Idaho Falls to-night and I'd better get going. Don't want to be too late or she'll give up on me."

He retraced his steps upstairs and Shelly quietly let herself out into the night.

Tom had a date. She should be glad. This was what she wanted . . . wasn't it?

# Chapter Five

He'd break his neck, she knew he would. "Tom, don't do it."

"Have faith," he shouted, pushing off on Philip's skateboard. "I used to be good at sports."

Wobbling, knees bent, sneakers turned out like a gangling ballerina doing a plié, Tom gathered speed heading for the monstrous ramp that had been unveiled to Shelly a few minutes earlier.

"Cool," Philip yelled, doing what seemed to Shelly like a frenetic version of the twist. "Hit it, Tom. Take off, man."

She didn't believe any of this, not that Philip sounded as though he was speaking a foreign language, or that Tom was apparently enjoying every second of this craziness.

"Duck," Philip ordered. "Grab the deck then take the ramp on a forward slide."

Tom's arms flailed before he managed to grab the top of the skateboard.

"You got it!" Philip rushed closer. "Now cruise in and take the corner curve with your feet forward. Awesome," he yelped.

The next awesome move Tom made landed him in a scrambled heap at the base of the ramp, his feet in the air, his arms crossed protectively over his head. The board shot upward, circled, and crashed harmlessly in a corner.

"Fantastic." Philip went to his knees beside Tom. "You're a natural. Geez, it took me months to get up the guts to try that."

Tom uncovered his face and gave the boy a sheepish smile. He inched carefully to a sitting position and grimaced at Shelly. "What do you think?"

She sat down abruptly on the floor, suddenly aware of weakness in her arms and legs. "Awful," she said. "Suicidal. How did you let Philip talk you into such madness?"

"Aw, Mom. Don't be a drag. I've been skating for years. I know what I'm doing."

"He does—"

Shelly stopped Tom with a withering stare. "Don't tell me you were using anything like this . . . ramp thing, in Cleveland. You'll kill yourself."

Before she could protest further, Philip leaped onto the board, pushed off, swept up the straight section of the ramp and executed a sharp flip at the corner. Shelly held her breath as he descended and shot to a halt a few inches from her.

"See," he said, triumphant. "I know what I'm doing. And I wear a helmet." He knocked on the white plastic contraption on his head. "And pads." Bulbous red bands cushioned his elbows and knees.

She leveled a glare at Tom. "And where are your helmet and pads?"

"He's getting them," Philip said in a rush. "We've ordered them. I wanted him to get some Vans, the high-top suede kind. Boy are they cool. But Tom says they're too expensive."

Shelly met Tom's eyes and hardly stopped herself from laughing. Guilt, like that of a child caught in some deception, turned his very mature face into that of an uncertain boy. He kept quiet and turned his hand over. Blood trickled down the palm.

"Vans?" she asked, her voice muffled from the effort at control.

He fiddled with a tennis shoelace. "Shoes," he said. "Specially made for boarding. I think it's Philip who wants a pair but I'm his excuse for raising the subject."

Philip busied himself around the ramp, smoothing its already silken surface.

"Mmm. Well, we'll just have to see about that," Shelly said, feeling herself sucked into the warmth and familiarity that existed among the three of them. A week had passed since she'd spent the evening out here and she'd had a lot of time to think. One thing she'd decided was that she needed and wanted Tom as part of her life and that it was possible as long as they accepted each other as they were. She was irritated by her curiosity over whoever Tom was seeing in Idaho Falls. He hadn't mentioned the woman and she hadn't asked about her.

"Hey, Mom. You try." Philip hauled her up.

"No way." Tom was instantly on his feet. "This isn't something for women."

Shelly raised her brows. "Says who?" The last thing she wanted was to get on the wretched board.

"Says me," Tom said and picked up the board.

"That's chauvinism," Philip announced, a smug grin plastered on his face. "Isn't that right, Mom?"

Maybe she shouldn't get into this. "Give me the board, Tom."

His mouth became a stubborn line and he made no move to comply.

"Look." She stood where Philip couldn't see her face and made owl eyes at Tom. "I think I'd just like to try keeping my balance. Nothing with the ramp. I'm not up to that."

Tom hesitated, then put down the board. When he tried to help her mount she shook him off. "I'll do better on my own." Promptly she turned into a flailing mass, her feet shooting in one direction, the board in another, before she fell in an ungainly heap.

Laughter did nothing for the pain in her rear or her elbows.

Before she could get up, Tom was kneeling beside her, smoothing back her hair, checking her face closely. "You okay?"

She winced, rubbing her bottom.

"Does that hurt?" Completely unconsciously, Tom rubbed the spot, too.

Shelly was all too aware of the familiarity of his touch but kept a straight face. "I'll survive."

"Of course you will." He held her chin between finger and thumb, looked a little too long into her eyes and kissed her mouth lightly. "But you do agree this is a sport you don't need to take up?"

"Uh—" He'd never kissed her lips before. His mouth was very firm, yet soft. "Okay, I agree. But you've got to agree, too."

"No way."

She'd forgotten Philip and now she turned to him, startled. What was happening to her... with the way she was reacting to Tom. Whatever it was would be dangerous if not squelched.

"What did you say, Philip?" she asked absently.

"Tom's a natural. He says we're going to practice together."

And what could she do about that, about the enthusiasm in her boy's voice, the brilliance in his eyes. Nothing. She didn't want to do anything.

"Don't worry, Shel," Tom said, helping her to her feet. "I'll look after the old bones . . . and our boy's."

*Our boy's.* Shelly felt her composure slipping. With Tom she felt what she never had before, shared interest in Philip. In his self-preoccupation, Ben had missed so much. "As long as you're both careful I suppose—"

"Tom." Cully, sixtyish, grizzled and toughened by a lifetime of hard work, put his head around the door. "Phone call for you over in the shop."

"Who is it. Customer?" Tom reached for his coat.

"Wouldn't say." A man of few words, Cully went as abruptly as he'd come.

"Won't be long," Tom said, giving Philip's shoulder a squeeze. "Take it easy, sport, okay? I'll be back shortly and we'll show your mom some more tricks."

Shelly moaned as the door closed behind him.

The next time she checked her watch twenty minutes had passed, and she frowned. The routine of the farm was becoming familiar, and she found herself worrying about the things associated with it.

Perhaps the call was from the Agriculture Inspection department. They checked the soil and the crop three times a year. An inspector was due out to check Conrads' before the new season's Russet Burbank sets went into the ground. For all Shelly knew he could already have been at the farm and might be contacting Tom with bad news.

As she began to pace, the door opened again and he stepped in, accompanied by a rush of cold air.

"Tom—" She stopped. He had received bad news. His face was very serious. "What is it?"

He buried his hands in his pockets. "Philip, why don't you practice here on your own for a while. Your mom and I need to talk. You understand, don't you?"

"'Course." Shoving off in the direction of the ramp, Philip was too engrossed to pick up the tense vibes in Tom's voice.

By the time Shelly caught up, Tom was striding across fields of gummy black mud. "Hold it. Slow down." Her sneakers sank, ankle-deep, with each step. "Look at your shoes. And mine."

He didn't appear to hear. "I want to get away a bit." They reached a fence and Tom climbed to sit on the top rail. Shelly stood at his knee.

"Is there trouble?" she asked him.

He rested his forearms on his thighs and let his hands dangle between his knees. "I don't know what to do."

Shelly's heart turned. "I knew it. Let me help you."

He gave her a puzzled stare. "What?"

"I'll help you, whatever the problem is."

His laugh grated. "You don't know what you're talking about."

The words stung. "I'm sorry. I didn't mean to intrude but you said you wanted to talk to me."

"That was Ben on the phone."

All her blood rushed downward. It had been months since she'd spoken to Ben. The last time had been fiery and she'd told him not to contact her again. Why had she assumed he'd give up that easily?

"Why did he call you?" she asked in a small voice. "Was he trying to reach me."

"Yes and no. Not the way you mean."

A brisk wind blew, brushing a pale sky free of cloud. Shelly lifted her head and let the coolness whip her cheeks. Despite a few remaining clumps of snow, she could smell spring...newness. Please, don't let Ben spoil the fresh start she was trying to make.

"He asked me to talk to you."

Shelly slid a hand into one of Tom's and he slowly closed his fingers, tightened them. She didn't know what to say, what questions to ask.

"Ben says you won't speak to him."

"No. The last time I did he lost his temper and threatened me. I told him then that it would be better, for a while at least, if we avoided each other." Her heart shifted.

"How do you work things out with someone if you won't even talk?" He looked at their joined hands and stroked the backs of her fingers.

Shelly wanted to drop the subject and go back to where they'd been, with Philip, such a short time ago. As usual, Ben had the ability to smash any peace she made.

"I don't want to work things out with him. I told you I hoped we could be friends again one day, but that there would never be anything more, not after what's happened between us."

"Can it be so bad?" He bowed his head so she couldn't see his face.

"It was," she said simply. "Bad enough to be beyond mending—at least as far as I'm concerned."

"Ben said you'd say that."

Oh, how she resented him. He would play on any sympathies to get what he wanted. "What else did he say?"

Tom jumped down and put an arm on each of her shoulders. "Would you do something for me?"

She fiddled with a button, unwilling to commit to anything.

"Ben asked if I could think of some way to make you agree to communicate with him again. Is there a way, Shelly?"

She shook her head. "You don't know it all, Tom. You don't know how many chances I gave him and how many times he . . . you don't know. I'm only starting to climb out of the mess I was in. Don't ask me to risk starting all over again. I can't, not even for you."

He started back, and she followed slowly, reaching his side as he neared the storage shed.

"Ben's my friend, too," he said, not looking at her. "I had to do what he asked me to do."

"I understand," Shelly said. All joy had leeched out of the afternoon. "And now you've done it."

"Not quite." He turned to her. "He wanted me to tell you something else. Very important, he said." The way his features twisted frightened Shelly.

"Tell me," she said. "Is Ben . . . is he all right?"

Tom smiled, a sad smile she thought. "Look at your face. You're scared for him. But you don't care about him, do you? Not even a tiny bit?" He held up a hand to stop her reply. "Don't worry, he's fine. He asked me to tell you he loves you. He said to say he always will."

IF THERE HAD BEEN any graceful way to turn down the Dillons' dinner invitation Tom would have grabbed it. There hadn't been.

"You sit where you are, Gladys. I'll get the pie." Lucky Williams got up and cleared dinner plates, bustling, overly energetic in her efforts to cover tension in the room.

Lucky and Irving Williams had also been invited for dinner and had managed to keep conversation going despite long silences from the Dillons, Shelly and Tom.

"How are you settling in at the school," Doc asked Shelly. Several glasses of wine had made his ruddy face glow.

"I have good days and bad," she said, pushing her water glass back and forth on the flowered tablecloth. A blue angora sweater, worn with navy slacks, made the most of her feminine shape.

"You shouldn't have expected a smooth road there," Gladys said, puffing up her chest inside the wrap-around apron she hadn't removed. "Bound to be some resistance to new blood."

Tom was grateful Philip had gone up to his room. The atmosphere was becoming more arctic with every second.

"What does that mean, Mom?" Shelly said. "I'm not new blood. I was born and grew up here. And I'm a good teacher so why should there be any resistance?"

"Philip doing all right?" Doc Williams kept a determinedly cheerful expression in place. "Kids take a while to make their way in a new school."

Gladys got up and put the kettle on. "You know what I mean about new blood, don't you, Tom? People around here don't take to new ways."

"I—"

"Now, Gladys," Fred Dillon said before Tom could finish. "Times change and we aren't that backward in Allenville."

"True enough," Lucky agreed. She passed around wedges of berry pie and cups of coffee. "I expect they're very glad to get some fresh ideas up at the school . . . for as long as they'll have you."

Tom glanced from Lucky, who made much of settling in her chair again, to Shelly, who had grown pale and silent. The slant of everyone's remarks had been steadily moving toward this point throughout the evening.

"You aren't still working on that Leonard house, are you?" Doc asked Shelly.

Shelly drank coffee and met Tom's eye.

"Ben called again today," Lucky said. "I told him we were all having dinner together tonight and he said how much he wished he could be with us." Tears showed in her eyes.

"Poor Ben," Gladys said, and Tom noticed that her hands trembled. He wanted to get away, to be anywhere but here.

Doc leaned toward Shelly. "You only have to say the word and he'll come. He said he could come and stay for as long as you like."

Shelly set down her cup. Her face lost all color. "You aren't being fair. Neither is he. And if you're going to keep this up I'm leaving."

"Shelly." Fred Dillon shook his head. "You can't expect us not to want what's best for you."

"You obviously don't know what's best for me. Stop pushing. It's over with Ben and me. How many times do I have to say it."

Gladys turned to Tom. "You're the only one who can reach her. You tell her."

He crossed his arms and bowed his head.

"Most women would jump at the chance of being married to a man like Ben," Gladys said, her voice rising.

Shelly laughed and Tom glanced at her. Hysteria? Or something else? How much hadn't she said about her marriage?

"It's this new generation," Gladys went on. "Time was when a woman was glad to walk in her husband's shadow as long as he looked after her."

Tom breathed in through locked teeth. This was one discussion no one would win.

"There are a lot of ways of interpreting being looked after," Shelly said.

"And what does that mean?" Lucky sat very straight. "Are you saying Ben didn't take care of you?"

Shelly raised her hands and let them drop into her lap.

"What kind of wife walks out on a perfectly good husband just because there are one or two little things he doesn't do exactly the way she wants them?" Lucky continued.

"Damn it." Shelly shot up. "Damn you all. Little things? What do you—"

"Shelly, don't." Tom caught her arm as she tried to pass him and eased her back into her chair. Then he leaned over her and made direct eye contact, willing her not to say things she'd regret later.

"You tell her, Tom," Doc said, puffing up. "She's got to come to her senses before it's too late. You can't expect a man like Ben to stay on his own forever."

Shelly laughed, a hard snicker that turned Tom's stomach. There was more she hadn't told him, maybe a lot more.

"It's time you took a look at yourself as a wife," Gladys said. "Ask yourself if you were so perfect."

"I wasn't perfect," Shelly said very softly.

"You hear that, Tom?" Gladys said. "And you know Ben. Don't you think she's being hard-headed about this?"

Tom looked at Gladys but said nothing. He thought he was going to explode at any second.

"Ben calls every day," Lucky said. "He's desperate about all this. He misses his family. You're denying him that, Shelly." She leveled a finger at her. "If you keep it up those calls are going to stop and you'll be the loser."

"Leave me alone," Shelly said. "I already was a loser—for years."

"Are you saying what happened was all my son's fault?" Lucky shoved her plate away.

"Shh." Fred Dillon patted her hand awkwardly. "Shelly isn't saying that."

"It's Philip I'm most worried about," Doc said. "You're not doing what's best for the boy."

Shelly's back straightened slowly. Tom felt her growing tension . . . and anger. "Philip's fine."

"No, he's not," Gladys said. "A boy needs a father as well as a mother. And he needs a routine where his mother's at home."

"Most women in this country work outside the home," Shelly said. "And I am here for him when he needs me. And I'm probably a better mother because I'm not stuck at home all day."

"You make being an ordinary housewife sound like a penance." Gladys's eyes glittered. "It's been good enough for me and for a lot of other women."

"I'm not putting down being a housewife," Shelly said. "I think it's wonderful and admirable and thank goodness there are women who enjoy it. But that doesn't mean it's right for me."

"It's what's acceptable." Gladys drummed the table now.

"Says who?" Shelly trembled visibly.

"You aren't bringing Philip up properly," Lucky announced. "You're being selfish and depriving your child of the solid home life he could have and deserves. Come to your senses, girl." Bright spots of color stood out on her strongly boned face.

Shelly got up again, slowly this time, and Tom made no attempt to stop her. "How dare you say I'm not a good mother. If there are selfish people around here, it's all of you. You don't want the nice order of your lives interrupted. If you really cared about us you'd try to help me do the best I can."

Doc thumped the table. "That's enough. You're going to do as you're told."

Tom gritted his teeth. Ugly scenes were outside his experience, and he felt trapped. Doc had definitely drunk too much.

"My son has apologized for anything he may have done wrong," he continued.

"*May* have done wrong?" Shelly backed away.

"He calls every day, and tomorrow I expect you to have the decency to talk to him. I told him you'd be at our house waiting to hear at about four. That gives you time to get there after school."

Tom couldn't believe what he was hearing. Every nerve in his body jumped.

"After school tomorrow," Shelly said, sounding deadly calm, "I'll be moving into my new home ... with my son."

"You'll be at our house," Doc said.

"I'm going upstairs to be with Philip now."

"Tom, talk to her." Gladys reached a hand toward him. "Tell her this is the right thing to do, to go back to Ben and forget all this silliness."

He shook his head. "It has to be her decision." Didn't they know they were driving her away from any shred of hope for reconciliation?

"No, it doesn't." Gladys shouted, and Tom recoiled. "You tell her. You know it would be best for everyone."

"Yes, Tom. Talk some sense into her," Lucky said.

He closed his eyes an instant. White heat pumped behind his lids.

"Tom—"

"Stop it." He stumbled to his feet, seeing Shelly's pale face distorted through the glare of his confusion. "Stop it, all of you."

"Tom," Fred said. "You do agree that Shelly should do what we're suggesting and give Ben another chance, don't you?"

That was it. All he could take. He strode to the door and threw it open. Shelly's little sob was something he only half heard. He was going to explode. "I don't know what I think, and I'm sick of this."

The door slammed deafeningly behind him.

# Chapter Six

Shelly's Jeep was parked by the fence. A hint of light showed at the living room window and through the glass inserts in the front door. Tom figured she must be in the kitchen.

He looked at the upstairs windows. Another light shone in the one to the left, in the room that was to be Philip's. Shelly's, with its tiny adjoining bathroom, was at the back of the house.

The light went out in Philip's room. Tom peered at his watch. Ten-thirty. If he'd intended to come by at all it should have been hours ago when Shelly was moving into the house, not when she'd be exhausted and thinking of getting some sleep.

He was a heel. Only a heel would walk out the way he had yesterday at dinner and then stay away. She had really needed him when she was beset by everyone...only he hadn't trusted himself with what he would say.

There was something he had to do and he might as well get it over with.

He climbed from the pickup, opened the gate and walked to the front door. If she told him to get lost he wouldn't blame her.

She didn't answer his ring.

Tom bent to look into the hall, shadowy and distorted through rough-cut bronze glass. The kitchen door was open, and dimly he heard music. He rang the bell again, waited, then set off around the side of the house.

At the kitchen windows he stopped and leaned a shoulder against the wall. Shelly sat on an unrolled sleeping bag in front of the stove, a headset over her ears. She held the cassette player in her hands. A radio, plugged into a socket behind her, must be responsible for the music he could hear. A fire glowed inside the stove sending shadows over her pensive face. She looked . . . lost.

"Geez, Shel," he muttered. "Still hardheaded." She wore pink sweats and her hair was pulled back in a rubber band.

The only possessions in sight were an assortment of dishes on a counter and several cardboard boxes. She'd said she intended to move today and had done it, regardless of the decorating not being completely finished or the fact that she evidently didn't have furniture.

If he tapped the window she'd probably be frightened, but he wasn't going away until they'd spoken.

He rapped with a knuckle and saw her jump. Quickly he rapped again. "Shel," he shouted and moved in front of the undraped sliding door.

The apprehension faded from her eyes. She pulled off the headset and got up to open the door. "What is it?" Nothing friendly had taken the place of her anxiety.

"Are you going to make this tough on me?"

Shelly rubbed her arms. She wore no makeup and her pale face showed fatigue. "I asked what you wanted, that's all."

He had no right to be irritated but he was smarting at the thought of his behavior yesterday and he'd grasp anything to divert himself from having to deal with the guilt. "Well," he said, leaning on the jamb, "I heard you're new in the area and I wondered if you might need brushes."

"Brushes?" She frowned.

"Oh, forget it. Let me in, will you?" He pushed past without waiting for her to agree.

"Well, hello. Why don't you come in?" She stayed where she was.

"This is hard enough without your sarcasm." He felt—mean, and helpless to do anything about it.

"I'm not making anything hard for you. I didn't ask you to come here. If you're uncomfortable, why don't you leave?"

He took a deep breath and slid his hat off slowly. "Let's not do this anymore."

"Fine with me. I'm beginning to feel I don't make any decisions in my life, anyway. I just stand around like a target while everyone takes pot shots at me."

There was no irritation left in him, no fight, only self-disgust. "I'm sorry, Shel. That's what I came to say. I didn't help you out yesterday and I should have."

She rubbed a hand over her face and stared out into the darkness. "They shouldn't have put you on the spot. And I should have done something to stop them from pushing you the way they did. I felt so trapped, so helpless. I couldn't seem to say or do anything right."

"And I didn't help. Damn, I wish I hadn't stormed out like that, like an angry kid . . . not when you needed me."

"Oh, Tom." She looked at him and tears shone in her eyes. "Here you are again, picking up my pieces. And you're telling me you're sorry you haven't done more. How did I get so lucky as to have a friend like you? Most people would have told me to get lost years ago." She laughed. "The moral of all this is—don't pick up magazines that you didn't drop."

He laughed, too. "No way. Always pick 'em up. You may get as lucky as I did." Careful, he'd better watch what he said. "If I hadn't been there that day I'd probably never have gotten close to you and Ben, and I don't even like to think about that."

She closed the door and held onto the handle. "Ben isn't a bad man. You don't think I'm trying to say that, do you?"

"Come here, you," he said, and she did so, slowly, pushing back escaped wisps of her heavy blond hair. When she got close she leaned on him and his heart seemed to stop. If she and Ben really were through, couldn't there be a chance for . . . ? But they were like brother and sister. That pattern had been set the day Shelly and Ben married. Some things couldn't be changed. If she had ever shown a hint of interest in him it would be different, but she hadn't.

Shelly put her arms around him and rested her face against his neck and the dangerous warmth began, yet he couldn't do anything but hold her.

"Thanks for coming, Tom. I felt so low."

At least he could do that much for her, make her feel accepted. "What did your folks and Ben's say last night about the way I walked out?"

"That I was upsetting everyone," Shelly said, bitterness weighting the words. "Mom said you were hurt because of what I've done to Ben. They've never asked what he did to me."

And neither had Tom. Not really. He closed his eyes and stroked the back of her neck. Muscles in his thighs turned rock hard with the effort of holding himself a few inches from her.

"Do you want to tell me about it?"

Her hands tightened, and she grasped his jacket. "I don't want you to think badly of Ben. He's only human, and in some ways not a very strong man."

Tom frowned. "He always seemed strong to me."

Shelly looked up at him. "Can you even imagine the kind of hero worship a pro football player gets exposed to? Or what it's like to have women throwing themselves at you?"

He swallowed distaste, afraid he knew what was coming. "Ben's not the kind to do more than look. Any man does that much."

"Yeah, I know how the saying goes—you may be on a diet but that doesn't mean you can't look at the menu. I never expected him to be an angel."

Tom put Shelly from him but kept his hands on her shoulders. "Ben wouldn't be unfaithful to you."

Her eyes fixed, then slid away. "He was. More than once. And I forgave him more than once, but in the end I couldn't take it anymore."

His embarrassment shook him. Ben was as close to a brother, a kindred male spirit, as he'd ever come to having.

"You don't believe me." Shelly turned from his hands and sat on the sleeping bag again. "I wasn't going to tell you because I didn't think you would. And I can't say anything to his folks or mine because they'd be crushed. So I guess it's back to going it alone. I will make it. And I will be happy again here. In time everything's going to be okay."

He took off his coat and glanced around the kitchen. No kettle was in sight but there was a saucepan and he filled it with water and put it on to boil. Next he rummaged in a box of food and found coffee.

"What are you doing?" Shelly sounded dispirited.

"Making us the coffee we both need."

"You don't have to take care of me."

"Yes I do. I want to. And I do believe what you said. Not because I would have expected it of Ben but because you're honest."

The thoughts and sensations hurt him. Somehow he had to make sure Shelly got over what had happened.

"Sit here." She patted the sleeping bag and he dropped down beside her. "How do you like the decor? Camp, huh?" She laughed but the sound was humorless.

"Give it a week or so and this place will be great. It's a solid house. Have you looked for furniture?"

She shook her head. "Dad insisted I take my old bed for Philip. I sold everything I had in Cleveland apart from some basics."

"It doesn't matter. We'll take the pickup into Idaho Falls and get what we can there, not that you'll be able to do everything in one trip, but we can catalogue order some stuff, too." If he kept busy and didn't think too much the disappointment wouldn't have a chance to fester.

A little noise made him look at Shelly sharply. Her head was bent forward.

"Shel? Oh, please don't cry. I'm so sorry it turned out like this with Ben. Try to forgive him again even if you can't get back together."

"That's not it." Her voice was muffled. "You make me cry, Tom. You're so good to me."

He winced and blew into a fist. If only she knew. He'd have to be even more cautious now. As fragile as she was, any suggestion that his motives for being there for her were other than those of a friend could blow her completely apart.

"Listen. I just want what's best for you, okay? I'll be whatever you want me to be. Call and I'll come." He was sealing himself in and he was helpless to change the pattern.

"Hold my hand," she said.

He threaded his fingers through hers. "You're going to be okay."

"I know. I'm so lucky. Do you know your mom and Mary stopped by earlier. They said what you did, that they'd do anything they could to help me."

"I've got a great family." That was true and he'd better not allow himself any self-pity because he was lumped together with them as far as Shelly was concerned. He had another thought. "You need to get out some."

"Around here? I don't think so. When I came back I knew I was settling into the life of the single parent in a small community, and I'm up for that."

"There're things to do in Allenville. Come to the dance out at the Elks on Saturday. It isn't any great shakes but it's a good time with nice people." What had made him say that? Did he have a masochistic streak?

Shelly brought her face closer and her eyes glistened. "I don't know why you bother with me. You really care, don't you?"

He nodded.

"You genuinely want to take an old divorced lady to a dance?"

He nodded again. He wanted more than anything to have an opportunity to be close to her.

"Then, thank you." She inclined her head formally. "I accept. At least no one can make anything out of *you* taking me somewhere. Not even my folks."

He kept an impassive expression in place. "That's right." If only she knew what people were already saying. But he'd invited her now, and he'd have to deal with any sly remarks that came his way afterward.

"What about the woman you're seeing?"

"What?" He leaned toward her, then remembered. "Oh, her. That's nothing serious."

An odd expression crossed Shelly's face, a kind of clearing. Had she disliked the thought of a woman in his life. He flexed his spine and started to move as steam curled up from the pot on the stove. She wasn't the jealous type.

She stopped him from getting up. "Tom—" her thumbs rubbed hard at the tendons in the back of his hands "—you always come through for me. One day I'll find a way to pay you back."

"There's nothing to pay me—"

"No. Please let me say this and don't be embarrassed if I sound mushy. I love you, Tom, really love you. There's never going to be anyone else like you in my life."

"Me, too."

He looked into her eyes, reading. Trust was what she meant. She trusted him, lucky stiff that he was. He bobbed to his feet and headed for the range. What he'd most like to do was get outside and run, before he choked on his own frustration.

PHILIP SCRAPED the last of his ice cream from his bowl and licked the spoon both front and back.

Tom smiled at Shelly and raised an eyebrow. "Maybe you can eat the spoon, too, Philip," he said. "I guess we didn't feed you enough."

They sat at the maple table Shelly had bought when Tom took her into Idaho Falls earlier in the week. The matching chairs had ladder backs and tied-on seat covers of dark blue corduroy. She loved them. That trip had been a good one. They'd found a bed for her and a dresser and a little over-stuffed flowered chair with no arms, which looked as if a designer had matched it to the pink-and-gray-check bed-spread she'd bought. Apart from a bookshelf and televi-sion set, the living room was empty but she felt no urgency to have everything done at once.

"Do I have to go to Grandma and Grandpa Williams's tonight?" Philip said, continuing to clean his glittering spoon. "Can't I stay here? I'm old enough."

This was the first time Philip had shown any reluctance to spend time with Ben's folks. Shelly glanced at Tom. "They're looking forward to having you, and we won't be late." She'd had many reservations since accepting Tom's invitation to the town dance, but tonight she was excited at the prospect of getting out.

"It's not that we don't think you're old enough to stay alone, sport," Tom said. "But humor us this time, huh? Make us feel it's okay to go out and that we don't have to worry about you."

Tom had eaten with them several times this week. Shelly watched him with Philip and thought, not for the first time, that at a quick glance they could be related. *We,* Tom had said. He was taking on more and more responsibility around here, and she couldn't help feeling a little guilty about that, even though she enjoyed the security.

"I'd better get changed," she said, checking her watch. "Mary said the women wear dresses but not too fancy." Tom's sister and husband were coming with them.

"And we'd better do the dishes," Tom told Philip who grunted and slid slowly from his chair.

Tom ruffled the boy's hair and smiled at him. At first Shelly had wondered if Philip would mind her going out on what sounded almost like a date. She needn't have worried. He'd said it was a neat idea and gone back to what he was doing. But why would he think much about it, particularly when the man was Tom.

Twenty minutes later Shelly was back in the kitchen, purse in hand. She'd opted for a mauve woolen dress with a cross-over bodice and softly flared skirt. It wasn't exactly small town, but nothing she owned apart from her casual clothes was. The dress had been expensive and so were the matching, very high-heeled shoes and narrow leather belt.

Tom turned from the sink and didn't seem to notice soapsuds seeping down his forearms. He stared until Shelly felt awkward. "Is this all wrong? Should I change? I wasn't sure what to wear." She started backing up.

He shook his head sharply and wiped at his arms. "No way do you change. You caught me off guard, that's all. Remember, you're still my childhood pal, only you turned into a swan on me. I'll have to fight off the guys tonight."

She smiled, letting out a sigh. "No sweat. The way you look, I'll be the one fighting off the competition."

They both laughed, but she eyed Tom as he rolled down the sleeves of his blue-and-green striped shirt. He wore it with dark gray slacks, and the square toes of his black boots glistened. She'd already seen enough of his physique without clothes to know how well built he was. Clothes that accentuated every long lean muscle only added an element of erotic mystery and guaranteed to make every female in sight want to touch.

Shelly busied herself making sure she had what she needed in her purse. What was she thinking about? Erotic mystery? Good grief, she must be turning into a frustrated divorcée.

The Williamses lived on the far side of town from Tom and Shelly. Their house was a sprawling ranch-style structure on a spread large enough to accommodate the medical center Doc was talking about building.

As usual, the door was unlocked and Shelly led the way into the house. "Lucky?" she called. "Doc?" How could so much be the same when so much had been irrevocably changed?

Ben's parents appeared in the entrance to their big comfortable sitting room. "Come in, come in," Doc said with a hearty warmth not reflected in his eyes. "Make some coffee, Lucky. Sit down, the pair of you, and I'll break out the brandy. You did say you were having dinner before you came? Philip, why don't you go into the den and see what's on television. You don't want to hang around with a bunch of old fogies. Sit down, Shelly, you, too, Tom."

When Doc paused for breath Shelly realized her mouth was open. Lucky rushed from the room and Philip followed more slowly, giving her one of his "what's up" looks. She and Tom stood where they were.

"Cold out there, I bet," Doc said. "Good night to stay home by the fire. Courvoisier okay with you, Tom?"

"Um—"

"Best, I always say. You won't want more than a drop, Shelly. I know you never were much of a drinker. But it'll warm you up." And he went to the liquor cabinet in a lighted wall unit and clattered around among glasses and bottles.

Tom turned to Shelly, raising his brows. She shook her head. "Er, Doc. Tom and I are meeting Jimmy and Mary in half an hour so we'd better take a rain check on the brandy, and the coffee. Thanks, though. We'll take you up on it another time."

"Not at all," Doc said, turning with a large brandy bubble in each hand. Each one held enough to put an average man to sleep. "Lucky'll be right in. You've got plenty of time."

On cue, Lucky hustled into the room with a tray and set it on a table near the fire. The room was comfortable and expensively furnished. Matching sofas and a love seat of supple brown leather made an intimate conversation area.

Shelly felt helpless but exasperated. Doc and Lucky were trying to delay them, and their tactics weren't even subtle. "Is it inconvenient for Philip to be here this evening?" she asked, more shortly than she intended. "I expect Tom's mother or mine—"

"Not at all." Doc rocked back on his heels and laughed. "Why would you think that? Philip's our grandson and our home is his, just as it is yours."

She swallowed, out of her depth.

"Doc," Tom said evenly, "we really appreciate the offer of coffee and so on, but we do have people waiting for us and we'd better go."

The Williamses looked at each other and Doc took a swallow from one of the glasses he held. He appeared to forget he still stood with one in each hand.

"We wanted to talk to you about this," Lucky said, clasping her hands tightly in front of her. "Now promise me you won't get angry, Shelly... or you, Tom."

"We aren't angry," he said in a tone that suggested he could get angry very quickly.

"Good, good." Doc glanced at his hands and put down the glasses. "Look, why don't you forget about the dance tonight. I could call the Elks and have someone tell Mary you can't make it."

Shelly narrowed her eyes, trying to read the man's expression. "Why would we do that?"

"Well," Lucky said, and passed her tongue over her lips. "Don't you think it might be a better idea to stay here this evening. I mean, perhaps it isn't a good idea for you to be, er, seen at a dance...."

Now Shelly understood completely. She sighed. "This is going to have to stop, you know."

"Now what do you mean by that?" Doc blustered.

"You're worried about what people will think. You still believe you can hide what's happened between Ben and me but you can't. I've already told anyone who asked that we're divorced."

"And I've told them it probably isn't for good," Lucky said sharply. "You wait and see. Ben will—"

"No, Lucky." Doc cut her off. "Enough said for now. I can see we aren't going to change her mind. I'm surprised at you though, Tom. I'd have thought you'd be more careful of your reputation."

The comment startled Shelly. "Tom's reputation? Why should his reputation be in jeopardy? There isn't a soul in this town who doesn't know Tom and I...and Ben have looked out for one another most of our lives, so what are you suggesting?"

"Leave it," Tom said. "Don't take any notice, Shel. And don't you worry, Doc, or you, Mrs. Williams. I'll take good care of her and make sure there isn't any talk. She needs to get out for once. And now, if you'll excuse us, we have to go. We won't be late picking Philip up."

Shelly followed him from the house without looking back.

They drove through town in silence and turned north for the last two miles to the club.

"Why would they say something like that?" Shelly asked. "That you should worry about your reputation if you're seen out with me? That's sick."

"Yeah," Tom said, staring straight ahead, a black straight-brimmed Stetson tilted forward to shade his eyes. "Sick."

SHELLY LIFTED THE HAIR from the back of her neck and smiled at him. Tom smiled back. Her cheeks were pink and damp little curls had formed around her face. They'd danced the first three numbers since they'd arrived without stopping.

"I guess you approve of the music," Mary said loudly when they returned to the table. A disc jockey with equipment resembling an airplane cockpit was providing the entertainment.

"I love it." Shelly slid to the edge of her seat and stretched out her legs. Long legs, Tom couldn't help noticing, shapely and . . . very narrow at the ankle.

"Tom?"

He glanced up into Cathy O'Leary's flushed face. "Hello, Cathy. How are you? You remember Shelly, don't you?"

"Yes," Cathy said, and Tom saw her smile tighten. "How long are you going to be in Allenville?"

Shelly sat straighter and crossed her legs, hitching her skirt a little higher to reveal the gentle curve at the back of her knee. As Tom moved his attention from the spot, he met Jimmy's eyes. A muscle jerked in his brother-in-law's jaw.

"I don't have any plans to move on," Shelly was saying to Cathy who was as diminutive as ever. She wore her reddish hair pulled into a knot that made the best of well-defined features.

"It's true what they say, then...about you leaving Ben?"

Tom shifted but stopped himself from interfering. These were the battles Shelly must learn to fight for herself.

"Ben and I are divorced," she said. "I assumed everyone in town knew I took Mrs. Osborne's job at the school. That should make it pretty clear that I intend to stay here."

"Hmm. I suppose so. We only wondered, that's all. Allenville's a bit tame after the bright life, isn't it?"

"This is my home. I like it here." The pink that suited her so well had faded from Shelly's face.

"You don't say. I expect you're careful what you tell the children, though?"

Shelly leaned forward. "I don't think I follow you."

Cathy inclined her head. "As a librarian I'm very conscious of how impressionable the young are. They can be influenced by what they read and hear and I'm sure the parents wouldn't want any flighty ideas put into the children's heads.''

He couldn't believe what he was hearing. Quiet Cathy rarely expressed an original idea and she invariably chose to stay on the fence on any touchy issue. Could her bravery be because of him? He ran a hand over his hair. It wasn't his fault if she had a thing for him, but if it was going to make her a threat to Shelly's peace of mind he'd better do something about it.

"How about a dance, Cathy?" he said, and got up to steer her away before he had to look at any of the others.

On the floor she gazed up at him with slightly parted lips and a beatific expression that made him squirm, but he kept his own smile in place and talked about inconsequential things. When the music finished, he gritted his teeth and held her elbow until the next piece started, when he danced with her again. By the time he escorted her back to her seat—at a table where Beattie and her pudgy, short-sighted husband, Chester, sat—Cathy was giggling and Tom managed to slip away while Beattie positioned herself for interrogation.

When he returned to Shelly, she was alone. Jimmy and Mary were dancing. "May I have this dance, ma'am?" He bowed to Shelly who promptly got up and held the hand he offered.

The entire floor of the room was wooden with tables placed in precise rows on three sides. Dusty red velvet drapes were looped back to the wings of the stage at one end. The disk jockey worked there, crooning out his unintelligibly suggestive monologue.

A slow beat pulsed, the base notes heavy. Tom hesitated then put one hand at Shelly's waist while he held her hand with the other, feeling stiff and formal. Dancing had always been a pastime he loved although he'd had little

enough opportunity for practice. The skill he knew he had
was natural.

Shelly moved effortlessly, her supple muscles undulating
gently with each sway of her hips. Tom wanted to pull her
near and close his eyes. Her dress was soft and clung wherever it touched. She did close her eyes and he let out a long
breath. He guided her carefully but the moves she made
were all hers. He'd never been more intensely aware of what
total femininity meant, or of what it could do to his flesh.

She opened her eyes but they didn't quite focus and he
knew she was completely involved in the music, the rhythm.
Without thinking he slid his hand to the small of her back
and just as naturally, she stepped toward him until they
pressed close. He crossed his arms behind her and she locked
her wrists around his neck.

He couldn't take it, if she went away again. God, what
was happening to him?

"Thanks for bringing me, Tom." Her lips brushed his ear,
and he blessed the lowered lights that hid the rigid contrac-
tion in his face.

"Thanks for coming." Where could they go from here?
How could he face time after time of being with her, and
maintain the lie he was living?

She leaned back and her hair swung away. "I haven't felt
this good in so long. And it's all because of you. You always seem to know what I need."

Her breasts pressed him softly through her clinging dress
and his thin shirt. The shaded vale there was something he
saw in his mind, and the fullness. What he also saw with his
senses was all of her, pale, smooth, molded to him as she
was now, pliant, inviting....

"Tom? Are you tired?"

He stared. "No, of course not. Are you?"

"No. But you looked . . . funny. And I know you have to be up so early every morning."

"I'm not tired. This is good for me, too. I don't get out enough." He sounded normal, didn't he?

Clapping startled him and he took a step away from her, but he didn't want to move away, not ever.

"My turn, brother." Mary grabbed him, laughing as the music speeded and he looked back in time to see Jimmy whirling Shelly away. Their eyes met for an instant and she was gone, swallowed in the gyrating crowd.

"Okay," Mary said making no attempt to dance. "I need some fresh air and I think you do, too."

He didn't argue as she threaded an arm through his and walked him firmly out to the parking lot.

"It's cold out here," he complained when she settled against a truck. "I'd better get our coats."

"No need. This won't take long."

"Oh. Do I hear a lecture coming? What have I done this time?"

Mary tilted her chin up to a moonless sky. "Nothing yet, but something tells me it's only a matter of time."

"Are you going to explain that before we both freeze?" Apprehension gnawed at him. He thought he knew what she was going to say. Mary had always been able to figure him out.

"I'll make it short, Tom. Only a fool or a blind person wouldn't have noticed what just happened in there. I don't think Shelly's caught on yet, but I doubt if it will take her long unless you back off."

He waited while she looked at him.

"You love her. And I don't mean just as a friend. You're *in love* with her."

Tom clasped his hands behind his neck and looked at his
boots. "I'm not going to deny it. Not to you. But I don't
have a chance with her, we both know that."

"Do we? You may be right but that's not the point for the
moment. She's trying to settle in and make a new life for
herself here. Complications, like having the whole town talk
about the two of you, are something she doesn't need."

"You don't think it's right for me to—"

"Wrong, Tom. Oh, you are so wrong. I've never thought
anything was more right, or that anything was more unfair
than the way things worked out. What I do think is that
you'd better be very, very careful how you proceed."

He frowned at her. "I'm not going to proceed, Mary. You
know I can't. Shelly doesn't feel the way I do. She never
did."

She shrugged. "That's something I can't second-guess.
What I can is what might happen to her character around
here if a scandal starts."

"I don't know what you're asking. I've said I don't intend to pursue her."

"Sure you don't intend to. But you're human. And I see
troubles ahead, that's all I wanted to warn you about."

THE CLOCK IN THE PICKUP showed eleven when Tom turned
in at the Williamses' gates.

"I didn't realize how late it had gotten," Shelly said. She
felt wonderful, more relaxed than she remembered feeling
in so long. "Philip's probably fallen asleep."

"We'll get him home quickly," Tom said. He sounded
distant and had been quiet for the last hour. Regardless of
what he said, she was sure he was tired.

"Tomorrow's Sunday," she said. "Don't forget we told
Philip he could come out to your farm and start learning to
plant. It's only a week or so away now, isn't it?"

"Yeah." He switched off the engine. "Would it be easier on you if I went in and got him? You could stay here and I'd tell them you're in a hurry to get home."

"Oh, no. You don't have to do that for me." She hopped out, folding her gray cashmere coat tightly about her.

Tom came to her side and put an arm around her shoulders. "This has been so special, Shelly."

He held her tightly. "It's been special for me, too." She tried to see his face, but the brim of his hat hid everything but the shaded angles of his jaw and the outline of his wide mouth, and they betrayed nothing.

"I guess we should get Philip."

"Yes." She covered his hand on her shoulder. Could he be unhappy, needy of her company but unable to ask? Or was it just the constant pressure he lived with that made him sound tense.

They stood there, and Shelly sensed he didn't want to end the evening.

The front door, swinging open, broke the silence and Tom started forward. He kept his arm around her.

"There you are." Doc's big body was silhouetted against the light. "We were about ready to send out a search party."

"Hi," Shelly said cheerfully, still conscious of Tom's silent presence. "I'd forgotten how town dances could hop around here. It's been a long time."

Doc chuckled and stood aside to make room for someone to come from behind him.

"Next month the three of us should go together. It'll be like old times." Ben Williams ducked his head as he stepped outside.

# Chapter Seven

Shelly stumbled, and Tom shifted his arm to her waist. He felt . . . disembodied. The man moving toward them was his best friend, yet he was a stranger. How had that happened?

A few paces away Ben stopped. His face was indistinct, but Tom saw the uncertainty in his eyes, the hesitancy of his smile. Ben looked only at Shelly.

"Come on in, all of you," Doc boomed from the doorway. "It's cold out here, and I don't need any more patients."

"Hi, Shelly," Ben said, his deep, slightly rough voice so familiar to Tom.

Shelly stirred at his side and he dropped his arm. "Hello," she said, then, "Excuse me. I'd better go and wake Philip. We need to be getting home."

Tom let out the breath he'd been holding. He had to say something to Ben, but what?

"How're you doing, Tom?" Ben watched Shelly go into the house. "It's been a long time. Too long."

"I'm good," Tom said automatically. "How about you?" This felt insane, this polite exchange.

"Hey, buddy. Damn, but it really is good to see you."

Ben, always the one to wade in and do what his emotions told him, covered the space between them and threw his immense arms around Tom.

Tom hesitated only an instant before he returned the hug, slapping Ben's back the way he'd done so many times before when they met after a separation. Over Ben's shoulder Tom saw Doc blend back inside the house, and the poignancy of it all rushed in. They shared so much history. The eroding away of the special bond hurt.

"Did you talk to Shelly?" Ben released him and glanced around.

"Yes."

"What did she say? D'you think she's ready to ease up on me?"

It was hard to hold himself apart, to remember what he now knew about Ben. What came naturally was to fall back into the easy closeness they'd known. "She hasn't been real keen to talk about what went on between the two of you." That much was true.

"No. She wouldn't be. But that doesn't matter now. I know she'll forget any disagreements we had in time. But, hell, I didn't expect her to go this far, or for it to take this long. I never thought she'd go through with a divorce."

"Yeah . . . no." Tom shifted his weight to one foot. Ben was as supremely confident as ever. That Shelly might mention his infidelity had never crossed his mind.

"I've got to have some time with her." Ben raised his face to the night sky where a silver-blue moon slipped from the luminous rim of a cloud. "And this is the place, Tom. This is where our roots are and where we're bound to come back when we're hurting. This is a place to heal in. I only arrived an hour ago and already I feel as if I'd never left."

Tom swallowed. Shelly appeared with Philip. What would she want him to do . . . what should he do? He knew what he wanted himself; to put them into the pickup and drive away, leaving Ben where he was. Much as Tom cared for his friend he couldn't brush off the anger he felt simmering and beginning to force itself into the open.

"Philip!" Ben's strident voice bellowed and he swept the boy off his feet. "There's my kid. I've missed you, son."

Tom pushed his fists into his jacket pockets. He felt Shelly's eyes upon him but kept his own gaze on Ben.

"Here you go, Ben." Lucky Williams came from the house, Doc a step behind, and handed her son some keys. "The Mercedes is yours for as long as you need it. Your father will take me any place I need to go."

"What are you doing here, Dad?"

Philip's sleep-fuzzed voice produced stillness. A wind had picked up, and tree limbs swished and tapped at the side of the house. Wood smoke scented the air.

"Coming to see you and your mom," Ben said after far too long. "And now I'm going to drive you home in your grandmother's car. You need to get to sleep while your mom and I have a chat. We'll talk tomorrow, Phil."

"I'll take Shelly home," Tom said and shut his mouth firmly. He yanked his hands from his pockets and had the sensation that he was polarized, waiting for a decisive current.

"No need," Ben announced. "Thanks for looking after my little family while I wasn't around to do it, but I'm here now. I need some time alone with them."

He did look at Shelly now. She seemed small, standing there, holding Philip's hand. But she said nothing, gave Tom no hint of whether she wanted him to intervene further. He wouldn't where he had no right—or where he wasn't wanted.

Lucky Williams's gray Mercedes sedan was parked to the right of the door. Ben walked toward it, ushering Shelly and

Philip with him as he went. They climbed in quietly, and the heavy door slammed dully behind them. Ben went around the other side. "See you, Tom," he called through the window, and the car swept from the driveway.

"Will you come in for something before you go?"

Tom started and waved dismissively at Doc. "No."

The pickup, when he climbed inside, was still slightly warm and held Shelly's subtle scent. He started the engine and drove to the road. Ben wasn't far ahead, and the red taillights of the Mercedes shone out like guiding beacons... or a warning to stay away.

The Williamses were happy tonight. So would the Dillons be. Ben was taking his family home. *Thank you for looking out for my little family.* Tom screwed up his eyes against a pain he knew wasn't physical.

He'd have to pass Shelly's house and either see them all going in or the car parked. When he did pass it was only seconds after Ben had pulled in.

Ben wanted to talk to Shelly alone. That meant he wanted to persuade her back into... If she forgave him, wouldn't it be natural for him to stay the night?

Sweat broke out on Tom's brow, along his upper lip. His shirt stuck to his back inside his warm coat. Then, as fast as the sweating started, the dampness turned cold on his skin. His teeth chattered until he clamped them together.

Where would Ben sleep?

Tom floored the accelerator, fishtailing the rear of the pickup. The truck shot forward, gathering speed until fences were a converging streak in the steel night.

"Damn you, Ben." Rage clamped Tom's fingers on the steering wheel like naked flesh on ice. He wouldn't be around the next time Shelly called, whether it was to say she'd decided to send Ben packing, or to tell Tom she would be resuming her marriage. They couldn't have anything together. When would he get that through his skull?

"God!" His headlights picked up the glittering eyes of a big animal and he slammed on the brakes. He never saw what it was he'd almost hit. The pickup slewed from the road and skidded against fifty feet of fence posts before grinding to a stop.

Tom sat, heart thudding, until his arms and legs decided to move again. Slowly, a persistent pounding behind his eyes, he turned the wheel and sent up a grudging little prayer of thanks that the vehicle wouldn't need more than some body work.

He was going home and staying there. He'd spent his last hours of hoping for what he could never have.

"I THINK HE LIKED the present, don't you?" Ben prowled around the kitchen while he spoke, touching, picking up, examining.

Shelly huddled in a corner near the sink, her arms tightly folded about her. At his father's insistence, Philip had gone silently to bed.

"Shelly?" He glanced at her sharply. "The skateboard was a good idea, huh?"

Philip had done no more than thank Ben politely for the expensive board. "Yes," she managed. "It's the kind he's been saving for."

Ben smirked. "I know. Dad told me."

"Oh." She bit back the temptation to say that if he had come up with an original idea for a gift for Philip it would have been a first.

"Nice little house."

"Thank you."

"Mom and Dad said you're buying it."

"Yes."

"Hmm. Do you have anything to drink in the place." His dark brown eyes fixed on her. "I'm jumpy, but I guess you can understand that, honey."

She couldn't suppress a shiver. Honey was the old familiar term of endearment that used to make her feel safe and fearless.

"Is it still bourbon?"

"Does it rain on the plain in Spain?" He laughed and her heart turned, just a little. "You remember what I like."

"I remember." She found the bottle in a cupboard above the range and went to the refrigerator for ice. She'd left Tom standing in the Williamses' driveway. Why had she done that? She must get to him, talk to him.

"I don't know exactly what to say, Shelly. On the plane and then driving from Idaho Falls I was so sure I'd know all the right things, the words you'd want to hear."

She gave him his drink and he sat at the kitchen table. Shelly retreated behind the counter as if it could keep her safe.

"I've missed you." He pushed the glass back and forth on the table.

She couldn't seem to think of anything to say. He hadn't changed. His dark hair was as thick as ever, curling over the polo neck of a bulky tan sweater. She tried to study him dispassionately. Ben had always been big and solid, even as a boy. Now, as a man who dedicated much of his life to toning and caring for his body, he was physically impressive. His shoulders and chest, incredibly powerful, appeared massive in the sweater and unzipped heavy green parka. His jeans strained over his thighs and calves. His hands alone were at odds with the almost overwhelming proportions of the rest of him. Big, they were nevertheless long-fingered, well-kept and graceful. Shelly's eyes fixed on the wedding band he wore. She looked away quickly. He hadn't worn the ring since shortly after their wedding. Dangerous in active sports, he'd said, and she'd never argued the point.

"I came because I had to," Ben said and when she raised her face he was staring at her. "I couldn't stay away any longer."

"There's no point in this," she said quietly, hating the tension she felt, the feeling that a trap could be closing on her again. "We said it all a long time ago. Let go, Ben."

"I don't want to." He had such dark eyes, intense, an asset many women hadn't failed to notice. And equally dark brows arched away from the straight bridge of his nose. His best feature was his mouth. Wide and full, it tilted sharply upward at the corners and formed deep dimples in his cheeks when he smiled. Ben was a perfect man to look at, and in many ways he was a good man, but he hadn't been a good husband.

"What will it take to convince you to at least consider trying to start over?"

It was beginning again, the constant pounding and niggling he'd subjected her to once she'd managed to convince him she intended to end their marriage. Leaving Cleveland was supposed to stop all that. She should have gone somewhere other than Allenville, some place where she could be lost.

"Shelly, answer me." He cleared his throat and said more gently. "Just tell me what I have to do to convince you I'm sincere."

"Nothing." There would be no way to get him to leave amicably. She sensed now that before the night was out they'd be reduced to the old raging at each other. "Let's not go through it all again. We're divorced, Ben. There's no changing that."

"But there is." He stood abruptly and had to grab his teetering chair. "People divorce and remarry all the time. Look, if you want to have a home here as well as in Cleveland, I understand. Getting here is no big deal. We could commute...not during the season, of course, but during the rest of the year. How does that sound?"

She couldn't believe he'd expect her to answer such a suggestion. Over and over she'd told him there could be no going back but he wouldn't accept that the decisions she'd made were irrevocable.

"Shelly? I want you and Philip back where you belong—with me."

"No! Please don't do this. Maybe one day we can be friends again. Right now I don't even feel that's possible. The hurt's still too fresh and I can't sweep it away. Hurt is something that has to heal."

"I told you I was sorry." He came to face her across the counter. "I was a fool but I've paid enough now, don't you think?"

He didn't have any idea how it felt to be betrayed. "I'm not interested in making you pay. But there's no going back, and you have to accept that."

"Damn it, I don't have to accept anything." His fist hit tile with a dull thud and Shelly flinched. "Give me another chance. That's all I'm asking for—a chance to be the kind of husband and father you said you wanted me to be."

His anger intimidated her, had always intimidated her. "It doesn't work for one human being to try to be what they don't want to be."

"Hell." He swung away so she was confronted by his back. "The same stuff. I try to give and you find fault."

"I think you should leave."

"I just got here."

"Please, Ben. Don't do this. There's nothing to be gained. I will not be bullied by you . . . not anymore."

"There you go again." He turned around and brought his face close to hers across the counter. "The innuendos. I've never threatened you or touched you in anger. But you manage to lay the veiled hint that I have."

Shelly stepped backward. "You haven't overtly threatened me. But what do you call it when you say things like 'Don't cross me or you'll find out who's the boss.' And how about the times you told me I was holding you back socially because I didn't like the things you like? How about your threats that you'd divorce me if I tried to interfere with your good time?"

He colored deeply. "I've always hated the way you do that. The way you drag up things I said a long time ago and use them against me."

"At least you don't deny that you did say them." That was progress. "And you said them more than once and not so long ago. But why fight about it all over again? Go on your way. Please. Let me get my life together again. I can do it, I know I can."

"Damn it all." He made fists. "You make it sound as if you're a mess and it's my fault."

"No—"

"Yes. As long as I can remember you've been blaming me for your shortcomings."

He was trying the time-tested ways of bringing her to heel, only she wasn't biting this time. "I don't have to blame you for anything anymore. All we are to each other are people who used to be married."

The expression in his eyes made her pause for an instant, her determination wavering. She didn't want to hurt Ben. He was hurting now but she couldn't help him, not and survive, herself.

He jutted his chin. "I want my wife and son back. Tell me what I have to do to get them."

Her limbs trembled. She should have foreseen this and tried to prepare but she'd been fool enough to think he wouldn't give her a hard time here, not where his folks were, and her own—and with Tom nearby. She'd been wrong.

"Tell me, Shelly."

"Nothing," she whispered. "It's too late."

Ben came around the counter and seized her shoulders. For a moment she thought he would shake her. Instead he simply pulled her so close she had to crane her neck to see his face.

"I didn't always do things right, okay?"

"Let me go."

"If you'd given me more time I'd have learned how to be a better husband and father." His voice grated in a way she recognized. He was close to losing control.

She didn't dare try to twist away. "I gave you more than enough time. You would never have changed."

The slight tightening of his fingers made her nervous. Had the shock of finding out he couldn't get everything he wanted revealed a side of him she'd never seen?

"I would have changed, I tell you. I'd have become what you wanted me to be and there'd have been no need for this. But I can forget, Shelly. We'll put it behind us and press on."

His mouth came down on hers before she guessed his intention. She fought, then, kicked at his shins until he inhaled sharply and lifted his chin. There was darkness in his eyes.

"If I scream, Philip will hear and he'll come. Don't cause that. Oh, Ben, you were never violent. At least I had that to hang on to." She felt the start of tears.

"I'm not violent, just pushed beyond what any man can stand. We made a pact. Till death do us part. Remember?"

"Or infidelity? Ben, I don't know why you won't let go. You didn't want me until I started to move beyond your grasp. If I'd stayed you'd never have become different. You'd have destroyed me." She pushed against his chest and he released her. "I don't want you anymore. Don't you understand? There's at least one woman who isn't pining to have you in her arms and in her bed—me."

"I don't believe you said that."

Her throat burned with the effort of holding back tears. "Get out. Go back to Cleveland and let me get on with my life. And don't come back—ever."

"I know you still love me—"

She raised her hand but he caught her wrist before she could find out if she was capable of hitting him.

"All right." His tone had become menacing. "I'm going. But don't think you've heard the last from me. I don't give up on what I want, do you understand?"

The force with which he thrust her arm from him half spun her around. "Just go."

"Oh, I will. But remember what I've said. Tonight was only the first of many visits." He walked into the hall. "I'll wear you down," he shouted, and the front door slammed.

Shelly waited until the low growl of the car's engine faded before she snatched up the phone and dialed. Twelve rings later Tom said, "Yes" in a flat voice she scarcely recognized as his.

"It's Shelly."

Silence.

"Tom, I'm sorry about the way the evening ended. When I saw Ben I couldn't seem to think what I should say or do."

"Don't give it another thought. Did you and Ben get anything sorted out?"

He was no different from everyone else, he wanted everything the way it used to be—neat and tidy. "Ben's probably on his way back to Cleveland. But don't worry about that. We'll cope with our disagreements and no one else has to be concerned." Ben was still a hero to Tom and she wouldn't dash the illusion.

Tom wasn't saying anything.

"Can we talk for a while?" She needed his steadiness, his warmth…the comfort he gave her in the knowledge that he was unchanging.

She heard him let out a long breath. "What did you want to talk about?"

"Old times, maybe. Nothing special. You know what a night owl I am. I thought you might like to keep me company."

"I have to be up early."

Shelly closed her eyes. "I'm sorry. Sometimes I forget how hard you have to work. Can we get together tomorrow? Take a picnic lunch up by the creek…the place we used to go?"

"No…not tomorrow. Why don't you get some sleep."

And let him get some sleep? She wasn't Tom's responsibility. Loneliness was something she'd have to learn to cope with alone. "Okay. You're right. Talk to you soon, huh?"

"Soon."

She was going to cry. Everything felt like a void. "Right. Well, I'll see you then."

"See you."

"And, Tom. I'm sorry about—"

"Forget it. I already have. Good night."

"Good night."

PHILIP OPENED HIS DOOR wider and held his breath, listening. Mom's room was across the hall and he knew she'd turned the light out because the line of brightness had gone from the bottom of her door.

At least she'd stopped crying.

He'd wanted to go down while his dad was there, while he was shouting, but he couldn't have done anything and Mom would only have gotten more upset if she thought he knew she was unhappy.

It was like all the other times since the divorce when Dad came around and got mad. Except maybe it was different. Tonight, he had yelled that he wanted them all back together again, and he'd said something about keeping the house in Allenville and going back and forth to Cleveland. What if Mom decided to get back with Dad? Grandma and Grandpa Williams said that's what would happen one day.

Philip took a step onto the landing. His stomach felt funny—mixed up. Dad had looked real strange when he brought the box in from the car. And he'd kept saying things like, "Pretty cool, huh?" and "That'll knock the other kids' eyes out," while Philip took out the new skate. Dad thought he was an okay kid, but he'd never done what other fathers did. But tonight he'd sounded as if he was trying to be like . . . they were buddies.

The skate was something. Exactly what he'd been planning to buy as soon as he had the money saved. The sick feeling in his stomach got worse. His feet were cold. What if Mom said they were going back to Cleveland? Those other times, before the divorce, when Mom had been sad and Dad had said they were going to be happy and for her not to worry . . . they never lasted. Philip rubbed one foot on his other ankle.

Why did he keep on wishing they could be together? It never worked.

He knew what he would do. Creeping, careful to stop and wait at each creak of floorboards in the old house, he made it to to the top of the stairs and started down, sliding heel after heel over the end of each step and holding tight to the bannister. He didn't want to go back to Cleveland. He didn't want to not see his dad, but he wanted to stay here.

Men don't cry. Dad said that to him. Philip's eyes felt scratchy. He could cry now because no one would see, but he wasn't going to.

The kitchen was all black shapes, and dark fingery lines wavered over the ceiling because the moon was shining behind the trees outside the window. He moved forward slowly, holding out his hands until he reached the wall phone.

Maybe Tom would be mad. It had to be real late. Philip hesitated, shivering. Tom said to call anytime he needed to. He lifted the receiver and waited, listening for a creak from upstairs. The dark felt thick and fuzzy and there wasn't any noise.

The phone rang so many times he started to hang up. Then the rings stopped and Tom said, "Yes?" Philip held the phone tightly. He could still hang up.

"Hello, who is this?"

"Philip," he said and hunched his shoulders.

There was a rustling and sounds as if Tom was sitting up in bed. "Philip? What's the matter?"

"Nothing."

Tom was quiet, then he said, "Tell me why you're calling. It's okay, don't worry, just tell me."

"Okay. Dad bought me a new skate, the kind I was going to buy."

"That's great."

"He's gone now. He went back to Cleveland."

"Your mom called and told me that. She said she and your dad would work out their problems so you don't have to worry. Is that why you called?"

He didn't know what to say.

"Philip?"

"Dad said he wants Mom and me back and that we could keep this house and come here sometimes. He shouted and got mad and Mom cried . . . like she used to." The scratchiness in his eyes got worse and he rubbed them. His nose began to run and he wiped it on his pajama sleeve.

Tom's breath sounded loud. "Do you want to go back to Cleveland? You're bound to miss your dad."

"I miss him. But I want to stay here. Dad . . . he likes me and Mom, but he sort of forgets us or something when we're around him. Mom's been happy since we moved here and—" He had to swallow several times. "Is it my fault?" he whispered.

For a long time Tom didn't answer, then he sounded different. "Kids aren't responsible for what their parents do. They just get caught in the flack."

Philip wasn't sure he understood. "Dad doesn't need me. It's Mom he needs, I think. Not all the time, but sometimes. Maybe if he and Mom didn't have me around they'd be okay."

The loud breathing noise came again. "Both your parents need you. They love you. It's just that they've been having a tough time for a while. I've got a hunch they'll work it out. They've been together most of their lives—since they were younger than you—"

"I don't want to go to Cleveland. I want to stay here and come tomorrow for the planting lessons...and be with you, Uncle Tom. I was going to teach Kurt some stuff on the ramp. I don't want to—"

"Hey, ease up, okay?"

"Okay."

"Everything's going to be fine, you'll see."

"Are we still going to talk about planting tomorrow?"

Tom cleared his throat. "Sure we are. What made you think we weren't?"

"I heard Mom say we shouldn't have come here. We aren't wanted."

"To your dad?"

Hot tears started falling. "To herself when she went to bed. She said we're a nuisance to everyone we touch."

"You didn't hear her right. I...we want you. All of us. And tomorrow you can come over and start doing some chores around here. It's time you learned how tough it is to live in farm country."

"No lie? I can come?"

"We had a deal didn't we? And you can bring that new skateboard and try it out."

Philip sniffed. "Kurt can use the new board, I don't want it."

"But you said it was...okay, whatever you say."

"You aren't just saying you want me over there because you're being nice."

"No way, kid. This is a business deal."

Gray light had begun to come through the windows. It had to be getting close to morning. Philip smiled. The tears had stopped. "Great. Mom'll bring me over. What time?"

There was a little silence. "Your mom doesn't have to come. She's got her own things to do. I'll be by for you around ten."

"Okay."

"And, Philip, I'll be in a hurry so why don't you wait out front so I don't have to come in?"

# Chapter Eight

Shelly pulled the Jeep to the edge of the track leading into Conrads' Farm and waited for a semi and trailer to pass. This must be a buyer trucking out his seed purchase. She remembered Tom telling her that he liked the cellars empty by mid May so this would be one of the last outgoing hauls of the year.

The semi swung onto the road and Shelly wrapped her arms around her steering wheel, staring ahead at outbuildings, the two-story farmhouse with Tom's barn behind and, a distance beyond that, Mary and Jimmy's house. And all around as far as the eye could see lay fields where barley and peas had been sewn and the dark soil that was steadily being opened, then closed over seed potato sets.

This was Tom's home, the only place he'd ever wanted to call his own. He had grown older as they all had, but he hadn't changed deep inside where it mattered. He was still honest and he still knew what he wanted and what was right. Would Ben have been any different if he'd stayed in Allenville?

Shelly drove slowly back onto the track. She'd taken two weeks to find enough courage to come looking for Tom. Oh, she'd seen him at times. Philip had been coming out after school to work with Mary's boys and the rest of the crew and she had picked him up each evening, but Tom had been distant and figuring out the reason had been simple enough. He must know she'd turned Ben away and now he was angry. Having him mad with her was more than she could take. Somehow she would make him accept what had happened.

The trucker would have picked up his load from the line of metal storage cellars to the right of the farmhouse. Shelly checked the fields, peering as she drove, until she located first one and then another tractor, each pulling a planter. Moving figures told her the workers were out there. With luck, Tom might still be at the cellars. He was always the one to deal with buyers.

She wound the Jeep along the track until she reached the first cellar. Before she could drive to the second, a green pickup appeared from between two of the low-lying buildings and she had to stop again. The pickup edged past and then she saw Tom walking in its wake, his hat tilted forward at its customary angle. His head was down as he leafed through some papers. She sat very still. This long-legged rangy man with his loose-limbed walk and broad swinging shoulders, was more familiar to her than anyone else in the world. Watching him brought her warm pleasure.

He looked up and stopped, took off his hat and pushed back his disheveled hair. Pretty soon it would be streaked by the sun and he'd look even more like the boy she'd known.

His hand went up in a wave and he strode to open the door of the Jeep. "Hi, Shel. You're early. I'll have to drive out and get Philip."

She switched off the engine and climbed down beside him. "I didn't come to get him, not yet. Who was that in the pickup?" She hadn't recognized it, or its driver.

"Department of Agriculture. They have to inspect and tag every outgoing load of seed spuds."

"Oh." She fidgeted with the zipper on her parka. "I wanted to talk to you. I think it's time, don't you?"

His big shoulders hunched inside a faded denim jacket. "Whatever you say. I didn't think we'd stopped talking."

"That's a copout, Tom Conrad, and you know it. You can't be warm enough in that thin shirt and jacket."

He inclined his head, smiling. "It's plenty warm if you're working, thanks, Mom. If you're cold you can come through a couple of the cellars with me. I need to check the cooling systems."

She followed him quietly into the nearest building. The door stood open and inside there was a smell of alder dust and the peculiar scent of earth and potatoes. He opened a control panel and flipped one switch after another. Fans whirred while he continued to check controls for the humidifier and air washer and the equipment used to keep the temperature at the necessary constant forty degrees.

"Getting ready for the next season of baby-sitting," he said absently, referring to the intense watchfulness every farmer kept over his stored crops.

Tom threw all the switches and closed the panel.

"Finished?" Shelly asked.

He looked at her over his shoulder. "I'm never finished. But I can usually choose to take five if I want to."

"Will you choose to now?" Muscles across her shoulders tensed for rejection.

His intensely blue eyes settled on her and she had difficulty not looking away. He seemed to be sizing her up, but as always in these moments, she had no idea what he was thinking.

"I can take off for a while now the load's out." He glanced around. "There's nowhere to sit in here."

Relief made her light-headed. "Could we go up by the creek? I've wanted to go ever since I got back, but it wouldn't be the same on my own."

His lips parted but he didn't speak immediately. His breath escaped slowly. "I guess that'd be okay. But we shouldn't stay up there too long."

Tom drove the Jeep. He left a message at the house to say he'd be back later. The old winding road to the creek was little more than a path overgrown with the spring's new growth of tender grass and fragile flowers on swaying stems.

In the parking place they'd used years ago, Tom edged the Jeep into deeper grass and switched off the engine. Shelly joined him in the crisp air and lifted her face to the fragrant wind. "God's country," she murmured. "Smell. Feel it?"

"I always do," he said.

She struck out toward the trees that lined the creek. A stiff breeze moved across the ground, shifting flowers and grass as the wind shifts an ocean, in changing currents.

A sudden soaring noise brought a cry to her lips and she hesitated, then laughed. "A meadowlark, Tom," she called. "Look." The bird ascended with its joyful song, its patches of yellow brilliant in the clear afternoon.

"We'd better get on." Tom reached her side and held her elbow the rest of the way to the creek. Like homing pigeons they found their favorite pine. Below, the water gurgled by, swollen by thawed snows.

Shelly moved to sit but Tom stopped her. "It's soaking."

"Fine." She took off her waterproof parka, spread it out and dropped to the ground. A heavy pink sweater and jeans were ample to keep her warm. The tree felt solid and familiar at her back. "I'll share," she said, tapping the coat beside her. "Take a load off your feet."

The tan, felt Stetson hit the grass before Tom plopped down. He leaned forward to struggle out of his coat then draped it around her shoulders.

"I don't need it, thanks," she said, trying to take it off. "You'll freeze."

"Garbage." He clamped an arm around her shoulders on top of the jacket and settled back. "This is balmy to me. Now talk and make it quick."

Shelly made an attempt at a whistle but the noise was a tinny squeak with a lot of escaping air. She didn't want to talk now, only sit here with him and pretend they were eighteen . . .

"Shelly, you aren't talking."

"I'm thinking."

"About what?"

He was comfortable to lean on. "Other times when we came here. Remember the high school prom?"

"Vaguely."

She elbowed him and craned to see his face. "You do, too, remember it."

He smiled down at her and ruffled her hair. "Like I said, I remember it vaguely. Indistinct stuff about you wearing a strapless white dress with little silver roses embroidered along the hem and silver sandals and your hair tied into a ponytail with a yellow ribbon. And, of course, Ben's pink bow tie and cummerbund and the way Mary got sick and couldn't come. Not a lot."

Shelly laughed. "That's the way it is for me, too. So clear it makes me sad. Why would it do that?"

"Because it's sad to realize you used to be so uncomplicated and so sure the world was a place just waiting to welcome you and make your path smooth. It's the loss of innocence that hurts."

She turned around and knelt facing him. "You're such a complex man. Is that what you do out in those fields, think about what it all means? You were always the smartest person I knew."

"Why didn't you wear a silver ribbon?"

She narrowed her eyes. "What?"

"Silver roses, silver sandals. Why a yellow ribbon?"

"Oh." She nodded, grinning. "You would think of something like that. I just happen to like yellow ribbons, okay? And yellow roses and daisies . . ."

He wasn't smiling anymore. "There was something you wanted to talk about."

"Okay." She spread her fingers on her thighs. "You're mad at me."

He looked blank. "I don't know what you mean."

"Ever since Ben was here you've hardly said two words to me."

"This is a busy time for me."

"Not so busy you have to be rude."

Tom's head rested against the tree and he turned sharply toward her. "I haven't been rude."

"What do you call it when you pick my son up outside my house without coming to the door? And when you ignore me each time I come to the farm?"

His adam's apple moved. "You're making something out of nothing."

"Well, maybe, but I thought I should bring you up to date on the way things are between Ben and me."

He lowered his eyelids a fraction and light caught the blond tips of his dark lashes. "It isn't my business."

"Yes, it is, in a way. We promised we'd be each other's business."

He shifted, hitching himself straighter. "This starts to sound like an old record, but all I want is for the two of you to be happy. You both matter to me."

"Did Philip say I sent his father away?"

"More or less."

"Do you think that's bothering him?"

"Yes. And that's something I'd already decided to talk to you about, but your turn first."

She pursed her lips, deciding what she could say that would be best for all of them without being a lie. "Ben calls me most days."

Tom leaned forward and rested his elbows on his knees. "He worries about you, doesn't he?"

"Yes." He worried about how he would get her to do what he wanted.

"So you're working on your relationship again."

Her throat felt closed. "Yes." It wasn't true, but she didn't know what else to say.

"Good." He smiled briefly and looked away. "Ben's a great guy, we both know that. And you've had too many good years together to throw the whole thing away."

Throw away? Didn't anyone around here consider that a step like divorce had torn her apart and that she wouldn't have taken it if she hadn't intended it to be forever? But let Tom relax for a while. In time he'd accept things as they really were.

"What did you want to tell me about Philip?"

"Have you noticed anything different about him?"

Shelly's legs cramped and she sat sideways, frowning. "He's been quieter than usual in the last day or two, but I'm not sure why. What has he said to you?"

"That's just it. He doesn't say anything. He listens to whatever I teach him about planting and seems to enjoy Kurt and Aaron, but he's not the same somehow." While he spoke he gathered a bunch of tiny white flowers and wound the stems together.

"You think it's because of Ben? That he misses him, I mean?"

"I'm not sure. He doesn't want—" He closed his mouth tightly and a muscle contracted in his jaw.

"He doesn't want what?" Her skin turned colder and goose bumps shot out on her arms.

Tom shook his head. "Oh, I don't know. I guess I was going to say he doesn't seem to know what he wants. I'm sure it's tough on him, loving you both. Divided loyalty is a tough one."

"Let's get back," she said, suddenly anxious to be with Philip. "This is my fault. I've been thinking too much about myself lately and not giving him enough attention."

"Hey." A strong calloused hand closed on her wrist. "Enough of that. I wouldn't have mentioned it if I thought you'd start blaming yourself. Listen, I think he's a bit unsure about a lot of things right now. All we need to do is keep an eye on him and be ready to listen when he's ready to talk, okay?"

She eyed him and smiled a little. "All *we* have to do? Philip isn't your responsibility. You've done far too much for us already."

"Because I've wanted to," he responded, standing and hauling her up with him. "Until there's someone else to back you up I'm saying I'm still here to do the job . . . if you want me."

For seconds she looked at his serious face before she wrapped her arms around him and hugged tightly. "Thanks. I feel greedy for taking what you should be giving to a family of your own, but I can't say no." She raised her face. "Some woman is going to be very lucky to get you, and so are the children you'll have."

THE PLANTING WAS DONE, finished yesterday with still a week of May to go. Tom trod between rows, kicking up dirt here and there. The weather was holding steady but there was always the concern about keeping the soil level high enough to avoid too much warmth or light.

An engine growled somewhere behind him. Jimmy had gone into town to pick up some parts for one of the tractors.

Tom heard harsh breathing and turned to see Shelly running as fast as high heels would allow in the narrow troughs of soft muddy dirt.

Slowly, he pulled his hands from his pockets. Her face was pale, her teeth gritted between parted lips.

"What's happened? Shel?" At two-thirty in the afternoon she should be at the school. He began to run toward her, his heart pounding hard.

"Is he here?" She reached him and he grasped her shoulders. Beneath his hands she trembled.

Tom knew who she meant but he had to ask, "Philip? No. He doesn't come until after school, you know that."

The tears in her eyes broke free. "Oh, Tom, I was just sure he'd come to you. He's gone. He didn't even go into class this morning so they thought he was sick."

He took off his hat and wiped his brow on a sleeve. "I'm not getting this. Philip drives to school with you in the morning, doesn't he? He only catches the bus home."

"I drove him but he didn't go to school. He must have taken off as soon as I was out of sight." She turned her head as if to focus through the tears. "He didn't say a word at dinner last night. And he didn't eat, either. This morning was the same but... You don't think someone could have—"

He fished out a handkerchief and gave it to her. "No, I don't. I think he's probably at home by now."

She held the handkerchief over her mouth. "He's not. I went there first. And I called my folks and Ben's. I didn't tell them the real reason because I didn't want to frighten them." Her voice rose and she clutched his arm. "He's gone. What if he's trying to get to Cleveland? Would Ben—"

"I believe Philip prefers living here, and I don't believe Ben managed to spirit him out of school without being seen," Tom told her with a ring of conviction that was as much for his own benefit as hers. "Let's find him."

The question was, where did they start looking? Shelly mustn't know how scared he felt. He led her to the house and told his mother what had happened. Alice, calm the way she was in any situation, said she wouldn't be surprised if Philip came to the farm on the bus, the same as usual. "Probably played hooky like someone else I know did a few times," she said, wrinkling her nose at Tom.

Tom tried to take courage from the recollection. "See how terrified they kept me around here?" he said, smiling at Shelly. "Mom could be right. And the bus should be by within half an hour."

She nodded but her lips were so tightly drawn there was a white line around them.

"How about some coffee?" Alice asked, drying her hands on a towel. Her sleeves were rolled up to the elbow for washing dishes.

As if she hadn't heard the offer, Shelly went to the window to stare out. "You can't see the bus coming from here," she said. "I'm going out by the road."

"I don't think that's such a good idea," he said. "He'll know something's wrong if you're there waiting for him."

Shelly rounded on him. "Something is wrong. I'm worried sick and when he gets off that bus he's going to find out he can't get away with this kind of thing."

"He's only a kid—"

"What do you know about kids? You don't—" She took her bottom lip in her teeth and shook her head. "I'm sorry, Tom. Forgive me, please. I really got a scare when Liz Russell asked why Philip wasn't in school. I went to pieces."

"Forget it," he said. She was right. What did he know about kids? He did know he cared about Philip...about Philip...and Shelly. He really cared for her, and the feelings weren't getting dimmer, despite all the promises he'd made to himself to wipe them out. Not that it mattered a whole lot what he felt, not as far as she was concerned.

Shelly went outside and he followed, watching her hair catch the light, her slender body move so fluidly in one of the tailored suits she wore for work. He was still getting used to this person who'd become something different in her other world, the one away from his.

"What time is it?" she asked, glancing up at him with those big soft eyes.

He caught her elbow and pulled her back. "Slow down. We've got at least ten minutes to wait." The suit was a creamy color worn over a pale blue silk blouse. He liked her in blue...in any color she wore. In the weeks since she'd arrived she'd filled out a little and even though he preferred her in jeans, he had to admit she looked wonderful in dresses and suits that showed off her unforgettable shape and legs.

"Tom?"

He started. "What?"

"I asked you...you aren't listening. You're worried, too." Anxiety loaded every word.

"No." He lied but he had to. "What did you ask me?"

"If you really think he'll be on the bus."

"Seems logical." He shrugged. "We've got to keep our cool over this, Shel. Philip's obviously got something heavy on his mind and one way or another we need to get him to talk about it.''

"I know."

They trudged down the track to the gates. Shelly put her hand in his, and he said nothing about the way her fingernails dug into his palm. She was totally natural around him. Tom raised his face to the May breeze that carried scents of earth and fledgling grass and a warm suggestion of new flowers. A beautiful day and the woman he—and a special woman at his side. But his stomach was a rigid wad that cramped his muscles. Philip had better be on that bus.

Standing in the dust and gravel beside the road, they stared in the direction from which the bus would come.

"What do we do if he's not on the bus?" Shelly said. She wound her hands together while she squinted into the distance. "Where do we look?"

"If we have to search we'll do it methodically. Start at the school and try to figure out where he'd go. We'll check the fields around there, and the creek. Did you search the house when you went home?"

She began to pace. "You don't think he'll be on the bus. I knew you didn't. We shouldn't be wasting time here."

What she needed most from him was reassurance and he was doing a lousy job. "Hold on. Don't . . . there it is."

A swirl of diesel fumes shivered in the air seconds before the yellow bus crested a rise and rattled down the gentle run to the farm. Time the old pile of junk was replaced, Tom thought absently. He folded and refolded his arms, rocking back onto his heels and doing his best to stay calm.

"There's Kurt," Shelly said in a loud voice as Mary's oldest boy jumped down, his brown hair standing on end as usual. He was growing fast, and his jeans showed two inches of white sock above high-top sneakers.

Tom felt Shelly shove her hand under his arm but he kept his eyes on the bus.

"Come on," she muttered.

Aaron leaped to the road and looked back.

Tom let out a slow breath. Philip was there, he had to be. Aaron yelled something and a bag hurtled through the door. He caught it against his middle.

"Oh, God." Shelly turned to Tom and rested her face on his chest. "That's Philip's bag. He's not there."

Tom put his arms around her while the bus trundled by. Kurt and Aaron, with a sprinkling of freckles over pointed noses, approached.

"How come you've got Philip's bag?" Tom asked.

"Mrs. Russell gave it to us to bring home," Aaron said, holding the red bag in front of him like a shield. "Philip didn't go to school today so I guess he left the bag there yesterday."

Shelly straightened and faced the boys. "You didn't see him at all?"

Kurt gave one of his sighs and said, "We said he didn't go to school. Anyway, you gotta already know that, Aunt Shelly."

Without a word, Shelly took off. She ran toward the Jeep and Tom ran after her. "Take the bag inside," he yelled to the boys. "And tell your grandmother to phone around and see if anyone's seen Philip. Tell her we're going looking for him."

The school yielded no clues. With three other teachers helping, the surrounding fields were covered and the creek for as far as it was reasonable to assume a boy could walk. And all the time Shelly grew quieter except for the sharp sound of the shallow breaths she took. Tom set his mind on a grim course that excluded imagining anything and kept the little search team moving systematically.

At five-thirty Lizzie Russell, Philip's diminutive elderly teacher spoke up. They stood on the steps of the town's tiny library. "Tom, this isn't looking so good. If he stays out all night we're going to be thinking about the cold. It still gets down pretty low."

Shelly made an odd noise and he rubbed the back of her rigid neck.

"Lizzie's right. So what do we do?" He already knew what should be done, what should have been done earlier only he'd hoped he wouldn't have to frighten Shelly even more.

"I'll go to the sheriff," Lizzie said, "and then we've got to round up every willing pair of eyes and feet in the area."

"Oh, no." Shelly scrubbed at her face. Her hair was a tangled mess, and the suit was now covered in grass stains and mud.

Tom agreed with Lizzie and sent her on her way. The other two teachers set out to start telephoning. "You should wait at your place in case he goes there," Tom told Shelly. "I'll get back to Mom and tell her to man the phone while I keep looking."

"No," Shelly said, lifting her chin. "He won't go there, but I'll get my mother to wait at my house, anyway. I want to be with you."

Tom didn't argue. If he gave her strength he was glad.

At nine-thirty he drove Shelly back to the farm. They'd scoured every track and path he could think of, passing other groups of searchers on the way.

Mary greeted them outside the house. She closed the door behind her as they approached.

"You've heard something." Shelly started forward, stumbling in her haste. "Has he been found?"

Mary shook her head. "Not that. It's just that I think I know what happened and why. Kurt and Aaron didn't want me to tell you because they'd promised Philip they wouldn't say anything.''

"Philip told them he was running away?'' Shelly seemed convinced this was what had happened.

"No. What they said was that Philip's been miserable at school for a couple of weeks. Evidently some of the kids are giving him a bad time, picking on him and so on.''

Tom narrowed his eyes. The wind had freshened and it tore at his hat and face. "Picking on him how? What's there to pick at?''

"Well...'' Mary glanced at Shelly, then looked at the ground. "Don't take this hard, Shelly, but kids are cruel, or they can be. Seems there's been an ongoing campaign to victimize Philip. Some of the kids think he needs to be put in his place. They want to make sure he doesn't get the idea he's better than they are—''

"Philip's not the kind of kid who—''

"I know, I know,'' Mary interrupted. "I'm only telling you what he's been getting from the other kids. They say things like, he needn't think he's a cut above them because his father's some big-time football player. There's been a lot of talk about him being a teacher's pet because you work at the school, and then they tell him his folks aren't real Allenville people because they moved away and...and they give him a bad time about the divorce. Shelly, there isn't too much divorce in a small town like this. Divorce still sets a family apart around here.''

"They've been torturing him,'' Tom said, half under his breath. "I'll fix that.''

"Not now you won't,'' Mary said. "Right now you'll keep on looking till you find the boy. Kurt said Philip reckoned he'd run away soon if the kids kept it up and that Kurt thinks he's hiding out somewhere. When you find him you've got to let him be the one to decide whether or not he wants help with the other kids. Boys have to grow into men, Tom, we all know that, and sometimes it means they need to deal with their own problems. He's looking for attention is all, I'd stake my life on it.''

"I haven't neglected him," Shelly said in a small voice.

"Nobody said you have," Tom said, a dull rage welling in him. "Where do I go next?" he asked Mary. "I'm running out of ideas."

The door opened and Alice burst out. "There was a call," she said, breathless. "Arnie Bender says he saw Philip."

"Where?" Tom closed a hand convulsively around Shelly's. "When?" Arnie drove the mail route.

"About nine this morning. He was turning in here."

"Here?" So where was he? They'd checked all the outbuildings, including the obvious one where the skate ramp was. "When Jimmy and the others come in, tell them to spread out and cover every inch of this place."

By eleven every muscle and bone in Tom's body ached and it was getting cold outside. Where the hell was Philip?

Shelly stayed doggedly with the search. They'd just left the rest of the group after rendezvousing by the shop. "We're going to make another loop around the outside of each building," Tom said and he heard his own desperation. "There have to be dozens of boxes and bins lying around. He could be in one of those."

"Dead."

Tom stopped. "What did you say?" The night seemed to seethe.

"Dead," Shelly repeated flatly. "If he's in a box or bin and he's been there all day and he isn't answering when people call, it must be because he's dead. He could be in a refrigerator. I've read about that happening."

"Don't you dare say that." He'd shaken her before he could stop himself. Horrified, he dropped his hands. "Please, Shel, don't say that. Don't think it."

She wasn't crying, just staring sightlessly at him.

"Refrigeration," he said, the word forming unbidden. Good grief—surely he wouldn't go into the cellars.

Without a second thought, he sprinted away, reaching the first cellar out of breath. The light, when he flipped it on, bounced glaringly from the white insulation coat inside. No sign of life in the empty building.

The next couple of cellars yielded the same result. On he ran until he reached the first of the only two cellars that still held spuds.

Shelly was at his side as he opened the door. "He wouldn't go in there. He's always telling me how you warn him and the other boys not to go near the stored crop."

"Yeah," he said, walking inside and throwing the light switch. "And don't you think that's why he'd come in here—because he knows we wouldn't expect him to?"

"But—"

"Philip! Are you in here?"

There was an eeriness about the lumbering hulk of spuds mounded the length of the building. The familiar smell didn't seem as pleasant tonight.

"Philip! You've made your point. We know you've got problems. If you're in here, come out so we can talk."

No response, only the whirring of the temperature control equipment. They waited but there was no movement.

"He's not here," Shelly said.

"There's still another cellar to check."

"And he won't be there, either. I'm going to have to call Ben. God, how I hate to worry him."

She was over Ben but she hated to worry him? Tom was too tired to do more than store the thought.

Shelly preceded him slowly through the door and he switched off the lights.

"Don't! Don't go."

Philip's voice hit Tom with a dull impact that brought nausea before relief.

## Chapter Nine

The roast smelled wonderful. Shelly pulled the pan from the oven and slid it onto the top of the range. She sucked in a breath and shook her stinging hands inside oven mitts that were wearing thin.

Sunday was her favorite day, even this one when Tom was coming for dinner and she was afraid he might intend to push for a confrontation at the school. Since Friday night he'd been seething and trying to get names out of Philip, who steadfastly refused to say who his tormentors were.

She checked pots of vegetables, smiling at the comfortable feeling all this gave her; the opportunity to cook a simple meal for a man who would appreciate the effort, the prospect of sitting with him and with Philip to eat and talk the way ordinary happy families did.

Families. She was pretending, playing a fantasy game. Tom was a friend not her husband or Philip's father. But still she was happy. When she and Ben had first married he'd enjoyed their quiet times at home, but too soon he'd become bored . . . and made Shelly feel invisible.

The front door banged and Tom's whistle accompanied the solid thud of his boots down the hall.

"Mmm." He came into the kitchen, his hat held over his heart, and closed his eyes. "Heaven smells like this. Hot beef and gravy and boiling spuds.'' His eyes opened as he grinned and leaned to lift a lid.

Shelly took the cover from him and replaced it. ''I didn't know you spent so much time on deep spiritual contemplation. Obviously you've come to some very important conclusions. Heaven is spuds, huh? Maybe you'll become the head eternal spud grower. Take off your coat.''

He grimaced. ''You just don't appreciate the finest things in life . . . and in the hereafter. Philip in his room?''

She checked the vegetables and turned down the heat. ''He's playing softball with the kids. Kurt invited him, and Jimmy came by to give him a ride. He should be back shortly.''

''That's a switch, isn't it?''

''What do you mean?'' She knew but she didn't want to discuss the subject.

''On Friday Philip just about killed us both with worry because he doesn't get along with the local kids. Today he's playing softball with them.''

One thing she refused to tell Tom was that she'd been watching the clock ever since Philip left, and that she wished she hadn't let him go. ''Kids bounce back. The sooner we get past all this silliness, the better.''

''I guess so.'' He didn't sound convinced. ''Here, I saw this and thought you might like it.''

From the pocket of dark gray slacks he produced a small package and tossed it to her. Shelly looked from the slightly rumpled white bag to Tom but he was busy taking off his jacket and stowing it on a chair with his black hat on top. His close-fitting turtleneck was also black and did nice things for his lean, well-muscled body. She hastily returned her attention to the bag and pulled out its contents.

"What is it?" A square white box lay in the palm of her hand. She'd almost forgotten the thrill of receiving an unexpected gift.

Tom stretched out a long arm to brace himself on the wall. "If you open it you'll know. And don't get excited because it's nothing much. I'm a poor farmer, remember."

She glanced at him sharply but he was smiling. "Right. That's what you are. You're also looking fantastic, my friend. There have to be dozens of women out there who drool over you only you don't take time to notice. We'll have to do something about—"

"Open the box."

For an instant she thought he might be irritated, but he continued to smile, and she relaxed. "Oh, Tom, how lovely." His gift was a pendant, an exquisitely formed yellow porcelain rose on a slim gold chain. "I've never seen anything like it."

"It's handmade. There's a place in Idaho Falls that sells them. I remembered seeing it so I ran in and got it yesterday."

She took it from the box and held it up. Prickling in her eyes made her blink. "You shouldn't have but I'm glad you did." At that moment she was happy and sad at the same time, and filled up with the way he made her feel needed and important.

"I didn't have to think very hard. You said you like cheerful yellow things." He took the chain from her hands and fastened it around her neck, his big fingers fumbling with the fine catch. "There, cheerful and yellow and obviously made for someone as beautiful as you."

A blush shot into her face. She couldn't meet his eyes. Feelings she couldn't understand bombarded her, and she covered embarrassment by standing on tiptoe to kiss his cheek lightly before putting the box back inside its bag and setting the package on a shelf. What did she feel? She wasn't sure . . . gratitude? No, there was something . . . Tension was doing odd things to her, that was it.

Tom was watching her. She felt his solid presence and smiled at him again while fingering the rose. Ben had never been like that, impulsively thoughtful.

The silence made her awkward but she couldn't think of anything to say. Clumsily she took out silverware and place mats and went to set the table. And all the time Tom stood, following her movements. Why didn't he say something? He was comfortable, that was all, and watching a woman cook and work around a kitchen was very natural to him. He wasn't the type who needed constant talk. Why did she feel self-conscious?

"What was that?" he said.

Shelly looked at Tom, then listened. There had been a soft click from the hall. "Must be Philip coming back. Philip!" She arrived at the foot of the stairs in time to see him reach the landing and go into his room. "Philip, are you okay?"

No response.

Tom stopped her from following. "Don't overreact. He'll be down when he's ready. If he needs a few minutes on his own for some reason, give them to him." The grim set of his features belied the logical instructions.

"Something's wrong." A squeezing inside Shelly turned to jumpiness. "He always says hi when he comes in."

"Let him be."

"Why? You're the one who wants to take on the school and everyone else in sight. Why the about-face?"

"I guess I'm trying to put myself in his shoes, okay? I came on too strong on Friday night and maybe I've put him on the defensive. He doesn't want me to interfere, does he?"

Shelly shook her head as she walked slowly into the kitchen.

An hour later she and Tom stood facing each other in the hall. There had been no sign or sound of Philip, dinner was spoiling and neither of them could decide what to do.

The phone split the silence and Shelly hurried into the living room to answer. Within minutes she was passing Tom and taking the stairs two at a time. "That was Jimmy," she said over her shoulder. "He wanted to know how Philip is. Another parent drove him after the game. Kurt got home and said they'd dropped Philip off and that he was hurt."

Tom arrived at Philip's room with her and turned the door handle. "Locked," he said. "Philip, open the door."

The only response was a muffled rustling from inside the room.

"Please," Shelly said, "let us in. I know you got hurt at the game." To Tom she whispered, "I can't understand why he's behaving like this. He's always been tough. Getting hurt playing sports is nothing to him."

"Philip," Tom called. "Open this door. *Now*." He stood with his head bowed, listening.

A snuffling noise came, then a hiccup.

"He's crying." Shelly stared at the door. "We've got to get in. Something's really wrong."

Tom pounded, waited, pounded again. "Philip, this is it. Open up." Seconds passed. "That's it." Without warning, he launched his shoulder into the door and it gave way. The top hinge splintered free, crackling like a felled tree and the lock shot loose.

Tom climbed into the room and Shelly followed, her heart pounding.

The light was off and the drapes drawn. She squinted at the bed, at the curled lump under the quilt. Tom started forward but she held his arm and shook her head.

Trying to make as little noise as possible, Shelly switched on the bedside lamp and rested a hand on Philip. "How're you feeling?"

"Go away."

She glanced at Tom who had moved closer. "Philip, I don't get this. If you've injured yourself it's no big deal as long as it isn't bad. Do we need to get you checked out?"

"No."

Tom ran a hand through his hair, then in one swift motion swept the quilt from the bed.

Shelly bent over Philip, then couldn't move, couldn't breathe.

Tom clamped his hands around her shoulders and moved her firmly aside. "Who did this?"

Philip tried to bury his face in the pillow but Tom sank to his knees and held the boy still. His left eye was swollen and rapidly turning purplish. Caked blood rimmed his nostrils and clung to a split in the center of his upper lip.

"Oh, my God," Shelly moaned, going to her knees beside Tom. "Someone hit you. You weren't hurt in the game, they hit you."

"I hit them, too," Philip said in a flannelly voice. He sat up and rested his forehead on his knees. His pale hair was grayed with dust and plastered to the back of his thin neck. "They said my dad's all washed up. They said—"

Tom sat on the edge of the bed and pulled him into his arms. "Who are 'they'?"

"No one. I can handle it." Philip drew in a sharp breath and whimpered.

"What's the matter?" Tom straightened. "Are you hurt somewhere else?"

"Here." Philip pointed to the arm he held clamped to his side. Shelly saw more blood on his palm.

When she turned the hand over she saw deep scratches embedded with grit. "They pushed you down?"

He raised his chin, a stubborn light in his one open eye. "I didn't cry, not then. Oh—" The arm pressed to his body stiffened convulsively and he rolled onto his side.

Tom stood up. "I'm going to call Doc Williams." His voice was cold, and Shelly peered at him. "Then I'm going to make some other phone calls." He shook his head at her. "Don't try to stop me. This has gone far enough."

PHILIP LOOKED around the room from where he lay on his bed. Grandpa Williams kept on smiling at him. His grandma stood beside his mom and smiled at him, too, although her mouth kind of trembled.

"I'm going to take you in for an X ray," Doc Williams said. He'd put a sling on one of Philip's arms, on the side where he hurt inside every time he breathed. "Could be just a sprain, but could also be a fractured rib. Can't do much about that but keep you comfortable, but we'd better take a look."

"I don't want to go anywhere," Philip muttered. He wished they'd all go away and let him sleep. Having his hands cleaned had hurt and so had the stuff his Grandpa put on his mouth.

"You'll have to do what Grandpa says." His mom didn't look so good herself. Philip hated the kids in this town...not all of them, just some. And he didn't understand the stuff they said.

Tom came back into the room. He was the best.

"I'm taking Philip in for an X ray," Doc said to him. "Routine. If he's got a cracked rib we need to be sure it isn't causing any other problems."

"I talked to Mrs. Butterfield," Tom said.

Philip scrunched down in the bed. Now things would get worse. Butterfield was the school principle. Philip was afraid she'd say it was his fault the kids picked on him, and when they found out someone had told her what happened, they'd figure a way to get at him some more.

"What did you say to Mrs. Butterfield?" Doc asked Tom.

Tom moved nearer the bed. "I said that I'm coming into the school tomorrow and we're going to get to the bottom of this. I expect the appropriate kids and their parents to be there."

"No," Philip said. "They'll say I'm a sissy again. I don't want—"

"That's enough," Shelly said. "We'll do what we decide is best for you. Tom's right. We can't let this harassment go on."

"I won't tell you who it was." He tried to sit up but he hurt too much.

"I knew something like this would happen." His grandma hadn't said anything before. He turned his head to see her. She had a handkerchief over her nose. "This is a small town and none of us can afford scandal. Shelly, when are you going to stop all this nonsense and go back to Ben where you belong?"

His mom didn't answer. She crossed her arms and her face looked all white.

"Mrs. Williams—"

"This is nothing to do with you, Tom," Grandpa said. "I know you mean well, but Ben's the one who should be looking after his family, not you. And he wants to do that if Shelly will just let him. I think you've gone quite far enough, my girl. You've got your husband's full attention and it's time you stopped punishing him and your son because you want to be the center of the world."

"I'm not looking for attention. What are you talking about? Ben and I are divorced. When are you going to accept that?"

"We aren't," Grandma said loudly. "I don't know what all this foolishness is. You used to be a sensible young woman. You aren't going to ruin two other lives for your own selfish reasons."

"Hey—" Tom pointed at Grandma "—don't talk to Shelly that way. What makes you think you can run other people's lives? Where do you get off blaming her for everything?"

Philip sank lower in the bed and hitched up the covers. His head ached. All around him everyone was shouting. All they cared about was themselves. He wanted quiet. He was afraid. This was where he wanted to be now, with his mom and Tom, but he wanted his dad, too, and not to be frightened any more.

"I've had it!" Shelly screamed. "Doc—Lucky, please go."

Doc Williams shoved things into his bag. "I'm not going anywhere until you listen to reason."

Mom went close to Grandpa. "The ones who need to get some reason into their heads are you two. Go. Butt out, and I mean it."

Philip put his fingers in his ears and hummed to make a noise inside his head and shut out their voices.

"Come on, Philip. Let's get you to your grandparents' car." Tom was bending over him, lifting him up. "You'll have the X ray and then I'm sure you'll be able to come right home and get back into your own bed." He raised his eyebrows in a way that said he understood how Philip felt. Tom would make it all right again.

Nobody said anything as they went out and down the stairs. Tom had wrapped the quilt around Philip and he began to feel drowsy.

"Mom's okay, isn't she?"

"Of course she is. Don't worry about a thing. We'll come with you and bring you home afterward."

Tom slid him into the back of Grandpa's big car and got in beside him. Everyone was so angry.

He leaned against Tom. "If Mom and Dad didn't have me they wouldn't fight."

"Garbage." Tom put his face close. "That stuff has nothing to do with you."

"Yeah, it has. At least, if Mom didn't have me she could live here and nobody would mind so much."

Tom eased him closer. "Shh, kid. Go to sleep. Grownups make their own problems. Kids get caught in the middle. Your mom and dad will get their act together."

"No, they won't." Tom didn't understand. Why didn't grownups understand things? "Did your dad like you?"

"I . . . yes, he liked me very much."

"But he went away and left you."

"Not because he wanted to. He was sick for a long time, then he died."

"My dad used to go away because he wanted to. And Mom used to cry."

"I'm sorry, Philip. Try to sleep."

"Why didn't Dad love Mom and me?"

Tom's eyes were shiny. Philip thought he looked as though he might even cry. "Your father loves you," he said. "Now be quiet and rest."

THE BEEF WAS a congealed lump in the pan. Shelly forked it onto a plate. "You must be starving," she said to Tom. "I'll make you a sandwich."

"I'm not . . . fine. As long as you have one, too."

As usual, he was concerned about her. "It's a deal. What a day. Now I've got a boy upstairs in bed with a cracked rib and in-laws who blame me for everything."

Wind rattled the windows and a staccato drumming of raindrops sounded. Tom went to look out into the darkness. "Shel, I called Mom while we were at the clinic." He continued to stare outside. "You shouldn't miss work, not now."

She walked slowly to stand behind him. "What are you saying?"

"Mom says she'll be glad to have Philip over at the house for a few days. If you agree, I'll take him with me tonight. It'll be nice for him to have Kurt and Aaron around, after school at least."

"What did you really mean about how I shouldn't miss work?"

He crossed his arms on the sill. Standing like that, with the formidable expanse of black stretched over his hard frame, he seemed very big . . . and unyielding.

"You've already been told too many times how gossipy this town is. Don't give the folks anything to use, such as how a divorced woman with a child can't be a reliable teacher. The names Jimmy got out of Kurt didn't surprise me. Those boys who beat up on Philip have parents who were jealous of you and Ben from when you were kids. They're eating up your problems and feeding the poison to their children."

She pushed a hand through his elbow and laid a cheek on his arm. "I don't want to go away from Allenville."

"You shouldn't until you're ready." He moved to put an arm around her.

Did Tom mean that he expected her to go back to Ben eventually? She sighed and felt her energy ebb even lower. "I've got to do what's right for Philip."

"Will you let me take him home with me for a while so you can keep up at the school? He might even like it out in my barn."

She didn't want to let Philip go. "Okay, but I'll miss him. Doc said he might need a week or so. Tom—" she waited for him to look at her "—you won't make a big deal out of what happened today, will you?"

His mouth set in a hard line and he didn't answer.

"I'm not sure—" The phone rang, sending a jolt through Shelly. She ducked under Tom's arm and crossed the kitchen to answer.

"Shelly?"

She closed her eyes and rolled to lean her head back against the wall. Ben's was the last voice she needed to hear. "Yes."

"Look, I know I'm not one of your favorite people right now so I'll make this short."

She opened her eyes, raised her head. He sounded different, tentative. Could his parents have called him about Philip? They'd said they wouldn't.

"Shelly?"

"I'm here. What do you want, Ben?"

She heard Tom move and looked up to see him opening the sliding door. She covered the mouthpiece. "Don't go out there. It's cold. There won't be anything you can't hear."

"I've been rotten the last couple of weeks," Ben said.

Tom closed the door carefully and remained standing with his back to her.

"What am I supposed to say?"

"That I'm forgiven. I'm trying to apologize and I never was very good at that."

A lump formed in her throat. Everything was too much. She was sad and confused and now Ben had to add his little twist. "It's okay."

"I miss you, Shelly."

"Ben, please—"

"Okay, okay. I promised myself I wouldn't do that. Sorry again. I wish you luck, you know that, don't you?"

Did she? Did she know anything for sure? "Thank you."

"Well, that's it, I guess."

"Yes."

"Is everything all right with you?"

"Everything's wonderful here. How about you?"

"Okay. Well, I'd better let you go."

Shelly took a deep breath. "Thanks for calling. Take care of yourself."

His answering sigh came down the line. "You, too."

She hung up.

"Why didn't you tell him?" Tom had turned around. He frowned deeply. "Ben should know if his son's sick."

Shelly walked to him and held out both hands. When he held them she said, "Why should I tell him? In the weeks since we came back to Allenville, you've been more of a father to Philip than Ben ever was. Love's more than a word."

# Chapter Ten

"Time was when folks let kids fight their own battles," Russ Carrol said, following Tom across the school parking strip.

"And the time was when parents didn't gossip in front of their kids and give them the idea that it's okay to be bullies."

Russ's beefy hand grabbed Tom's shoulder roughly. "Who are you to talk about how kids should be brought up?"

"Don't—" Tom swung around slowly and knocked Russ's arm away "—put your hands on me. If you've got any sense you'll go home and think about what was just said in there. Your boy got Philip where he couldn't be seen by anyone else and incited a fight."

"He threw the first punch."

"Yes he did. And I'm proud of him for his guts. He wasn't about to let the kids call him names...or insult his father."

Carrol adjusted the straps on his overalls and fixed Tom with a narrow stare. "You run along, Tom. You got what you wanted in there, or you think you did. My boy won't be touching the Williams kid again."

The semi-hidden threat didn't slip by Tom. "You got something else in mind, Russ? Planning an attack on another little family as threatening as Shelly Williams and her boy? Maybe I'm your next target, is that what you mean? Well, go ahead, buddy. I'm big enough to take it.''

"Sure you're big enough, but I wonder if your lady friend is. She can still find herself out in the cold if word gets to the school board.''

Tom had reached for the doorhandle on the pickup. He withdrew his fingers slowly. "My lady friend?''

"Ah, don't play dumb with me. Ain't many bodies in town doesn't know you and Shelly Dillon have something going.''

Why had he assumed the prattle on that score had ceased? "Want to expand on that? And it's Shelly Williams now.''

Russ shrugged elaborately. "Ain't nothing I can tell you that you don't already know.'' He laughed unpleasantly. "Old friendships can be convenient, I guess. Sometimes makes it easy to slip into another man's shoes . . . and his bed.''

"I—'' Tom made a fist and uncurled it just as fast. This creep probably hoped for a fight. "The only piece of truth in what you just said is that Shelly and I are friends. I don't like my friends' reputations smeared.''

"Who's smearing?'' Russ's expression changed to one of innocent surprise. "Just repeating what I heard said. Hugging and kissing. Buying gifts in Idaho Falls. Spending nights at her place.''

Tom made a move toward him.

"Just repeating what I heard,'' Russ said, retreating. "Trying to be neighborly so's you can deal with any talk. Maybe you'd better warn your *friend*, too—before someone else does.''

Russ walked away, and Tom made no attempt to stop him. Disgusted, drained, he got into the pickup and stared through the windshield at the sagging school fence. What had gotten into the people around here? He started the engine. How he would manage to keep the talk from Shelly, he didn't know. Damn, what if he couldn't?

BEATTIE GREEN STARED woodenly at Shelly. Seated at her son's desk, she was one of a number of parents who had listened through the school open-house presentation with crossed arms and blank faces.

"Please feel free to look through your student's desk," Shelly concluded, "and to wander about the classroom. I'll be available for any questions you may have."

She dusted chalk from her hands and smiled around. At first no one moved, then they all got up and filed out as if they were puppets on a single set of strings. Shelly watched them go, until she was left alone with the smell of pencil shavings, old books and warm dust behind the popping radiator. She could see the parents congregating outside the classroom, talking in whispers and glancing back at her.

The speaker high in the corner crackled to life. "Parents, we hope you've enjoyed this session." Mrs. Butterfield's plummy voice faded in and out. "Spend as long as you please in the classrooms but don't forget to stop by the library for coffee and to buy goodies at our bake sale."

Shelly walked numbly between rows of scarred desks, lifting chairs on top as she went. Why had they come if they weren't interested in what their children were doing? And why had they been so cool? Beattie she could understand, after what happened with her boy and Philip the week before. Although she might have had the decency to be apologetic. And why had she brought Cathy O'Leary who didn't have a child? What had happened here tonight with the parents?

Gradually the muted conversation in the corridor faded. Shelly went to the staff room to collect her coat and walked out to the Jeep carrying a bag loaded with papers to correct.

"Shelly, we'd like a word with you." Beattie materialized from the shadows, Cathy trailing at her heel.

"Of course," she said, deliberately pleasant. "I'll just put this load down." She unlocked the Jeep and shoved the bag of papers onto the passenger seat.

"It's time we had a chat," Beattie said, hands clasped, a bedraggled purse dangling from one wrist. "Cathy and I decided we should say what's on a lot of peoples' minds."

Shelly looked from Beattie to Cathy. "I take it this is a school matter?"

Cathy shifted from foot to foot. "The children of this town are important. They're our future, our most important resource."

Original clichés, Shelly thought. She said, "I couldn't agree with you more. That's why I'm a teacher."

"Why did you come back here?" Cathy's voice rose. "Aren't there schools in Cleveland that need teachers?"

Letting her uneasiness show would be a mistake. "Cathy, why are you here tonight? You aren't a parent."

"What happens to the young people of this town is important to me," she said, defensiveness sharpening the words. "It's up to every concerned citizen to take an interest in what goes on in this school. And sometimes it takes someone who can be more objective to make the right decisions."

Shelly's legs shook a little and she locked her knees. This confrontation had been planned. She detested conflict, particularly when she didn't understand the reason.

"Cathy also came because she's close to me," Beattie said, sounding pompous. "There are times when it's nice to have the backing of your own kind. She and I understand each other—we've got the same roots. But you wouldn't know what that means."

Shelly stood very straight and shoved her hands into the pockets of her raincoat. "Well, I guess you and I don't have the same roots, apart from having been born and brought up in the same town. We have nothing in common apart from that, thank goodness. But I must say I'm glad you've stopped pushing Cathy around, Beattie, or have you?"

"What does that mean?" Beattie lifted her clasped hands higher.

"You victimized Cathy when we were children. For as long as I can remember you called her names and picked on her. And she always seemed to be looking for ways to become a pet worthy of an occasional crumb or pat from you. I never could understand why bullies gather admirers, but it happens."

"I don't know what you're talking about," Cathy said. "You talked like that when we were kids—high and mighty."

"Mmm. Did Beattie persuade you to come along tonight because you're smarter than she is?" Agitation trembled in the night now. "And did you agree because you're still hoping for a crumb or two of Beattie's magical attention? Fascinating . . . it really is."

"Don't you answer her, Cathy. I'll tell her, then she won't be so pleased with herself." Beattie stepped close to Shelly, who didn't give in to the urge to move backward. "You're not wanted here. We want you to move on. Go back where you came from or anywhere else you please, but don't stay here, not if you don't want a lot of trouble."

Shelly turned cold. "What are you talking about? You don't have the right to tell me what I should or shouldn't do."

"Oh, I think I do. You're unfit, that's what you are. We all talked about it and decided you're unfit."

It was Shelly's turn to close the distance between her and Beattie even more. "Unfit?"

Beattie did retreat. She backed into Cathy, who shuffled up beside her. "Unfit to teach children, you are," she said in a voice that rose higher and higher. "The people of this town don't want their children's minds polluted. And I said I'd be the one to tell you."

Shelly flinched as if she'd been slapped. "This is crazy. Cathy, you're intelligent enough, what is Beattie talking about?"

Cathy bowed her head. "You'd be better to do what she says and not ask any more questions."

"That's right," Beattie said. "You clear out and take your prissy troublemaking boy with you. Tattling on my boy over nothing. Stirring up nonsense with Mrs. Butterfield. But that's not the half of it. That's not the real reason we can't put up with you here."

"Are you going to tell me the real reason? Or am I going to get into my Jeep and try to forget we ever had this conversation?"

"You're a bitch, Shelly Williams." Beattie screamed more than spoke. "We don't hold with the likes of you in Allenville. Running out on your husband and turning him away when he tries to get you back. You always were a slick one and now you think you're going to bring your fast ways into our school where our children can get the idea it's all right to be like you."

"Beattie—"

"You hold your tongue. If you aren't out of the school and out of this town, I may have to go to the school board."

Shelly trembled steadily. She took her hands from her pockets and rubbed them together. "You, Beattie, are a vicious gossip. There isn't a person in this town who doesn't know that, and there isn't a person on the school board who will listen to your ranting."

"Hah!" Beattie pushed her hand through Cathy's elbow and started dragging her back. "They'll listen when I tell them what you are. Morally unfit to teach children!"

The first drops of a shower fell on Shelly's face. She blinked. Each breath she took hurt her throat.

"That shut you up didn't it? No arguments to that one." Beattie and Cathy hurried away.

The rain fell harder and harder. By the time Shelly roused herself enough to climb into the Jeep, her hair clung to her face and water dripped steadily inside her collar.

On the way through town she stopped and called Alice Conrad to say she wouldn't be by to see Philip. She had visited him after school in the afternoon, before returning for open house.

"Shelly," Alice said, "I don't know how to tell you this but I'd better, even though Tom says he doesn't want you worried."

"It's all right, Alice, I already know. I just had a conversation with some people who couldn't wait to tell me what's going on."

"In that case, I expect you'll understand if he's, well, you know." Alice sounded miserable.

"I understand," Shelly said and hung up.

By the time she reached the house her windshield wipers couldn't keep up with the sheeting downpour. Steering into the driveway, she almost hit Tom's pickup before she saw it. She switched off her engine and put on the emergency brake. He'd come because he knew she needed him.

Completely soaked, Shelly squelched into the house, shaking her hair and grimacing as she kicked off sodden shoes and worked buttons free on her raincoat.

"Tom!"

Shrugging out of the coat, she padded a soggy course to the kitchen where the light shone through the open door. "Tom, where are you?"

His denim jacket lay half on a chair, half on the floor. His hat was under the table.

"Shel? That you?"

His voice came from the front of the house. Relieved, she hurried back to the hall, stopping again just outside the living room. He was sitting in the dark.

"Tom, are you in there?" She reached a hand inside and turned on the overhead lamp.

"Yeah, I'm here. Taking a rest. Don't mind, do you?"

"Of course, I don't mind." She smiled, pushed her dripping hair back and went in. "Thanks for coming..."

Stripped to the waist, he sprawled on the new blue couch. A damp ring spread from his wet shirt where it had landed on the carpet in a screwed-up heap.

The hand that trailed on the rug held an empty glass.

# Chapter Eleven

Tom rolled his head from side to side, narrowing his eyes as if trying to bring Shelly into focus.

She'd removed the glass from his hand before going to make coffee. Now the trick was to get some of it into him, which wasn't going to be easy as long as he remained where he was.

"I tell you it's sabotage." He closed his mouth and turned his face to the back of the couch. "Someone did it to me."

Shelly, kneeling beside him, sat back on her heels and set the coffee mug on a table. "Sabotage? What are you talking about? Look at me and explain."

His answer was a snore. Frustrated, she covered her face with both hands. If she had the energy she would cry.

"W'as the matter?"

She started and looked up into his droopy eyes. "What's the matter with you? You don't drink, Tom. Why would you come over here and get drunk like this?"

"Phil . . . Philip's at my place. I had to get out."

"Sit up." She stood over him. "And drink some coffee. You're not making any sense."

He crossed his arms over his chest and grunted.

Shelly took one powerful arm in both of her hands and tugged. "Sit up." Not an inch of him moved, or even stirred. "Damn you, Tom Conrad. I've had all I can take for one day."

"You?" A booted foot hit the floor, and he struggled onto an elbow. "You've had a bad day." He swayed forward and she pushed him back.

"Okay, let's calm down." She sat beside him, slipped a hand behind his neck to support his head and brought the mug to his lips. "Drink, and that's an order."

He did, grimaced and coughed. "Don't care," he muttered. "Third of everything gone. They got back at me. Got . . ." His eyes closed.

Shelly waited, shaking him gently. A sense of foreboding grew steadily.

He lurched against her and the coffee spilled. "Cully found it first. Walked out there and went knee-deep."

She managed to put the mug down again. Something was terribly wrong with Tom, and it didn't spring from her problem. Half-sitting, he held on to her now.

"What did Cully find?" If Tom hadn't said his hired hand's name, Shelly wouldn't have remembered what it was. "Tell me." His head was a dead weight on her shoulder.

He raised his face until their noses were inches apart. She swallowed at the smell of rum. "I told you. The breakout from the irrigation system. Cully said . . . we went back and it's no good."

Shelly put a hand on each side of his jaw to stop him from bowing his head again. "The irrigation system is broken? Where? Explain what's wrong, please. I'll help, you know I will."

"Help!" He snickered. "Whatcha gonna do, wear waders and see if my spuds turned into fishes? I got a flood. Someone busted a water gate somewhere, or did something to the pipes, and I got acres of spud soup."

The impact of what he'd said slowly took shape. And the meaning of what Alice had said on the phone. Rather than referring to Shelly's concerns, Alice had been talking about this. Instinctively, she eased Tom's head onto her shoulder once more, stroking his damp hair and murmuring senseless words. Tears sprang into her eyes, tears at the injustice of what had apparently happened. She didn't have to be a potato farmer to know what flooding meant. Wipeout. It rarely happened, but when it did the damage and loss of revenue could be crippling.

"Tom, listen to me. This is no good. You can't go to pieces. Your mom needs you, Mary and Jimmy and the boys." She wanted to say *I need you*. "It'll work out, I know it will."

He jerked upright, out of her arms, and slumped against the couch. "What d'you know about it? It's Ben that should be here. I oughta call him. I'll do just that." Stopping him from getting up was unnecessary. One wobbly move and he landed back where he'd started. "Good ol' Ben. My pal. Couldn't take enough of what I wanted. Never enough. Now he's taken everything."

Shelly massaged her cold face, trying to think, to make sense of what he was saying.

"It was okay for me to have less. I never minded that." His eyes closed slightly. "That's a lie. I minded a hell of a lot. I still mind."

"Ben doesn't have anything to do with what's happened at the farm," Shelly said, gripping Tom's knees and trying to hold his gaze. "How much acreage—"

"He does, too. You never knew. I never told you, but I'd bet everything..." He tipped his head heavily onto one shoulder. "Everything I have left, that is. I'd bet he knew what it was like for me. Big, bluff Ben. Smiling while he...he knew how I felt even if I never said so."

This made less and less sense. Her first impulse was to call the farm and have someone come and take Tom home. But that would embarrass him and put more pressure on Alice and the others.

"Listen. I'm going to help you lie down. You can sleep in the spare bedroom until you're sober enough to go home. Have some more of this coffee."

"Don't want coffee." A big hand splayed over his face. Shelly longed to hug him, to take away all the hurt. "Ben's gonna pay, do you hear me?"

His voice rose, and Shelly drew back. Anger tightened his face while a suggestion of tears stood in his eyes. Tom never lost control. He had tonight.

"Let me help you upstairs." Her heart beat harder and faster.

"This was gonna be the year when we made real headway." His shoulders heaved, then dropped. "Not anymore. Thanks to good old Ben, that's all so much pie in the sky."

"Knock it off." She took his hands in hers and tried to pull him up. "You're scaring me. Ben doesn't know anything about flooding. He doesn't know what's happened to you."

A sudden yanking landed her on her knees between Tom's thighs. "I'm not scaring you," he shouted. "I would never scare you. Ben's doing it. Like he messed up everything before. He should have looked after you and Philip. He shouldn't have that boy."

Shelly felt faint. Too much stress for too many hours was taking its toll. She sank down between his legs and rested her forehead on his thigh. "I don't know what you're saying."

"I know how I got van...vandalized. I'm taking it in the gut for what Ben did. He did things that made you have to leave him. If you hadn't had to do that you wouldn't be here where..."

"Oh, please," Shelly whispered, "say what you're trying to say. I'm so tired."

The hand lay still on her neck, its warmth seeping into her chilled skin. "Someone had to look after Philip...fight for him. I didn't mind that. I wanted to do it. But it's Ben's fault. If he'd looked after you there'd have been no need. The people here were looking for an excuse to get at me and they found it. I showed them up, and they paid me back."

"If you know that, you can prosecute." She was still held fast but she managed to look at him. "We'll go to the sheriff."

"Won't be able to prove anything." His voice slurred to an indistinct drawl. "S'Ben's fault. Everything."

"You can't blame him," she began, but the pressure on her neck slackened and his hand fell away. Shelly touched his face, "Tom?" He was asleep and slowly sliding sideways.

Getting him upstairs was out of the question. For a long time she stood looking down at him, oddly young, vulnerable in his sprawled pose. His hair had begun to dry and the lighter streaks glimmered among the tousled straight wreck that had grown longer than usual while he'd been so busy with planting. The same glimmer showed along the bleached tips of his lashes as his eyes moved beneath closed lids.

All she could do was to make him comfortable where he was. From the upstairs linen closet she collected a pillow, a blanket and a towel.

He moved a little as she lifted his head but instantly settled into the pillow. *Tom,* she said over and over in her mind. Could she and Philip be the cause of someone destroying part of his crops?

She needed him so, but she should leave him alone to get on with his own life.

Working off his boots proved more of a challenge than she'd expected. By the time the first one plopped free she was sweating. She rested, dragging off his wet sock and drying his foot. She paused. Slowly, she traced the sharp shin bone, passed her fingertips lightly over the start of hard calf muscle beneath skin covered with dark blond hair. Long, strong legs . . . like the rest of him.

She finished drying his foot and pulled the other boot until it came away with a sucking noise. Again she disposed of a dripping sock and went to work with the towel. She would not allow what she'd started to feel to happen again. If she were honest she'd admit she'd felt it before, but she couldn't face that, not with Tom, who'd already suffered enough at her hands.

He was too tall for the couch and there was no choice but to settle his legs and let his feet hang over one end.

His body was dry by now. Shelly touched his chest where the dark hair flared wide. Dry enough . . . and solid. Her breathing turned shallow. The jeans were wet. She swallowed, glancing at the rain-darkened waistband that rode low on his narrow hips.

Quickly she spread the blanket over him. A few hours in damp jeans wouldn't kill him.

"Tom," she whispered. "Can you hear me?"

He groaned and threw an arm over his head. Shelly sat down on the floor beside him. He was a beautiful man, inside and out, and she could . . . she could so easily give in to feelings she recognized too well.

Carefully she kissed his naked shoulder, spread a hand on his chest and rested her cheek there where his heart beat steadily. She closed her eyes and felt a surge within that was

almost a blow. This could not be. She would not let it be or
ever let him know what had become so clear tonight.

Shelly backed away. She'd married Ben. Tom was her
friend, and Ben's. These feelings weren't what she'd thought
they were.... He must never know. Oh, God, he mustn't
even guess she'd ever looked at him and wanted . . .

Tomorrow they'd talk and she'd help him figure out what
had to be done at the farm. If all she could offer was sympathy and support that would be enough for Tom. He was
a giver, not a taker.

"Shelly!"

She rushed back to him but he slept on, his lips moving.
His mouth was perfect. Why hadn't she always known how
perfect his mouth was?

Tom was lonely, too. She shuddered. They were two normal adults. Loneliness could drive people into situations
they couldn't handle. Rather than shame her he'd probably
respond if she let him know how she felt.

He ought to have someone of his own—and be out of her
reach permanently.

# Chapter Twelve

"Tom— Eat something before you leave. Talk to you later. Shelly." He read the note again before putting it in his pocket and going to the kitchen.

The inside of his head beat like a bongo drum and his dry mouth was something he'd prefer to spit out. What had he done here last night? Good God, what had he said to Shelly?

His shirt hung on a hanger on the back of the kitchen door, and his socks were spread over the tops of his boots near a heating vent. A fizzing, popping sound drew his eyes to the coffee pot. The smell made him feel sick. He'd left the farm at six and stopped to buy a bottle of rum, then he'd come here.

The farm. He slipped heavily into a chair and rested his head on the table. Bits and pieces came back. Cully knocking on the barn door; squelching through the north fields... Black earth puddled with scum-rimmed water.

He had to get home.

Minutes later, a box of crackers under his arm, he locked Shelly's front door and walked gingerly to the pickup. Wind and rain buffeted him, and every step jarred his brain.

He climbed in and opened the crackers. Cramming several into his mouth, he switched on the engine and backed from the driveway. Twisting his neck hurt. The crackers were dry and salt crystals burned his tongue. He would never, as long as he lived, touch another drop of booze.

What had he said to Shelly?

Every dip and bump in the road brought a fresh dart of pain. He rubbed a hand over his stubbled chin, massaging aching jaw muscles. He must have ground his teeth while he slept. A shower, a shave and some aspirin were a must before he went about initiating the steps of flood cleanup and started calculating losses and what to do about them. He thought of Betty away in school. No way was his little sister going to suffer because of a vendetta against him. Please, don't let it be so bad he couldn't recover.

A sturdy bay, tethered to the porch railing in front of the house, was the first thing Tom really focused on as he stopped the pickup.

Jay Barthrup's horse. Jay was the local ditch rider responsible for patrolling the canals and opening the reservoir gates to release water.

Tom struggled from the cab, pushing against the wind to reach the house. Before he could mount the steps, Cully and Jay emerged from the front door.

Cully's thin face seemed shriveled. "Been waiting for you, boss. Jimmy's gone on ahead but we said we'd wait till you turned up."

Beneath the brim of his sweat-stained hat, Jay's dark eyes made a slow pass over Tom. "Rough one. You okay?"

He'd brought the crackers from the cab. Now he tried to stuff them into his jacket pocket only they wouldn't fit. "Yeah. Mad as hell but okay." Why try to hide that he'd tied one on and that he was a mess? "You planning to check the gates today? Don't reckon you'll find much."

Cully grunted and Jay said, "Already checked 'em. Not that we can do a damn thing about it. Ain't no doubt in my mind that two gates were opened since the last time I

touched 'em. The one near Three Pines and the one soutl
of that. With the water level as high as it is, wouldn't tak
that long to build up enough pressure to cause a ditcl
breakout, and we got a dandy right at Sims' Ridge. Mei
have been on it since Cully called last night and the water'
stopped up. They think the ditch was given a hand, if yo
know what I mean.''

Tom stared at the distant Tetons, indistinct in today'
drizzle. The wind drove the rain into his face and he wipe
his eyes. "Sorry I left you to it, Cully. Is that where Jimm
went? Up to the ditch?"

"Yeah. He's pretty shook up, too."

"Sure he is. We're all going to feel the pinch aroun
here . . . if that's all we feel. We may go under altogether."

"Nah," Cully said. "We've been through worse than this
Tighten the old belt, and we'll get through again."

Tom wasn't so sure. He'd overextended on new equip
ment, and the two loans he was already paying off made hir
reluctant to go after another. But it was too soon to knov
what he'd do.

Another pickup, this one red and beaten up, rolled to
stop, and Russ Carrol slid out. A battered green baseball cap
was tipped back on his head, and a brown plaid coa
strained across his belly. His face was creased into a som
ber mold.

"What's he want?" Cully said under his breath.

"Mornin', Tom," Russ said, strolling up to the group
"Heard about your trouble and came over to see if there'
anything I can do."

Tom's head gave a mighty thud and he half closed hi
eyes. Just what he needed. "There's nothing, thanks, Russ
Except a prayer or two, maybe."

"Know what you mean." The man settled his weight on one foot. "But I reckon I might be able to do something useful. You got time to talk?"

"I should go check out the damage."

Russ shifted to the other foot. "Suit yourself. Just tryin' to be neighborly."

It seemed that Russ had developed a thing for being "neighborly," but Tom's curiosity got the better of him. "You two go ahead," he said to Jay and Cully. "I'll find you."

Once the two men had left, Tom faced Russ. "Okay. Thanks for coming over. What's on your mind?" As he spoke a shutter clicked in his brain. *They were looking for an excuse to get at me.* Had he said that to Shelly and made her feel to blame?

"You listening, Tom?"

He took a deep breath and concentrated on Russ's shiny face. "Sorry. What did you say?"

"I was talking about the breakout. Who expects a thing like that? Must have been a weakness there."

Tom narrowed his eyes. As far as he knew, details of the breakout weren't common knowledge yet. "Must have been," he said, intently watching Russ's shifting eyes.

"Reckon you'll have trouble hanging on."

Tom's stomach made a slow revolution. He didn't want to hear the truth out loud. "We'll make out. May take time to catch up, but Conrads has had its share of trouble before and we're still here."

Russ cleared his throat. "You know them acres you got fallow by my place?" he said.

"Yeah." Tom's spine tightened. "What about them?"

"Well—" Russ shrugged, not meeting Tom's eyes "—I been looking for more land and I wondered if you might be interested in sellin'."

The suggestion took a second to process. Sell some of his
land . . . "No. I'm going to need every inch I've got."

"I know, I know. But the money, Tom. Think of the
money you're gonna need to clean up those flooded fields
and fill in for the income you won't be getting."

"I'll take my chances." The vulture had arrived a little too
on cue. Tom fixed him with a hard stare. "Didn't your father approach mine years ago about buying that land?"

"That's neither here nor there," Russ said offhandedly.
"I'd be willing to lease it back to you and the rent wouldn't
be high. You'd get the best of both worlds . . . a bit of new
capital when you need it, and the use of the land."

"And you'd own it. That'd make you feel real good,
wouldn't it? And how long would it be before the rent went
up, or you decided you wanted to use the land yourself?
That's prime acreage, and you know it."

Russ bristled. "You thinkin' for me? I didn't say I'd do
any of those things. Anyway, I don't see that you've got
many choices. Where else you gonna' raise money? I know
you've got loans already. That's the price of expanding so
damn fast." He reddened. "But that's your business. All
I'm doing is trying to help out. I heard the ditch went on
Sims' Ridge and I came right over. Guess it don't do no
good to be neighborly."

Tom's heart beat faster. Damn the pain in his head. But
it wasn't so bad that he'd missed the slip. Could Russ have
been told exactly where the breakout was? He doubted it.
Few people would even know there was a Sims' Ridge or
where it was located. Taking this buzzard by the throat
would feel great but it wouldn't accomplish a thing.

"I'd give anything to know how those three gates got
opened and closed yesterday." It was a shot in the dark but
neighborly Russ was no great brain and he might make another mistake.

"Two," Russ corrected obligingly and coughed. "I think I heard it was two, though there's no way of proving those things is there?"

"No," Tom said, very low. "I don't suppose there's any way at all. And now, if you don't mind, I'd like you to drive that pile of junk of yours off my land and never come back."

Russ's flabby jowls turned puce. "Shows what a man gets for trying to help." But he passed a hand over his mouth and the hand shook.

Without waiting for him to leave, Tom strode around the house, heading for the barn. What he needed now was to be alone, and to accept that he had to put all this behind him and pick up the pieces. He also had to find a way to stop hating.

SHELLY MADE AN EXCUSE to duck out of an after-school staff meeting and drove as fast as she dared to Conrads.

Tom's pickup was parked in front of the farmhouse. She peered across the fields and made out moving figures to the north. They would be doing whatever must be done to salvage some of the mess. Her skin prickled. Last night was something she'd never forget: Tom's desperation, his wild talk. And there were other things she wouldn't allow herself to forget or fail to guard against.

She'd intended to talk to him but in this moment her courage fled. Better not to get too close to him for at least a little while.

The front door wasn't locked. Shelly knocked and walked in, finding Alice in the kitchen.

"Philip's over at Jim and Mary's," she said as soon as she spotted Shelly. She smiled but her eyes showed strain.

"Alice, I'm so sorry about the flood."

"So am I." Alice sorted silverware into a drawer, dropping the pieces noisily. "I'm sorry about a lot of things."

Shelly closed the distance between them and put her arms around the other woman. "You've always been so strong. It's okay to cry."

"I've cried," Alice said. "Now it's time to get on with what has to be done. We'll make it. It's Tom I'm worried about."

"I know." Shelly stepped away. "He's taking this so badly. Not that I blame him."

"It's not only the way he's taking this that bothers me." Alice looked at her sharply. "Do I have to explain what I mean?"

Shelly shifted uncomfortably, unsure exactly how much Tom would have revealed about his antagonism toward Ben. "He's angry, Alice, and unsure about what the future holds. I know what he'd like to have me do, but I don't think that's a possibility. Too much has happened in the past."

"Are you sure of that?" Alice's mouth thinned. "It's never too late if something's truly worthwhile, and I think this is."

"I can't argue about it." Shelly shrugged, feeling helpless. "I'd better go and get Philip. It's time I got him back home and back in school. He'll be fine now, if he's careful."

"Aren't you going to talk to Tom?"

Shelly pinched the bridge of her nose. How could Alice begin to guess the complications that might arise if she didn't keep some distance between herself and Tom?

"Please," Alice said. "For my sake. He's in the barn. He's been there for hours."

Without responding, Shelly went, dropping her keys into her coat pocket then holding them tightly there.

The afternoon was windy and clear, innocent as if the rain of yesterday and this morning must have been imagined. She knocked on the barn door and waited, her hair whipping across her face. Tom's indistinct, "Come in," gave her a shaky feeling. Please don't let him be drunk again.

In jeans and an unbuttoned blue check shirt, he sat on the floor surrounded by papers. His feet were bare and he hadn't shaved. He looked... Shelly swallowed. He looked wonderful.

"How's it going?" she asked and felt ridiculous.

Tom stood up and stepped over the papers. "At this point I don't know. It's all still sinking in, and I keep going over the same figures again and again." He gave a small mirthless laugh. "They don't improve with time."

"I know I've said this before, but I'm sorry. Was it really sabotage? Or don't you know?"

"I'm sure it was. So's Cully, Jimmy and Jay Barthrup. But we can't prove anything. I've been poring over these for hours." He pointed at the scattered papers. "It's going to be the pits, but if we pare back to the bone I think we may just make it. What hurts most is that we were due. This was going to be the year when we started to breathe easily."

Shelly folded her arms awkwardly. "Alice said she's worried about you. She seemed to think I could cheer you up."

The look he gave her was odd...the familiar straight blue gaze, but with something else underneath, something she couldn't fathom.

"Did Mom say why she thought you could cheer me up?"

"I guess—" she hesitated and walked to the wall of books "—I guess you must have told her how you want Ben and me back together. At least, I think that's what she was talking about."

"Maybe."

"You're angry with me. You think this is my fault. Isn't that true?" His silence grated. She faced him. "In case you haven't heard, I've got troubles, too. There was an open house at school last night. Beattie Green and Cathy O'Leary let me know how Allenville views me."

The gradual paling of his face shocked her. He must have already heard the gossip. Could he feel his reputation was threatened by his association with her?

"Tom, why don't you say something? Last night I was told I was morally unfit to teach children."

He sat on the nearest chair and covered his face, saying nothing.

"I'm sorry," she said. "I'll leave."

She never made it to the door. He leaped up and cut her off. His face was strained, the lines about his eyes and mouth pulled tight. "You're not going anywhere. This has been coming for a long time and we'd better deal with it."

Trembling inside made her light-headed. "You let me know how you felt last night. Not that you haven't said it in a dozen different ways before."

He frowned. "What did I let you know last night?"

Shelly sighed. He didn't remember. "You don't approve of me. And you blame me and Ben for what happened here at the farm yesterday. I can't argue, Tom, because I think you're probably right and I feel so rotten. I will help...I do have some money—"

"I don't want your money!" He clamped her shoulders in his strong hands. "And you are so far off about so many things, I can't believe it. Did Beattie and Cathy say they were on your case because you're divorced?"

She flinched at his vehemence and put her hands on his chest. "Yes...they said I was morally unfit. I told you that."

He shook her gently and she dug her fingertips into his warm skin. Beneath her hands the hair on his chest was coarse.

"It isn't because of the divorce," he said, almost in a whisper. "Why haven't you figured out...I had a little chat with one of my neighbors, too."

She looked into his eyes and away again. His intensity clawed at her. "They think you're a traitor to the local cause?" she said.

"They think we're having an affair."

Shelly blinked and opened her mouth. The air seemed thin. She couldn't breathe but she smelled Tom's clean scent and with the tightening of his grip she was pulled closer. Slowly, watching her hands, she let them slip to his sides. The texture was smooth there. He was embarrassed, and she was the cause.

"No...they can't think that. It's outrageous." Weariness weighted every muscle.

"Is it?"

She must have misheard him. "What did you say?"

"Why is it so outrageous for people to think there's something between us? We're always together and often with no one else around."

"We've known each other since we were kids," Shelly said, but the words felt and sounded hollow.

"You and Ben knew each other from when you were kids—and then married. There's no magic cutting off of natural chemistry between a man and a woman just because they've been friends for a long time."

What she heard was a quiet desperation, and she didn't understand him. "But there isn't anything between us. What you want most is for me to go back to Ben and make our marriage work."

"Is it?"

Nothing moved. The points of their contact, his hands on her shoulder, hers at his waist, felt electric . . . fused. Shelly tried to form words but couldn't speak.

"I'm going to say my piece and then you'll just have to decide what to do about it. Is that okay?"

She nodded. Her mind seemed to move very slowly.

He released his hold to circle her neck lightly. Once, twice, he stroked his thumbs over her collarbones. There was no doubt about what his eyes showed now . . . painful uncertainty.

"When we were in our teens I never really examined my feelings . . . about you. You and Ben and I were a unit and we always would be. Shows how innocent I was. Oh, all the signs were there but I never had a whole lot of time to think, and maybe I didn't want to. Remember your graduation from college?"

She nodded again.

"Shelly, next to your wedding day that was the worst day of my life. That was when I knew I loved you."

"Oh, Tom." She tried to hug him but he held her away.

"Don't, Shel. Don't do anything that'll change things that shouldn't be changed. I can't take being near you anymore, and not being close enough. At twenty-two, when I finally let myself admit what I felt for you, I was wiped out. You'll never know the anger I took out on every inanimate object in sight. But I was wrong. I had no right. You and Ben fell in love and married and that's the way it goes. I learned to accept it.

"But I wasn't ready for you to come back and say you were divorced. I couldn't believe you were here and I was supposed to drop into the role of good old friend and supporter. Do you have any idea what that's done to me in the past couple of months?"

"I—"

"It's been hell, and I've waited too long to tell you. If I've upset you, I'm sorry, but I'm human and I can't go on this way. Please don't . . . I couldn't stand it if I thought I sickened you. I know this has to be a shock, but I've got to believe you'll understand and forgive me. If you need anything, you know I'll be there for you, but I'm going to have to put some distance between us, for my own sake. You'll want that now, anyway."

She pulsed faintly, her body, every nerve ending. "I don't want it."

Silence slipped in again, a great palpable silence.

She bowed her head but Tom used a thumb to raise her chin. "What did you say?"

"I said I don't want any distance between us."

He held his bottom lip in his teeth and stared at her hard. "You don't mean . . ."

"Yes, I do." Why couldn't this be an easy thing to do, to tell him what she felt? Why must it seem unnatural and dangerous? "For a long time I didn't realize what was going on with me. You were here, my best friend. Then everything changed but I still didn't fully understand that what I felt for you wasn't so simple."

He sighed. "And it isn't so simple, is it?"

"No. Tom, what do we do? I can't . . . how can this be happening? We can't just announce that we . . ."

Tom framed her face with his hands and smiled. Gently, slowly, he kissed her brow, kept his firm mouth pressed there while he wrapped her in his arms.

Shelly slipped her own arms around him beneath the shirt. He was solid, real, and she wanted to forget there were people out there, and situations that robbed any pure joy from the moment.

"We have to think. It would be so easy . . . so damn fantastically easy to go ahead and not think about what all this would mean to a lot of other people." He eased her head into the hollow of his shoulder. "I can't believe you feel the same way I do. And I can't even enjoy it."

She understood, but all the words had to be said. "There wouldn't be any going back, would there? And if things didn't work out we'd have less than we had before."

He released her. "There's no going back from here anyway. We know how we feel. The only question is what we decide to do about it . . . if anything."

Shelly blinked. When had the tears started. "I'd better go and pick up Philip." Tom's hands were in his pockets, his face turned away. "We'll talk, okay? And think. We've got to be sure what we decide is right."

"Okay," he said.

As she opened the door the wind caught at her, slapped the hem of her skirt about her legs. She looked back at him and raised a hand to wave.

Tom shook his head. "Go quickly, Shel."

She closed the door, but not before she heard him say, "I've always loved you."

## Chapter Thirteen

"I'm going to take care of it, sweetie."

"Pops...this isn't your problem, it's mine." Shelly held the phone tightly. The scuttlebutt had finally infiltrated the Dillon household, and her father was reacting with the protective instincts she would have expected.

"What affects my family affects me," he said. "You can imagine how your mother is. She'll settle down, but if the likes of Beattie Green think they can point the finger at my girl, they're mistaken."

Shelly visualized her father, crippled by arthritis, constantly fighting pain, and she chewed the inside of her mouth, furious with herself for bringing him more discomfort.

"Shelly?"

"Yes, Pops. I'm here."

"It was Walt Green who blabbed to your mother about you being a bad influence on the children. That whole family keeps afloat on the goods they get from us, and they never completely pay off their bill. I'll deal with them, d'you hear?"

"I hear." At any other time she might try to dissuade him from using leverage on her behalf. Today she didn't feel strong enough to argue. "But don't get upset, okay?"

"I won't. You hold your head up, girl. There's not a body in this town has a reason—"

The doorbell distracted her. It had to be Tom. Today was Saturday, and she hadn't seen or heard from him in three days.

"Pops, someone's at the door. I'll talk to you later." She hung up and hurried into the hall. She'd hardly slept or been able to concentrate on anything since she'd left Tom at the barn. Today Philip was visiting with Kurt and Aaron.

The bell rang as she opened the door.

"Hi."

Ben. Her legs felt like water. "What are you doing here?" She looked for Lucky Williams's Mercedes but saw a rental car parked by the fence.

"Coming to see you and Philip," Ben said, his dark eyes mirroring his insecurity. The never-ending wind tossed his curly and overly long hair wildly. "May I come in?"

Shelly hesitated. "I thought we'd more or less agreed to stay away from each other. At least for the foreseeable future."

"That last visit was a fiasco. I've already told you I was sorry for that. My folks don't know I'm here, so they won't add the kind of stress they did last time. And when I leave I'm going straight back to Cleveland. Can we talk?"

"I don't know." He couldn't know, couldn't guess the pressure she was under, or how badly she didn't want to see him.

He propped an elbow on the doorjamb and gave a wry smile. "Please. If I have to beg I will, but I don't think you want that. All I'm asking for is a little time with you."

What point was there in arguing? If she turned him away flat she'd feel guilty later. "Come in."

She returned to the kitchen, leaving him to close the door. He trailed in and stood awkwardly in the middle of the room. "Mind if I take off my jacket?"

She shrugged. Why couldn't it have been Tom who came?

"I've had plenty of time to think lately." He took off his navy cotton parka and held it in both hands. A pale blue turtleneck clung to his massive physique. He was a show-stopper and she was ordinary. His reason for continuing to pursue her eluded Shelly.

"Philip isn't here," she said. "He's out at Tom's place. He and Mary's boys are good friends."

"I'm glad. Boys need friends."

And they need fathers, Shelly thought. "He's beginning to settle in nicely." Thank goodness the sling was off Philip's arm. If Ben found out his son had been hurt, and why, Shelly had a feeling she'd be knee-deep in more controversy than she already was.

"When will he be back? I'd like to see him, too." Ben wadded the jacket. "I miss him. I miss you both."

Shelly looked away. "He'll be there most of the day unless I arrange to get him early. Coffee?" She might as well try to keep this pleasant.

"Thanks. Maybe I could go out and pick him up later."

And come face to face with Tom and his family? Shelly didn't respond.

"I've felt bad about the way I behaved when I came before. I shouldn't have said or done the things I did. I'm sorry."

"I know. You told me on the phone." She spooned coffee into a filter.

"Is there a chance we could be friends? I don't want to lose touch with you."

Why had it taken the loss of her love to make him decide she was important to him? "I'd like Philip to have a good relationship with you, Ben."

He was quiet while the percolator started to bubble. Shelly took out a mug, hesitated and reached for a second one. They had too much shared past for her to totally abandon him if he was suffering.

"Shelly—"

Again the doorbell rang and they glanced at each other. Before she could stop him, Ben went to open the door.

"Hi, Tom," she heard him say. "Come on in."

Shelly clenched her fists. She couldn't stand it. Ben and Tom in the same room with her.

Tom preceded Ben and when she saw him a breath caught in her throat. Dark smudges under his eyes testified to his having had as little sleep as she in the past few days. But added to that was an expression of tense confusion.

"Ben just dropped in," she told him quickly. "He says he can't stay long so it's a good thing you came by or you might have missed him." It sounded lame but she couldn't do any better.

Tom stood between her and Ben, his back to Ben. "How are you?"

She ached to go to him. "I'm existing," she said, praying he'd understand that she was telling him how much she'd missed him. "The days have seemed long lately, and the nights."

"How are things with you, Tom?" Ben asked, apparently oblivious to the charged waves in the air.

"Lousy," Tom said without turning around. "We had a flood and lost pretty near a third of the crop."

Ben slowly lowered his hands. "God. Tom, I'm sorry. What a bummer. Is it going to be tough . . . ? Hell, what am I talking about, of course it's going to be tough on you."

Tom continued to stare at Shelly, and the hunger in his eyes stripped her nerves. He'd come to tell her what he'd decided about the two of them. She longed for them to be alone.

"I'm making coffee," she told Tom. "Do you have time for some?"

"I'll make time."

"Hey," Ben said finally. "How about a walk, Tom? It's years since you and I got to talk about old times."

Shelly gripped the edge of the counter. Tom would refuse, he had to.

"Sure," he said. "We won't be long, Shel. Keep the coffee hot." With that he led the way through the sliding door to the backyard.

THE YARD WAS BIG and needed work. Tom hooked his thumbs into his jeans pockets. If he'd had time he'd have tried to do something about a vegetable garden for Shelly, but time was something that would only get tighter for him.

"I love this place," Ben said. They'd walked to the back fence where, side by side, they leaned and looked out over miles of uncultivated land.

"Yeah. So do I."

"You couldn't believe I'd leave Allenville for a place like Cleveland, could you?"

Tom turned and propped his elbows. This was crazy. He'd come to talk to Shelly, the woman he loved, and here he was chatting with her ex-husband. "Not at first. But later I did. I had some pretty unreal notions when I was younger."

"We all did. And some of us didn't grow up fast enough in the end."

Tom glanced sideways at his friend's set face. He was talking about what had happened between him and Shelly. His throat closed.

"It was all so glamorous," Ben said, almost to himself. "Newspaper interviews, TV spots. Parties, gifts—you name it, I got it, and I didn't cope so well." He spread his big hands. "I was a boy from a small town. Sure, there'd been all kinds of attention in college, but nothing like you get in the pros. I bought all the trash about how wonderful I was and ate it up. Shelly suffered. I'll never forgive myself for that. I took it for granted that she'd always be there no matter what I did. I should have known better."

Tom cleared his throat, uncomfortable with this different Ben who'd never been big on humility.

"When I lost Shelly I lost the only worthwhile thing in my life," Ben said.

There seemed to be nothing to say. Tom watched Ben and couldn't miss the sheen in his eyes. This was no act.

"I'm supposed to be a fighter." Ben averted his face. "In the last few weeks I've had to face up to whether or not I've got what it takes to hang in with the biggest fight of my life, and I think I do."

So that's what was happening. Ben was declaring his intention to get Shelly back. And he innocently confided in Tom because he would never figure him as competition.

"What do you think my chances are?" Ben asked.

Tom raised his chin to the sky. "Only Shelly knows that."

"I'm sorry," Ben said, clapping an arm around Tom's shoulders. "You're worried to death about the farm, and I'm piling my problems on top. Look, don't take this wrong, but I'd be glad to help—"

"No."

"It'd be a loan. An investment, if you like. We've already got a fair amount invested in each other in a lot of ways."

Tom wasn't this kind of man. He wasn't made of deceit, and he couldn't stand the guilt that was swelling until it threatened to choke him. He straightened and gave a grin that cost him more than Ben would ever know. "Thanks. If I get desperate I'll let you know. But we're going to pull it out, I feel it in my bones."

"You sure? I meant what—"

"We'd better get back in and have that coffee."

THE BOY HAD GROWN, Ben decided, grown a great deal. His son was a tall, angular sprout with dark eyes like his and Shelly's blond hair, and he scarcely knew him.

"I thought you might like to see where your mom and I used to come with Tom when we were growing up."

"Mom and Tom brought me here before." Philip dropped to sit on the creek bank and swung his legs.

Of course, they would have. Ben sat beside him. "I guess we should have come here years ago, only I never thought of it."

"No."

Was it too late? Had he lost his wife and son completely? He refused to believe that was true. "How's school?"

"Okay. We get out for summer in a couple of weeks."

Picking Philip up from Mary Thomas's house and bringing him here had seemed a great idea, the ideal chance to be alone and catch up. The notion was losing its appeal.

Water gurgled below, swirling around rocks, dipping, catching at a leaf here and there. A peaceful place full of good memories, but a bad choice for today. Ben couldn't think what to say next, and looking at the water dash past, as he had long ago in happier times, only made him wistful.

Philip plucked blades of grass and let them slip between his fingers. Long fingers like his own, Ben noted and glanced at bony wrists protruding from the sleeves of a jeans jacket. His heart gave an odd and unaccustomed twist. This was his child. If he didn't watch it he'd cry and then it really would be all over.

"This is where I want to be." He'd said it before he could stop himself.

"Where?" Philip looked up at him.

Damn, he'd like to get to know his son if he could only be given a chance. He'd made a colossal mistake, a heap of them, but couldn't you hope to be forgiven if you were really sorry?

"You want to be where?" Philip prompted.

"Here in Allenville," Ben said, staring ahead and plowing on.

Philip let out a gusty breath.

"I want to be here with you and your mother."

"You and Mom are divorced."

At least the response hadn't been a flat statement that Ben wasn't wanted. "I know, son, and I'm sorry about that. But I don't want you worrying your head about it. If anything's going to change there it'll be up to your mom and me to decide. Regardless, I'm considering moving back to Allenville."

He could almost hear seconds ticking away before Philip said, "You're a football player."

"That doesn't mean I can't do something else. What if I open a business here?" Please let him get a sign, some hint that Philip would like to have him around.

Another long pause settled around them.

"D'you think it'd be a good idea?"

"Dunno." Philip shrugged and destroyed more grass. "What kind of business? There isn't much to do around here if you don't farm."

Ben couldn't help smiling . . . and he couldn't help the thrust of pride listening to Philip brought. He was a bright, forthright boy.

"How about a new fast-food place? There's only that one greasy spoon in town and the burgers at Ole's bar. We could even try a bowling alley. Don't you think that would go over? There's got to be a need for more entertainment and washed-up football players usually end up..." He clamped his mouth shut. That was the last thing he should have suggested. Philip could interpret the comment to mean that he wanted to come back home because he was finished in Cleveland.

"The café doesn't do much as it is," Philip said. "Maybe it wouldn't be so good to compete with what business the Greens do have."

"And maybe it would do them good to have some competition." This wasn't going right. If Philip was enthusiastic about having a father around again he hid it well.

"Whatever you think." Philip bobbed to his feet and smiled at Ben, but his eyes were wary. "We oughta get home. Mom gets worried if I'm late."

Ben got up. He was getting the brush-off, not that he intended to give up. "Your mom knows you're with me so she won't worry, but we'll go if you want to. I should get back if I'm going to catch my plane anyway."

"Yeah." The boy almost ran back through the trees to the rental car.

Half an hour later they arrived at Shelly's house and Ben reached over to push open the door for Philip.

By the time the boy reached the porch, Shelly had come through the front door and stood, arms crossed over her slender middle.

Ben got out of the car and looked at her over its roof. Still so lovely, so gentle. "I'd better get going. Plane won't wait."

"Safe trip." She waved and he saw again his Shelly, the quiet girl he'd defended from the town's bully kids, the prettiest girl at the high school prom, the most beautiful bride...

"Thanks." He slid back behind the wheel, fumbling for the keys, barely able to see. Under his breath he said, "I'm not giving up."

## Chapter Fourteen

This was one day she'd like to wipe from her memory. Shelly
drove the wide road through town toward home, slowly
passing the Frostop root beer sign, the rundown Teton View
Motel with its ten cabins, with the showy forecourt display
of golden rod nodding in late afternoon sunshine.

Landmarks she'd seen all her life and come to ignore were
new again. Metal elevators stood tall against the sky, gray
ghosts in the shimmering haze and spilling trails of brilliant
grain along the asphalt.

The final stress for the day had come in the form of a
querulous call from her mother who begged to see Shelly
and Philip. Unable to refuse, she had gone, listened to Mom
swing between rage and tearful self-pity, and then, at Pops'
request, allowed Philip to spend the rest of tonight and tomorrow with them.

The pale road swept by, the fences, scrub grass. What
must Tom be thinking? As if preserving propriety, he'd left
when Ben went to pick up Philip.

Shelly drove the Jeep over the last creek that brought her
house into view and almost jammed on the breaks. Sun
glittered on a blue pickup standing in her driveway.

At a crawl, her foot hovering between the brake and the
gas, Shelly drove the last few hundred yards and parked.

Tom stuck his head out of the pickup window and stared at her. Even at a distance there was no mistaking his frown. He climbed from the cab, threw his hat onto the seat and came over to rest his arms along the open rim of her window.

Close up, his stress was evident again, and his eyes were searching hers. "Where's Philip?"

"Mom and Dad are upset. Talk about you and me is all over town and it finally got to them. We had a discussion and I think they feel better, but I could tell Pops wanted Philip with him. They're very close."

He raised a hand and pushed back her tousled hair, hooked a curl behind one ear.

Shelly automatically leaned her face against his palm. Everything had changed between them. Even this simple caress proved that.

Tom opened her door and lifted her to the ground. "I tried to stay away but I had to come. I can't work or think straight while I don't know what you're thinking."

She eased his hands from her waist. "Why didn't you wait for me inside." He had his own key.

His laugh lessened the tension fractionally. "And have you expect to find me passed out on your couch again?"

He followed her inside and into the living room. There was a stillness, a waiting.

"How did it go when Ben brought Philip back?"

She took off her cardigan and sat on the couch. "He didn't stay. Just dropped Philip and took off for the airport."

Tom stood with his weight on one leg, his hands on his hips. His sun-streaked hair glinted as he bowed his head.

"I don't think he'll be back...not for a while," she said.

"Don't bet on it."

She looked at him sharply. "What makes you say that?"

"Ben. He made it pretty clear to me that he's planning a fresh offensive. He wants you and Philip back."

"I think . . . I'm not sure what to think about that, but it doesn't matter. It's over."

"Doesn't Philip want to get together with his father?" Tom's blue eyes focused on her. "Did he say how it went between the two of them."

Shelly wished she didn't have to remember the way Philip had closed up on her when she'd broached the subject. "He didn't want to talk about it. But he mentioned that Ben said something about coming back to Allenville to live." Her heart beat harder, as it had when Philip had told her.

Tom sat down heavily beside her, his wrists limp between his knees. Automatically Shelly laid a hand on his arm and he trapped it there.

"Did Philip sound as if he liked the idea of Ben moving back here?"

"He didn't sound like anything. He's had too much to cope with for an eleven-year-old. But think about it, Tom. Ben in Allenville permanently? Is that likely?"

"I hope not." He stroked her fingers. "Do you like the idea?"

She rounded on him. "You know I don't. Why would you ask a thing like that?"

He smiled slightly. "To hear what you just said—and sound mad that I'd think otherwise."

"I'm glad you're happy."

"I'm not. Not yet. Shel, it's fess up and get on with it time. I'm past pussyfooting around. The months since you came back have been the most painful in my life, they've also been the best. For the first time I could think of you as a woman . . . without feeling guilty."

Tension mounted under her skin. Putting her arms around his neck was the most natural thing in the world, and kissing him, even if only tentatively.

Tom grew rigid and she arched her neck to look at him. The next instant he'd jerked away and stood up.

"What is it?" Blood rushed into her face. "I didn't mean to push—"

"Please, Shelly. I can't kiss you and go away. Not now. And it's the first time we've done more than give each other a friendly hug or pat. Can't you feel that, the strangeness?"

She smoothed her full silky skirt and tucked in the matching pink blouse that had wriggled up at the sides. "I feel it."

"We've been friends for so long, *were* friends for so long. But it's all different." He stood over her, feet planted, and she let her gaze travel up his long denim-clad legs, over his lean hips and flat belly, his broad chest. "What is it going to be? Are we going to risk it all, or just play footsie until we both go mad?"

Shelly hooked her fingers into the sides of his belt and stood up until they faced each other, a scant inch apart. She tilted her chin. Her soft breasts tensed against his hard flesh, and she drew in a sharp little breath. An instinct to put space between them was thwarted by Tom's splayed hand in the middle of her back, urging her even closer.

He let out a shuddering sigh and lessened the pressure. Once more he stepped away, and Shelly couldn't move. She watched his face, every line and angle, each deepening emotion that passed over his features. A beloved face.

"Tom, help me, please. I feel ... I ..."

"I know." He reached to hold the tips of her fingers. "You feel adrift and so do I. So I guess we go slow, sweetheart."

She felt light, floating. *Sweetheart*. The first term of endearment he'd ever called her. Was the barrier too wide to climb through? And if they tried, could she please him, or would this night be the biggest disaster of her life?

"You're trembling."

She laughed. "I'm scared."

"That's okay. I'm nervous, too."

"Not for the same reasons."

Carefully, the motion so painstakingly slow, he stroked her hair, the side of her face, her neck—and rested his hand on her bare skin just beneath the lapel of her blouse where the swell of her breast began. She shivered a little. Where he touched, she ached.

"Tell me why you're scared," he said, his fingers passing a fraction lower inside her blouse.

She closed her eyes. He would understand. "My ego isn't so big anymore. It never was but it got some hard knocks."

Her teeth sank into her lip, and Tom's gut went into a spasm. She meant that after Ben's betrayal she'd decided she must have done something to cause his defection. Damn Ben.

"You are so perfect, Shel," he told her. "You drive me wild. I've dreamed of touching you, of undressing you and lying with you. Sometimes I'm doing the damnedest things, planting, talking to buyers, and there you are. I can't even think straight when I'm like that."

She heard him, but barely. She parted her lips and leaned into him. He wouldn't judge, compare, only accept.

Her softly parted lips, her warm body pressed to his, almost undid him completely. His control was slipping. Stiffening his neck he brought his mouth down on hers, lightly, and let himself drift. Sweet, she tasted so sweet. Shelly's mouth opened and she reached closer and closer until it was as if there was no place where her body stopped and his began. Let him do this right. Let him have what it took not to go too fast.

The softness destroyed any hope of holding back.

Tom's mouth changed, turned hard, crushed down over Shelly's until she gasped. The tips of their tongues collided, and she returned the mad foraging . . . and felt him fumble with the buttons on her blouse.

He paused, cupped the fullness in the silkily erotic fabric. "You're bare under this," he said, taking a breath that seared his lungs. "I want to feel you against me." Her nipples tensed and he bent to kiss first one and then the other through the fabric. Wet circles formed over the dark areolas beneath. His arousal thrust against his jeans bringing exquisite pain.

Shelly shuddered, laid open by tingling fire. Tom's face was familiar yet strange: the face she knew, but changed by this new thing they'd never expected to have together. "I want to feel you, too." Her husky voice caught. She pushed on him, but he only smiled at her and continued to knead her breasts and make her blouse damp and clinging.

"Tom, let me." Throbbing, low inside, weakened her knees but she held on and forced enough space to undo the buttons on his shirt and slide it from his wide shoulders.

Trembling gathered in his muscles. Her hands, her fingers, stroked his skin; long, fluttering strokes that drove him crazy. The instant it took to shrug his arms from his sleeves was too long, and he clasped her to him again with a sense that he might have drowned if she'd been suddenly gone.

She reached around his waist and held on, pressing into his powerful length. His breath was hot on her neck where he kissed her again and again. Using the strength in his hard thighs, he backed her to the wall and pinned her there. He held her hands each side of her head, while his fevered eyes stared into hers and passed over her face and downward.

Shelly strained against him in a gesture that was an offer, the final offer. He couldn't stop now.

The top buttons on her blouse were undone. Trapping both of her hands in one of his, he pushed material aside to lift a breast free. Holding the soft weight, working the nipple with his thumb, he watched her eyes darken, her lips part, before he bent to kiss gently, so gently the effort drove his hips against her.

He was hard, all of him, hard and demanding, and she didn't want to wait anymore. Swiftly he disposed of the blouse. Then she felt what she could no longer stand to be denied, the solid expanse of his hair-covered chest softly crushing her naked breasts.

She was close but not close enough. Tom dropped his hands and let her cling, let her arms be the ones to hold them together like one flesh.

He pushed her skirt up easily, then glided his fingers over her bare and satiny thighs to the lacy ridge at the legs of her panties.

Shelly moaned softly. His thumbs pressed on into the unbearably exquisite spot that drained away her strength.

She sagged a little but didn't let go. He parted her thighs and gripped her hips, pulling her higher until she lifted her knees and wrapped her legs around his waist.

He couldn't see. Red and black passed before his eyes. Her skirt bunched around her hips and her panties slid beneath his reaching hands.

"Tom, you need—"

"I need," he whispered. "Hell, how I need." She was ready. The wall supported them both but he still had a driving strength that was enough for both of them.

Hiking her even higher, he dragged his belt undone and worked his jeans down. Shelly's fingers, finding him, drove the breath from his lungs.

"Now," she said.

The penetration was swift and their forging together abandoned, wrenching moans from deep within him.

He filled her and she welcomed him, surrounded him, squeezed her eyes shut against the rush of joyful tears.

She'd closed her eyes and he watched the pulling back of her lips from her teeth, the arching of her breasts. In his head was the red hot shimmer of mindless and passionate fulfillment.

There was an instant of pulsing stillness.

He was heavy, wonderfully heavy and damp. His hair, where it rested on her neck, was wet. She felt the beat of his heart against hers.

"God, I never planned it like that, Shel," he said and his voice broke. "I wanted it to be gentle and—"

"I wanted it just the way it was." She slowly slid to stand on the floor but kept her hands on his rock hard buttocks. "But I wouldn't mind if we went up to bed now. If you've got time."

He opened eyes that were still glazed and smiled lazily. "I've got all night."


TOM WAS EDGY. Yesterday he and Shelly had decided this was the best way to go ahead. Beside him in the pickup, Philip sat, looking through the window and chattering about how soon he'd be able to skate again.

"A couple more weeks," Tom told him. "Doc Williams said you shouldn't risk it too soon."

When he'd left Shelly, as she set out for her parents' place, they'd agreed that the next day Philip should go to the farm after school as usual. Later, around the time Shelly would normally pick him up, Tom was to drive the boy home instead and the three of them would discuss some of the changes that were going to take place in their lives.

He looked sideways at the blond head. It would work. Philip liked him, and there would never be any question of Ben being totally cut out of the picture.

Tom shifted in his seat. Pretending not to be apprehensive about what lay ahead would be pointless. He and Shelly had discussed that Philip had probably heard some of the suggestions about his mother and Tom. They were going to tell him that although the rumors hadn't been true before, they were now. Tom felt heat rise in his face.

The front door of Shelly's house stood open and Tom put an arm around Philip's shoulders as they walked in.

"Mom! We're home."

The boy went ahead of Tom into the kitchen.

Tom walked more slowly, rehearsing lines in his head and trying to close out the mounting desire he felt just at the certainty that he was about to see Shelly again.

He entered the room and stopped, his mouth drying out.

Ben stood by the sliding doors, his hands sunk deep in his pockets. Shelly sat at the table. She bowed her head while Tom looked from one to the other and held on to the door.

"Shelly, are you—"

"Ben came." She raised her face and he couldn't be sure what he saw, confusion, desperation?

"I came home," Ben said. "Allenville is where I belong. I never should have left."

# Chapter Fifteen

"Want to talk about it?"

Tom jumped. He hadn't heard Jimmy come into the shop. "Hi. I just got a call from the outfit in Montana. Looks like they're really interested in upping their order for peas." No way did he want to talk about what was really on his mind.

Jimmy used the toe of a boot to scrape a crate close to Tom's littered desk. He settled his compact body on the edge and took off his battered tan hat. An imprint of the band stayed in his close-cropped gray hair.

"Good news," he said. "About the peas." Jimmy wasn't a man of many words.

They were limping along businesswise. Nothing to spare, but making it—barely. "D'you talk to Cully about getting an inspection? Drainage is going well and the Department of Agriculture will want to check things over after the flood."

"I talked to him." Jimmy cleared his throat. "I was in town this morning. Picked up that fishing rod I promised Kurt."

"Yeah?" Tom knew what was coming. The latest chin-wagging about how Ben got back in town yesterday and the speculation that had to be circulating about what would happen.

"Did you see Ben yet?"

"Yeah. Yesterday afternoon."

"How'd that make you feel? Knowing he intends to stay?"

Tom rocked back in his chair. "You're going to make me discuss this, aren't you?"

Jimmy's weathered face colored. "I'm not blind, Tom. Neither is Mary, or your mom. We all know how it is . . . we know you and Shelly got pretty close there."

"Got pretty close?" Tom narrowed his eyes. He didn't like the past tense and sooner or later the truth was going to have to come completely out in the open. "We are close. Ben's being here isn't going to change that . . . not that I think he'll stick around long. He's not the type to enjoy living with his folks and twiddling his thumbs."

"He's not—" The blush in Jimmy's cheeks darkened, and he coughed. "Hell, this is none of my business."

Tom brought his chair to the upright position with a crack. "Hold on, there, Jimmy. Not so fast. Ben's not what?"

"Ask Shelly." Jimmy got up.

"I'm asking you."

"I thought you knew Ben moved back in with Shelly." Jimmy jammed his hat on and cursed under his breath. "Shows what happens when a guy doesn't keep his mouth shut."

Tom got to his feet and supported his weight on the desk. "You've got it wrong. You must have." When he'd left Shelly's it had been because Ben asked for some time alone with his family. Tom had gone reluctantly, expecting her to call him later. When she hadn't he'd assumed the meeting had gone late and she'd been too tired.

"Maybe I did get it wrong," Jimmy said. "It was Doc Williams who said Ben was with her. He was over talking with Mrs. Dillon. But maybe he only meant...no he didn't. Damn it all, Tom, he said Ben had moved in with Shelly. And it's all over town. I can't let you walk into that like a fool. And now I gotta go."

He left without another word, his boots scuffing the dusty boards.

She wouldn't. Tom slid heavily into his chair. Shelly wouldn't take Ben back, not after the weekend. But she hadn't called...

The phone, ringing now, jarred every bone in his body. Rubbing his eyes, he lifted the receiver. "Yeah."

"This is Shelly." She was whispering. "I'm calling from school, and I've got to keep this short. Tom, you do understand, don't you?"

He felt sick. "Understand?"

"About Ben? I've never seen him like this. It isn't what I want but I couldn't just turn him out until he's ready—"

"You *can't* turn him out? You mean it's true. He's living with you again?"

"Yes, but—"

"But what? What was all that we had together? A game?" His heart and head pounded. "I thought we were making a commitment."

"Give me some time, Tom. Please. I've never seen Ben so low. He needs me, and I won't kick him when he's down."

She was brushing him off, putting him back where he'd always been, runner up to the starring team of Shelly and Ben. "No," he said quietly. "Don't you kick Ben when he's down. Kick me instead."

"Tom, you know what you mean to me. If you love me, you'll trust me. We'll be together again—"

"When you feel like a change? Like hell!" He hung up.

SHELLY DRAGGED into the house. Something in the kitchen smelled good, only she wasn't hungry.

"Here she is." Lucky Williams, a wooden spoon in one hand, hailed from a spot by the stove. "And Philip. Hello my pet. Grandma decided to come over and make dinner for you and your mom and dad. Your mom works too hard."

Ben stood by the sink washing dishes. Shelly had never seen him wash a plate in her life. Bemused, she looked from one to the other.

"Hi, honey," Ben said, but he sounded edgy. He was no fool. This was play acting and he knew it. "Mom insisted. I said I could manage but she wouldn't hear of it."

"Can I go to my room?"

Shelly glanced at Philip. His face was pale and tight-lipped. She hadn't given him any excuse for bringing him straight home rather than allowing him to go to the farm as he did every day.

"I thought you might give your poor old dad a hand with this." Ben smiled and Shelly felt sorry for him. He really did hope he could pull this off.

"Okay." Philip walked slowly to the sink and picked up a dish towel. He let it hang and made no move to touch the draining dishes.

Lucky set down the spoon and undid her apron. She raised her brows at Shelly. "Um, Ben, I expect Philip would like to get some homework done before dinner."

Ben turned around, dripping soapy water on the floor. He looked from Shelly to his mother, who gave him a significant stare.

"Sure," he said. "Sure, Philip. You go on and do your homework."

Philip was barely out of the room when Lucky tossed aside her apron and planted her fists on her hips. "I don't know what you're thinking of, Ben. You know you have things to talk to Shelly about. And it can't be done in front of Philip."

"Mom, I can handle—"

"You can handle it? If you were so good at handling things, both of you, we wouldn't all be in this mess. Now, stop hedging, Ben. You and Shelly have to work out how to stop...well, you know. Fred Dillon's dealt with Beattie and a few others. But not every big mouth in Allenville owes money at Dillons'. It's up to the two of you to do the rest."

An overpowering lethargy dulled Shelly's mind. So Ben knew about her and Tom. It wasn't his business, but she should have been the one to tell him. She owed him that much.

"I'll be back at . . . what time did you say you were meeting Tom?" Lucky gathered her purse and jacket. A horn sounded outside. "That's your father. I told him not to come in because there wouldn't be time."

"Tom's meeting us at Ole's at eight. It only takes fifteen or twenty minutes to get there. Say seven-thirty?"

His mother nodded, smiled at Shelly and muttered as Doc blasted his horn again.

The front door slammed behind Lucky, and Shelly hung on to the hem of her cardigan. She would let Ben do the talking.

"Mom volunteered to come back and stay with Philip while you and I go out."

She shook her head. "You said we're meeting Tom at the tavern? Ben, what . . . ?" She didn't know what she wanted to ask. It was all a mad muddle in her head.

Ben dried his hands, then, without warning, he slammed the wadded towel into the sink, spraying water. Shelly watched the cloth billow, soak and sink.

"Ben—"

"We're not standing still for this." His chest heaved and he marched back and forth. "Some things never change. You and Tom and I have been fighting off the creeps in this town for as long as I can remember. Well, it's time they learned you choose your enemies more carefully than you choose your friends...if you want to stay in one piece. And this is as much our town as theirs."

Shelly blinked. "I—"

"No, Shelly. This time you aren't on your own with this filth. You should have told me weeks ago and I'd have come and sorted it out then. I'm sure Tom's done his best but he's too damned nice."

Defensiveness stirred her. "Tom can be tough if he has to be. He doesn't take any—"

"Yeah, yeah. But with this we need tough as in *real tough*, honey, and that's my forte."

She breathed in and out slowly. There was something she didn't understand here. Ben was supposed to be defensive, angry at her and Tom. That wasn't what she was hearing. Did that mean he was glad for them? No, not that.

"How in hell do these people dare to suggest that you and Tom have something going? Geez, how low can you sink? You know what I think? I think they know Tom's got principles they can't even dream of having, and they hate him for making them feel inferior. You're just the convenient pawn. Only I've got the solution all worked out, so don't you worry."

Shelly opened her mouth and closed it. He was defending Tom, and her. Ben loved Tom, trusted him and looked up to him, and he stood ready to take on this entire town if anyone tried to disagree with his assessment of his friend.

Oh, God. She sat at the table, already set for dinner...for three, and propped her chin. Regardless of right and wrong, and what had brought Ben and her to this point, she felt like the arch heel, and so would Tom if he knew.

*Tom.* "Ben, what do you mean about meeting him at Ole's?"

"A brain wave, honey. I didn't have all my marbles knocked loose on the field. Persuading him to come wasn't easy but I wore him down. All I really had to do was get at him with how we need to protect your reputation, and he agreed. We're going in there as a threesome, presenting a united front. Let 'em all make something of that."

"Oh, Ben. We don't want any trouble." She didn't want to go. She didn't want to sit there with Tom, pretending, meeting his eyes and knowing he believed she'd betrayed him.

"No trouble. Leave it to me. I'm going to be good old Ben, ready to talk about life in the pros. Drinks all around to celebrate our new beginning."

"I don't want to go." Her head and back ached. She should tell him, now. Get it over with. She needed Tom.

"Those bastards." Ben went to his haunches beside her and put an arm around her shoulders. "How could they do this to someone like you? If I didn't know how badly you want to stay here I'd suggest packing up and getting out."

Shelly straightened, and Ben instantly removed his arm. He was trying so hard to do everything right. Her eyes smarted.

Dinner was pot roast, Shelly registered that much but didn't taste the food. And she heard Ben talking to Philip, but not what they said. Too soon, Lucky Williams returned, and Ben was insisting he be the one to drive into town.

How easily old habits slid into place. Ben had never liked to be driven. As they sped along Shelly stared at the gray-

ing landscape. She couldn't think of anything to say, and
Ben was also silent.

"I told him we'd meet inside," Ben said as they parked in
front of Ole's.

"Remember when we tried to get a drink in here when we
were all nineteen?" Ben pushed open one side of the warped
double doors. The smell of stale beer, cigarette smoke and
grease blasted out, and Shelly wrinkled her nose.

"You and Tom tried. I was too scared."

"Oh, sure. Regular milquetoast, I don't think. You were
only waiting to see if we got away with it. There's Tom."
Ben grabbed her hand and strode across the smoke-laden
room toward a booth.

Shelly's heart slammed against her ribs. She could see
herself through Tom's eyes, herself and Ben holding hands,
with Ben grinning from ear to ear. Her knees locked at each
step.

"Tom!" Ben bellowed, meeting him as he rose from his
seat and wrapping him in a bear hug. His hand, pounding
Tom's back, made her flinch.

Tom had his smile in place, but over Ben's shoulder he
stared steadily into her eyes. She didn't look away until Ben
had released him and waved her into a seat.

"What'll it be?" He addressed Tom who hadn't bought
a drink.

"Ah, a coke would be fine."

"Coke!" Ben laughed so loudly Shelly cringed. The bar
was full, and she knew every face. "Rum and Coke maybe.
This is a celebration. Leave it to me."

He left without asking Shelly what she wanted.

Tom's hands were folded on the table. She studied them,
the long strong fingers, the broad palms; hard workman's
hands. He was watching her. Slowly she met his eyes. His

attempt at wiping away all expression fell flat. Hurt was there and . . . desire.

"Tom—"

"Don't. There's nothing to be said."

She swallowed, feeling other eyes upon them. Conversation was a steady drone with interjected bursts of laughter. Behind the bar, Ole looked as he always did—rotund, rosy, slightly sweating, his wire-rimmed glasses constantly in need of wiping or pushing up his snub nose. At the moment he was craning up toward Ben and laughing. Ben the charmer—who never gave up on what he wanted.

"Tom! Shelly! How about seeing you here!"

Jimmy materialized without Shelly seeing his approach, and beside him stood Mary.

"Jimmy," Tom said, and glower was a mild word for the way he looked at his brother-in-law.

"Hey!" Ben returned and slid three glasses onto the table. "Jimmy and Mary Thomas. Great to see you two. Join us. I'll get you a chair, Jimmy."

Mary took her place beside her brother and sat on her hands, her shoulders hunched. Shelly guessed they'd come to give Tom support.

Ben swung a chair to the end of the table, waiting for Jimmy to sit and hailed for, "Two more, Ole."

Shelly took a sip from her glass and realized Ben wasn't any more composed than she was. He'd bought rum and Coke all the way around without asking preference. Jimmy and Mary's drinks arrived—two more of the same.

"Mary and I decided it was time we had a night out," Jimmy said after a protracted silence.

"Uh-huh." Tom's tone dripped disbelief.

"We're going to put the lid on this thing," Ben said in a low voice, leaning forward. He downed his drink and waved his glass at Ole. "Mary and Jimmy know what I'm talking about?"

"They know," Tom said, his glance sliding toward Shelly.

*No they don't. And neither do you.* Somehow she'd talk to him, make him believe things weren't as they seemed.

Ben initiated loud conversation and laughter, mostly his own, although Jimmy made a creditable effort. Tom hardly touched his drink and talked less, while Mary appeared bent on pretending she wasn't present.

"I'm looking at the space the Leonards' vacated," Ben announced when there was a silence. "Called Renny Carrol on it today."

Tom's response was to down the contents of his glass and call for a refill. Beside him Mary shifted, moved her drink and began shredding her napkin.

"So what d'you think of that?" Ben beamed around. "What this town needs is a little class. Italian, I thought. Good food in nice surroundings. Classy but not too upscale."

Jimmy muttered something, then winced and turned to Mary, who continued to shred her napkin as if she hadn't noticed her husband's glare.

Why did this have to go on?

Ben leaned over the table again, as if he were in one of his huddles and sharing a play, only this time, he was quarterback. "Let 'em make something out of this, huh? Don't think everyone in the place doesn't have an ear cocked in this direction. Tom, if they had any notions about keeping up the gossip about you and Shelly, this'll fix it."

She wasn't going to make it much longer.

A roar of laughter went up across the bar. Shelly looked past Ben and saw two men arm wrestling. A cheering ring surrounded them and, from the way upturned beer glasses emptied, she figured their contents never made a stop in the mouth.

"Okay, Nipper! You win, again."

A brawny man in a red check shirt slammed his opponent's fist to the table and leaped up, downing a beer as he did so. "Who's next," he yelled amid a rumble of refusals. He turned and stared directly at Ben. "How about you, Ben Williams? Want to put your money where your mouth is?"

Ben continued to smile but his eyes turned cold. He didn't answer.

"Scared you won't do so hot?" Nipper Wallace, known as a troublemaker, worked for the local power company.

"Yeah," came a weaker voice, its owner camouflaged in the throng.

Ben made a move and Shelly clamped a hand on his wrist. "Leave it. They're drunk."

"Ya chicken, Ben? Worn out these days? Washed up?"

Before anyone could stop him, Ben was on his feet and crossing to stand toe to toe with Nipper.

"Hell," Tom said under his breath. "Some things never change. Let me out, Mary."

She stayed put. "Ben'll deal with it."

Ben took what seemed like less than a second to thump Nipper's hand to the table. He did it with enough force to lift the man from his chair.

"I wasn't ready," Nipper howled, rubbing his biceps and flapping his hand. "Lousy cheat. I wasn't set."

"Let me out!" This time Tom didn't wait for Mary. He scrambled onto the table and leaped over. Jimmy was a step behind but they were too late. Nipper had already made one of the biggest mistakes of his life when he threw a punch at Ben's rock hard middle.

"Oh, no," Mary moaned. "Stop it."

Shelly slid out of the seat and rushed to the bar. "Ole, do something!"

As she said it, Nipper's feet left the floor and he fell sideways in a heap. Splintering wood and breaking glass orchestrated the action.

"I'll do something," Ole said. "Send a bill when it's over. Sheriff would be too late."

But when Shelly looked over her shoulder, her stomach rolled. Nipper was on his feet and, ranged behind him, was a shambling group of toughs, mostly made up of some of the itinerant work force employed by the farms.

"The sheriff," she said urgently to Ole. "Call him."

He shook his head. "No need. They're just blowing off a little steam. Gets dull for young bucks."

Nipper had thrown the first punch, Ben the second. What happened next became a blur and Mary, clutching Shelly, was all that felt real.

"We can't do anything," Mary said. "I knew we shouldn't have come."

"It's my fault," Shelly said in a low voice. She trembled violently.

Mary shook her head. "It's a lot of people's fault but it can't go on. You'll have to make a decision. Or is it true that you've definitely gotten together with Ben again?"

The crack of Ben's fist hitting a man's jaw made Shelly wince. Immediately several new opponents piled in. Chairs slid in every direction. "Oh, God... No, I'm not getting together with Ben. It's tough right now, that's all. Something's wrong with him only he won't say what it is."

Tom had waded into the middle of the group and Shelly's hands flew to her cheeks.

"You mean Ben's sick?"

"No, not that. Something else. He's beaten down somehow."

When the tide turned in the fight it turned fast. Ben's immense size and strength added to Tom's lean speed and quick hands had taken their toll. Jimmy, smaller, but wiry and tough, did neat and thorough work. But it was the unexpected piling in of Russ Carrol, whom Shelly hadn't seen in the bar, with Chester Green and Walt Smith that seemed to snuff the enemy's last fire. Already tiring, the troublemakers started backing away as soon as they noticed increasing numbers in the opposition.

"Will you look at that," Mary said, her voice full of wonder. "Russ Carrol helping a Conrad. And Beattie's husband . . . and Walt. I never thought I'd see the day."

Nipper Wallace and his cronies were melting slowly toward the door and drifting outside, muttering all the way.

Tom and Jimmy, with Ben in the middle, an arm around each of their shoulders, walked toward Mary and Shelly. Blood drizzled from Jimmy's nose and Tom had a cut over his eye. Ben appeared unhurt.

"Jimmy!" Mary moved to dab at his nose with a napkin.

"We showed 'em," Ben said, breathless. "Don't worry, Ole. Send me the bill. Beers all around."

Shelly touched Tom's arm. "Let me look at your face. You've got a cut over your eye."

He glanced at her and away. "It's nothing."

She put a hand behind his neck and pulled his head down. He resisted for an instant before lowering his face. His gaze remained averted.

"That needs cleaning. Could even take a stitch."

"Still looking after your old friend?" He looked at her then, and she dropped her hands. A challenge, disgust, what was he leveling at her with that stare?

Ben, thumping Tom's back, took his attention from Shelly.

"Do something," Mary whispered urgently in her ear.

Shelly wound her fingers together. *Do what? Make an announcement here and now? Tom and I are lovers.*

"Geez, that was a gas," Ben said, evidently oblivious to Tom's silence and the watchful awkwardness of the others. "Well," he continued. "I don't know about the rest of you, but I'm not as young as I used to be and I need my beauty sleep. Maybe I need to rest up a bit after the fracas, too. But I'm not admitting weakness here."

He held Shelly's hand and headed for the door. "Serve 'em up on me, mind you, Ole."

*Tom, understand and give me time.* If he read her thoughts, his closed face gave no sign.

"And where do I send the bill?" Ole called.

Ben opened the door for Shelly. "To Shelly's and my place."

## Chapter Sixteen

She'd been right. There was the light. When he was upset, Tom always went out to the old shop that served as his office. Before she left the Jeep by the road to walk up the long driveway at Conrads', Shelly had checked the time. One in the morning. If he'd been at the barn, getting to him without waking Alice Conrad would have been more difficult.

For as long as possible she stuck to the main track. Now she veered to the left across uneven ground, peering about her in the darkness to avoid falling on some unseen object. The wind kept up a steady whine, and the temperature had gone down enough to make her jeans and cotton sweater too light to keep her from shivering.

Shelly went not to the door of the shop, but to the window in the partitioned room that was Tom's office. Standing on tiptoe, she could see in.

Clinging to the sill, she saw him and tears rushed into her eyes. She loved him, but he thought she was a user.

Tom sat, cross-legged, on the floor close to the stove. He'd lit a fire and flames sent flickering patterns over his blank face. He stared back at the glow. From where she was, Shelly could see a dressing on the cut over his eye. He moved, hunched over, the navy blue polo shirt he wore stretching across his shoulders. His jeans were old, faded by the sun of more than one summer. She glanced at his bare feet and smiled a little. His boots were tossed aside. He had always liked to go barefoot.

Waiting wouldn't make this easier. She went to the door, opened it without knocking and stepped inside.

He stared at her but he didn't appear startled.

"Tom, can we talk?"

He stirred and reached to poke another piece of wood into the fire. "Where does Ben think you are?"

"He's asleep."

Tom pulled his bottom lip between his teeth and she read his thoughts. He believed she'd come from the same bed where Ben slept.

"Tom, he—"

"Go back to him . . . before he misses you."

"He won't miss me. He sleeps in the spare bedroom, and where I am isn't his business."

"That's not the way it looked tonight."

He was being unreasonable. She'd come to him. He had to know that wasn't easy after their earlier parting. "Are you going to listen to me?"

"I don't think so. It's all been said."

"Damn you." She stood over him. "Nothing's been said. You haven't let me get a word in."

"What's to say? Ben needs you and, to quote you, you won't kick him when he's down. End of discussion. I've got to get on with my life."

Shelly dropped to her knees beside him. "Is that why you're out here in the middle of the night when you have to be up at five? Because you're getting on with your life?"

"I . . ." His jaw worked and his eyes darkened. "I came out to go over some books."

"Oh, sure. Why not tell the truth? While I was at home, dying inside and trying to figure out how to reach you, you were here eating yourself up because you're mad at me...and hurting."

"Shel...go home. We made a mistake, now let's try to pretend it didn't happen."

If he'd slapped her she couldn't have felt more stung. "Mistake? What happened between us was no mistake and you know it."

"Stop it." He swung toward her and gripped her shoulders. His features were taut, his lips drawn back from his teeth. " Your husband's at home asleep. You just told me that. You don't belong here."

"My *ex*-husband. He's no more than an old friend to me now, one who's in need. His contract with the team isn't being renewed, Tom. I finally got it out of him. He came running back here because we're the people he's always run to when he was wounded."

Tom bowed his head and dropped his hands. "You mean he's finished with football?"

"Yes. Last year he didn't play that much. The old knee injury flared up. I thought he'd be kept on for another year or two. I think he did, too, and that's what's rocked him so badly. He feels he's been used up and thrown away."

Tom grimaced. "Poor Ben. Hell, he always seemed to have the world by the tail. I guess no one gets to take success for granted. So now he's going to open a restaurant in Allenville and become a local celebrity, huh?"

"So he says, but he's not cut out for it. He'll play with it for a while before he gets bored, that's all."

Tom got nimbly to his feet, dragged on his socks and boots and walked to his desk, leaving Shelly where she knelt. "We've got one thing to be grateful for."

"What?" Shelly scrambled up and approached his back.

"It looks as if no one has to know we ever went as far as we did."

Her vision blurred and she blinked. "Tom, I want you."

He flexed his shoulders. "Don't say that. Go, I tell you. This is hard enough."

"No." Her breathing was shallow. "I won't go. I can't rescue Ben, not this time, not ever again. He'll be all right in time and then he'll go on his way. We'll be here—together."

His chest rose and fell unevenly. "You're dreaming."

"No!" She reached for him but he moved away.

"Yes, Shelly. I made up my mind while I sat here for hours. Ben needs you, he'll keep on needing you. And you're too deeply attached to him to turn him away. I can't take the rejection over and over again."

"We became lovers, Tom. I can't forget that, can you?"

He looked at the roof. "I've got to. It was just a need thing, anyway. We were too lonely people consoling each other. It could just as well have happened with someone else—for either of us."

Her breath caught in her throat and with it, pain. She heard her own sob. "Someone else? You think I...you think I just needed sex to make me feel good for a few hours and you happened to be handy? You rotten...I hate you."

Blindly, she stumbled to the door and threw it open. The wind stunned her with its strength. "You fool," she said, and it hurt to talk. "I love you so much."

When she ran, it was without direction, wildly, gasping, not caring where she went. He'd told her their lovemaking was a casual thing. She tripped, tried to regain her balance, and slammed to the ground. And before she could lift her face from the dirt, big hands were around her waist, turning her, and she looked up into Tom's shadowed face.

"My God," he said. "Oh, Shelly. I'm sorry. Forgive me, please." He supported her head and brushed back her hair. Grit sprayed her face.

Her cheek smarted. Both knees and the palms of her hands throbbed. She didn't care. "You think I used you?"

"No, no. I said...I've been in agony, Shel. I thought you'd taken him back." He crouched and pulled her against him. "Where do you hurt? You fell so hard. I shouted at you but you wouldn't listen."

She didn't bother to tell him she hadn't heard. "I'm okay. Don't worry. I'll go more carefully."

"You said you loved me."

She closed her eyes. "We say a lot of things when we aren't thinking."

"You were thinking. You meant it."

What little shred of restraint that remained broke, and the tears started. She curled into his body, between his legs and wrapped her arms around his waist.

"Don't, Shel. Please don't." Tom held her tightly, stroking her hair, then slowly got up, pulling her with him. He carried her away from the shed.

"Where are we going?"

"Home," Tom said against the top of her head.

"I don't want to go back there."

"My home."

She raised her head and saw the looming shapes of the house and the barn beyond. "What about the fire in the shed?"

"It'll be safe. Shh. Be quiet awhile. You're shocked from the fall."

In the barn Tom turned on a single lamp beside the couch and tipped up her face to look closely at her cheek. "Just a nasty scratch. If we clean it it'll be okay." He made the same pronouncement about her hands and turned his attention to her hair. "You've turned gray overnight. We'd better wash it. And shake the worst of the dirt out of your sweater."

She didn't care how dirty her hair was, or her sweater.

"Can you climb the stairs? I'll carry you."

"No." She went ahead, up to the open loft. It was the first time she'd been there. His bed was big and low with no headboard, but soft and inviting looking beneath its old-fashioned family patchwork quilt. How like Tom, to surround himself with simple special things that reflected his heritage.

He stood behind her. "Should I make you a hot drink? Tea or something?"

She hid her smile before she looked at him. He was caring for her and not knowing quite how it should be done. "No, thanks."

He rubbed his hands on his jeans. His awkwardness made her intensely protective of him.

"The bathroom's through there." He nodded to a door on the left. "There's a bathrobe on the back of the door. I'll see what I can do with the sweater while you wash your hair."

She pressed her fingers to her temples. How did she say it? How did she ask him to be with her?

"Are you all right? Do you need to lie down now?"

His anxiety cleared the doubt. "I need you to help me wash my hair."

He stopped moving his hands.

She opened the bathroom door and switched on the light. Again, everything was simple, white tile walls, fixtures and floors, all squeaky clean. Without checking to see if he'd followed, Shelly ran water into the sink and washed her hands and face, drawing in a sharp breath at the stinging of her skin.

Still without looking back, she took off her sweater and held it behind her. After an instant's pause, fingers touched hers and the sweater was gone.

"Do you have shampoo?" This time, with her weight braced on the sides of the sink, she lifted her face and met Tom's eyes in the mirror.

"There." He inclined his head to a shelf beside the mirror but reached over her for the bottle and unscrewed the cap, never taking his eyes from her face. "Put your head down," he said at last.

At first he was clumsy, his big fingers tangling in snarls the dirt and gravel had made, but his confidence grew, and the vigor with which he rubbed and rinsed.

"This is impossible," he said finally. "I can't get the soap out. Wait there."

She did, smiling softly to herself. Under his hands her body had awakened.

He returned. "Here, this'll work." Water sluiced over her head from some receptacle, which he filled again and again until his fingers squeaked through her hair and he said, "Good. Got it."

He'd also gotten her. While he wrapped a towel around her head, she stood up and she didn't have to look to know the bra was soaked, and the band of her jeans in the front.

"Oh, Geez." Tom grabbed another towel and patted her face and shoulders. He paused, glancing to where water ran between her breasts. "I might as well have put you in the bath."

When her fingertips made their own way to his rough jaw, his lips parted and he dropped the second towel. "It isn't going away, is it? We've got something together, Shel."

Reaching behind her, she undid the bra and let the straps fall from her shoulders. "We sure do. And it's *never* going away. I won't let it."

His attention was on her breasts, the way they moved when the bra dropped to the floor.

"Don't leave me again," he said, his voice hoarse. "I can't stand it if we have to be apart."

"We're going to sort things out." She needed the strength of his arms, wanted to feel his skin on hers. "Take off your shirt."

He worked it over his head, and fine-toned muscle flexed and contracted beneath tanned skin. Shelly didn't wait for him to toss the shirt aside before she pressed her breasts against the erotic texture of coarse hair on his chest.

Tom groaned and she arched her back, kissing him deeply while her hands roamed his body.

Abruptly he stilled her, clasping her wrists and holding her away. "Let me look at you."

"Tom, please." She strained toward him but he would have none of it.

"My love." His smile held a hint of wickedness. "Is there any rush?"

"Tom!"

The smile softened, only slightly. He backed from the bathroom to the bedroom and released her. He stood with his hands on his hips, his eyes alternating lazily from her face to her body.

Trembling, she unzipped her jeans and bent to slip them down. Tom's sudden movement, his hand sliding beneath the weight of her breasts, took her breath away. She reached for him but he shook his head. For now he wanted the pleasure to be all Shelly's.

Her breath came in small gasps as she continued to undress. He kept his hands on her, teasing her nipples until the intensity of feeling made her grab for his fingers.

He laughed, deep in his throat, and sat on the edge of the bed. "Not fair, huh?" But his face was flushed, and corded muscles stood out in his neck. A shiny film covered his skin.

She kicked aside her shoes and stepped out of her jeans and bikini panties.

Tom's smile faded. "You are something. You are...come here."

She went, naturally, wanting to be naked for him and to be whatever he wanted.

He pulled her astride his knees and kissed her lips softly, parting her lips, nibbling. And he kissed her chin, her brow, avoiding the grazes, and on, down her neck, over each shoulder. His lips made slow, decreasing circles on her breasts until she couldn't bear the waiting.

"Tom, I want to lie with you."

"Mmm. You will." His voice was almost dreamy, thick. "There's no hurry."

*There is, my love.* But he was kissing her again and his hands were caressing her body. She drew in a hissing breath and squeezed her eyes shut. The sensation drove deeper and deeper until she hovered on the edge.

He didn't speak. Standing, he drew off the rest of his clothes and threw back the covers on the bed. In one sweep he maneuvered her onto cool sheets, knelt between her legs and continued with his mouth what he'd started with his hands.

He slipped his arms under her body, clamped her to him and rolled over. When he made love to her, it was with Shelly above him, smiling down, meeting his passion with her own.

The light was still on but it might have been dark. She couldn't see anymore, only feel. They moved as one, on and on, deeper and deeper. She wished they need never stop, but then it came, the hot rush, the final joining...the falling of two love-tired bodies to lie, heavy together and sated.

"WHERE HAVE YOU BEEN? It's four in the morning. I was worried sick." Ben stood in the hallway, his hair tousled, and wearing only pajama bottoms.

Shelly's key had been in the lock when he opened the door.

"Keep it down or you'll wake Philip," she said, and then, "Tom's with me."

Ben backed up, frowning, as Tom joined Shelly and shut the door behind him. He put a hand on her shoulder. "Ben, we've got to talk. Can we sit down?"

"What is this? What's going on here?"

"Shh. Don't shout," Shelly said. She pushed her fingers between Tom's on her shoulder, trying to draw strength from him.

Ben ran a hand through his hair, staring at them, and she saw the instant when he guessed the truth.

"Ben, let's—"

"You and Tom." His eyes ran from her clean-scrubbed face to her rumpled clothes. "You and Tom. Why didn't I...how could I have missed it. You two are..." He advanced, caught Tom by the collar of his jean jacket and hauled him around Shelly. "You smarmy son of a bitch. You pretended to be my friend."

"Knock it off!" Tom smashed Ben's arm aside, and they stood glaring at each other, only inches apart.

"Please," Shelly said. "Please don't do this." She shook so badly she leaned against the wall for support.

"Shelly isn't your wife," Tom said, low but clear. "You're divorced, and she's only putting up with your being here because she feels sorry for you."

"You told him." Ben shot a narrow glance at Shelly. "I haven't told anyone else. I needed a day or two before it hit the papers, but you told him."

"You would have told Tom, yourself," she said, feeling no regret. "And that isn't the point. Tom and I are...we love each other. You have to leave, Ben. Stay in Allenville if you want to. That's your prerogative, but don't interfere in my life anymore."

Muscles bunched in Ben's jaw. He turned his back on them. "You're going to regret this. Both of you. I'm going to take Philip away from you, Shelly. I'm going back to Cleveland and taking him with me."

"You can't do that."

"Ben, think man," Tom said.

Ben swung around. "Oh, I'm thinking, *friend*. And you won't like what I've come up with. I'll get sole custody of my son back, and do you know why?"

Shelly felt rising sickness. "You're irrational."

"I'll get him back because no court is going to uphold a mother who has an affair virtually in the presence of an eleven-year-old child."

## Chapter Seventeen

"There's a letter for you."

Ben hesitated by the front door of his parents' house. "It can wait, Mom. I'm going to see Tom."

His mother walked slowly down the hall and handed him an envelope. He put it in his pocket, waiting for her reaction to his announcement.

"Why are you meeting with him?"

"It's time," he said. "He and Shelly have teamed up against me and I want him to understand I mean business. He's got no right to interfere."

"I can't believe this is happening," she said, and he noticed for the first time that she'd grown old. "Your father and I and Shelly's folks . . . all we wanted was for you kids to be happy. We kept hoping you'd get back together. We did our best to help. Now, I don't know if we were right."

He opened the door. "Sorry you feel that way. I happen to think you were right, not that Shelly and I will ever patch things up. But I'm not leaving my son with them. Why should Tom Conrad have everything that's mine?"

Before his mother could respond he went outside, leaving the door open. Tom had agreed to come into town, to Green's Diner, the only possible neutral meeting place apart from Ole's.

Ben arrived first, sat down in a booth and ordered coffee. The sooner he accomplished what had to be done in this town and got out, the better.

Tom's blue pickup slid to a stop outside the steamed-up windows.

"Morning, Ben." Tom loomed over him, tall, maturely spare where he'd once been thin—and good-looking, dammit.

"Yeah." Ben held his mug in both hands and looked at the greasy film on the coffee.

His hat tilted low over his eyes, Tom dropped his big, loose-limbed body into the other side of the booth and ordered orange juice and coffee.

The waitress went away, returned and left again, and still no word passed between them.

Tom took off his hat and drank the orange juice.

"How long?" Ben asked when he could trust himself not to choke on the words.

"How long what?" Tom asked, frowning.

"You and Shelly. How long have you been lovers?"

A faint flush tinged Tom's cheekbones and he shifted in his seat. Ben ground his teeth together. Tom Conrad was a hick trying to play sophisticated games and he wasn't good at it.

"You don't have the right to interrogate me," Tom said. "You don't have any rights in this. But I don't mind telling you that Shelly and I didn't rush into this. We both thought about what it would mean for a long time."

"Sure." He didn't believe it. "When did Shelly tell you she wasn't happy...in our marriage, I mean?"

Tom cocked his head. "I don't follow."

Why had it taken all these years to see through this man's honest front? "I'll take it slowly, Tom. After all, you didn't get the advantage of higher education, did you? You prob-

ably need more help working things out than some of us."
He lowered his gaze. Damn, he shouldn't have said that.

"How true," Tom said, his voice clear and steady. "So
why don't you take your time and keep the explanations real
simple."

Now wasn't the time for Ben to feel remorse over the op-
portunities Tom hadn't had. He was doing just fine. "You
betrayed me," Ben said, and his blood pumped faster. "You
took advantage of Shelly's unhappiness to get what you always wanted."

Tom folded his arms and leaned back. "Well, that proves
one of my theories. You did know how I felt about her,
probably before I knew it myself."

"I knew. But she married me, not you. That's not the
point. She came to you when she was trying to make up her
mind what to do about us and you told her. Divorce
Ben... then come to you. After a decent interval."

"No, I didn't know—"

"Oh, yes you did. If it hadn't been for you, she'd never
have gone through with it and we wouldn't be sitting here.
Shelly and I could have overcome what difficulties we had."

Tom leaned across the table, knocking his mug and slop-
ping coffee. "You call infidelity a *difficulty*? You ran
around on her. And don't think she was aching to tell me. I
had to pry it out of her because she's loyal, even after what
you did to her."

Despite the warm mug, Ben's hands turned icy. "I told
her I was sorry for that"

"Big of you." Tom hissed the words.

"We all make mistakes." There wasn't an excuse, but
there also wasn't any changing what he'd done. He was
tired. "She would have forgiven me in time if you hadn't
helped her make up her mind to end the marriage."

"I didn't. What makes you think I did?"

"She always came to you with problems. It was always, 'I wonder what Tom would say' and this time you said plenty. You took away my family."

Tom stared at him until he turned his head away. "You're off your rocker, Ben. If the football contract had been renewed, would you be here?"

Not that. He wouldn't think about that. "All these years you must have been waiting for the chance to get your hands on my family."

"Answer the question, Ben. Would you choose Shelly and Philip and Allenville over another crack at stardom?"

"Cut it."

"I'll cut it. I'm leaving. But I didn't have anything to do with your divorce. I didn't even find out about it until a year afterward." He stood up and tossed money on the table. "This is a fight you're not going to win—I'll see to that if you force the issue. Leave Shelly alone."

"Like hell." The fire had seeped out of him and he made himself raise his chin. "I'm fighting for Philip, so you'd better both be ready. Maybe Shelly won't want to risk that. I'll win, Tom. I always do."

Tom leaned over him, brought his face close. "Know what? I'd like to hate your guts, but all I feel for you is pity." He looked down at Ben for several heavy seconds before he walked out.

Pity. Tom felt sorry for him. Ben tried to summon up anger but he only wished he could sleep and forget. His life was falling apart. Dragging, he left the diner.

He could go to the school and wait for Philip to come out. Who'd stop him if he decided to drive away with his son?

Sun beat down. Air-conditioning kept the Mercedes cool, but he'd forgotten his sunglasses, and he squinted through scintillating glitter on the hood.

He parked where he could see the school yard. The kids were at recess. Not so much had changed. The same random heap of old tractor tires swarmed with bodies, and the same hoop on the wall was assaulted by leaping would-be basketball greats. He looped his arms over the wheel and rested his chin. Was there a kid over there who dreamed of becoming a star in some sporting arena? Was there a rare one who'd be good enough as he had been. If there was he prayed that kid wouldn't make the same mistakes he'd made himself.

Ahead lay the scarred fence leading from the yard to the road. Ben stared until the rutted ground became a blur with the gray boards and scrubby bushes. That's where all this had begun. What he had or had not become professionally was something different, but the fabric of his personal life had changed forever on this dirt.

*Would he be here if he still had a chance at the big time?* To hell with Tom Conrad. What did he know. This two-bit hole-in-the-road town was all he knew.

Ben sighed and checked his pockets again for sunglasses. He couldn't kidnap his own son. All that would do would be to put him in a worse light when it came to a custody fight.

The letter his mother had given him was crumpled. He pulled it out and looked disinterestedly at the envelope. Before he'd left Cleveland, he'd arranged to have his mail forwarded.

Slowly he smoothed the paper, reading the return address over and over before slitting open the envelope and withdrawing the two sheets of paper inside.

He read once, then again and again. A whoop rose in his throat—then died. The sheets crackled in his closing fist. His breathing speeded and he looked back at the kids in the school yard. This was what he'd wanted and had not even dared to hope for... a new chance to be a household name. Damn it, what kind of man was he? One who was human and ambitious? Yeah, but he was going to have to face up to some other things and make some decisions...and soon.

SHELLY WALKED into Tom's outstretched arms. "It's only just beginning," she told him. "But Ben's not going to win. We don't have a thing to be ashamed of and—"

Tom's kiss cut off the rest of whatever she might have said, not that she remembered what it was.

When he raised his face, she inventoried his features. Whatever came, whatever she had to cope with would be worth the effort as long as she had this man beside her.

"Why would he ask to see us out here at the farm?" She'd started analyzing every move Ben made. "I expected him to say he wanted to talk at his parents' place."

Tom rested his forearms on her shoulders and pressed his lips to her brow. "Maybe he thinks my humble home will give him the advantage. He can sneer at what I don't have and make a point of it to you."

"I love this barn," Shelly said. "And I don't think Ben's that low. Right now he's smarting, but he'll settle down."

"Will he?" Tom went to stoke the stove. "I hope you're right. Shel, there are a few things we haven't discussed."

"Like what?"

He straightened, still holding a log. "Like the farm's going to make it but I'm not on financial easy street. I can provide for you and Philip, but it won't be what you're used to for a while—"

"Stop. We'll be fine." They both knew she had her own income but that wasn't the issue here. "We don't need a lot."

Tom smiled. "I figured you'd say that. But we've got to figure out living arrangements. And then there's going to be the big one—we aren't in the wrong but this town is going to talk. I can handle it, but can you?''

"Yes. Tom, I was divorced long before I came back here. I'm a free woman. And you're a free man. We've got every right to be together. We'll cope.''

He fixed her with his speculative stare. "And Philip?''

"We'll make it work. For all of us. Whatever comes, we'll stand together and we *won't* be beaten, or let what we have be spoiled.''

He smiled slowly until the light came into his eyes. "I prayed you'd say that. Hell, I love you.''

She took a step toward him and stopped. "Ditto,'' she said, breathing deeply. "Don't look at me like that—not now. I can't concentrate when you do and we've got Ben to deal with.''

Tom's smile turned lazy. "Right now he doesn't seem quite so important.''

"But he is,'' she said hastily.

"Mmm.''

Shelly saw something move and looked through the window. "Ben's here. He's talking to your mom and Mary.''

"Outside?'' Tom dropped the log.

"Looks as if he's been in the house.''

"Damn. He's not going to hassle my family.''

"No, no,'' Shelly said as Tom made for the door. "He's coming this way and your mom looks okay. She's going back inside.''

Tom opened the door as Ben arrived on the threshold. They stood, staring at each other, until Shelly's nerves jumped.

"Let's get on with this, Ben,'' she said, winding her fingers together. "Tom, have him come in.''

When she stood side by side with Tom, Ben a few feet away, the first flash of real sympathy for her ex-husband hit hard. He looked at them with a mixture of bewilderment and awkwardness. For an instant his face showed naked insecurity.

Tom sought and found one of her hands. He held it in both of his. "What were you doing at the house? You've got no right to upset my mother and sister."

"They are friends of mine. I've known them since I was ten, remember? I stopped by to say hi. Anything wrong with that?"

"Depends on your motives."

Ben gave a short mirthless laugh. "And my motives are always suspect, huh? Think what you want to. Alice and Mary are special people, and I don't want them to think I'm not as fond of them as I always was. I should have come to see them sooner."

This was all irrelevant. Shelly moved her feet, and muscles in her legs tensed. He was softening them up, getting ready to move in with his next salvo and hoping shock value would catch them off guard.

Tom rubbed her cold fingers hard. "We've contacted lawyers in Idaho Falls," Tom said. "I went in there this afternoon and talked to a couple. We're not making any definite commitments to anyone yet, but we'll be ready when you are."

"You won't—"

"Ben." Shelly pulled her hand from Tom's. "We can work things through. I've always cooperated with your rights to see Philip. When I said I wanted to come home to Allenville, you didn't argue."

"I hoped if I didn't put up a fuss you'd find you missed me and come back." His sad smile twisted her insides. "Didn't work, did it?"

"Shelly's taken good care of Philip. He hasn't been exposed to anything he shouldn't have been," Tom said. "But

we'll let the lawyers deal with that. I just want you to know
that we won't be intimidated.''

"I need to sit down." Ben flopped into a chair that
groaned under his weight. He covered his eyes. "Hell, I'm
tired.''

"Aren't we all," Tom said, but he paced. "We want to
hear what you've decided to do and—''

The door swung open and Philip came in.

Ben leaped to his feet. "Hi, son. I thought you were out
with Kurt and Aaron.''

"I saw you come.''

Shelly wound her fingers together again. Philip was thinner, and taller. Next week he'd be twelve and he was
changing, but his age didn't account for the dark circles
under his eyes or the too old expression, the tightness in his
face. While the adults fought on, her son had to stand on the
sidelines waiting to be told what was to happen to him.

"This is a grown-up conversation," Ben said, and his
smile didn't soften the words. "I'll talk to you before I go.''

Talk about his life, Shelly thought, tell him what had been
decided. What did *Philip* want? She'd never asked him what
he thought about all this.

Instead of leaving, Philip took up position in the middle
of the room. "I'm not leaving," he said. "I thought about
it and I've got something to say in this, don't I?''

Shelly glanced from Ben to Tom. Tom smiled slightly as
if trying to reassure Philip. Ben looked blank.

Philip's heart beat fast. He knew they were here to talk
about him. They were going to talk, then tell him what they
decided. And then there'd probably be a lot of time at court.

"What I want should count," he said, trying to keep the
wobble out of his voice. "When you're a kid you're supposed to keep quiet and let the adults talk about what's best
for you. Only you're all upset about...about something else

and I don't see why you should get to use me because you're mad at one another.''

"We're not using you," his mother said. She moved toward him but he shook his head. He loved his mom. She was the best, but she had her own stuff right now and he had to look out for himself.

"Son," Ben said. "This isn't something you have to worry about, okay? Tom and your mom and I need some time alone. When we're through, I'll come and get you."

Philip told himself he wouldn't cry. Only little kids cried. "I'm staying."

"Philip—"

"No, Mom. I'm staying. I've gotta say some stuff. Then I'll go away and you can talk."

"Now, young man, I think you're overstepping the mark." Philip remembered that his dad always started like that, kind of quiet and tough. That was before he lost his temper.

Tom came over and put a hand on the back of Philip's neck. "Say your piece, Philip. We'll listen."

He was glad Tom kept holding on to him.

"Go on," Shelly said. "What is it?"

He swallowed and swallowed again. The fire in the stove was warm at his back but he felt cold. "You're gonna fight over me, aren't you? You're gonna have lawyers and stuff again, like in Cleveland, and there's gonna be a fuss."

Tom's grip tightened. "Not if we can help it."

Neither Shelly nor Ben said anything.

He looked at his dad. "I love you." It felt funny to say it, and his dad's face turned weird—all tight. "You never did a whole lot of things the other kids' dads did but you were okay. I miss you when I don't see you for a long time."

Ben tipped up his face as though the tall ceiling was interesting. "I love you, too, Philip," he said.

"Yeah, well, this is what I wanted to tell you all." If they got mad, they got mad, but he couldn't stop now. "Kurt said I was like a...he said he'd heard kids were like pawns when their parents got angry with each other. You know, like in chess—"

"We know what he meant," Ben said. His eyes looked misted. "Kurt's a smart kid."

"Well, I think you should do what you want about yourselves and not try to hurt one another with me. It makes me feel—you shouldn't only care about someone because it might help you get what you want."

Shelly started to cry. Philip looked at his sneakers and wished he'd never come. They wouldn't understand.

"Don't, cry, Shel," Tom said. "Philip needs to get this out and we need to listen. Go on," he told him.

"Don't cry, Mom." He started to hold out a hand but she didn't notice. "I want to decide where I want to be. Like I said, Dad, I love you, but I don't want to go back to Cleveland. I'm starting to belong here now. Even the kids are getting to be okay, and I like it out here on the farm. When I grow up, I want to be a farmer like Tom."

Tom made a little coughing noise and cleared his throat. Philip wondered if he was saying anything right, or if this would make it all worse.

"I want to stay in Allenville with Mom and Tom," he said, and wasn't sure if he'd spoken loud enough to be heard. "I want to stay here."

They were quiet for a long time. Philip looked up at Tom. He smiled.

"Okay," Ben said. "I'd better say what I came to say, and Philip might as well hear. He may want to take back one or two of the good things he said about me afterward, but I'll risk it."

No one else spoke while Ben took an envelope from his pocket and slid out some sheets of paper.

"This is something I'd given up on. It's from my agent. He's been trying to reach me on the phone but he didn't know where I was. I called him this afternoon. Evidently he wrote hoping the letter would find me before it was too late. It did."

"When I got the news that my contract wasn't being renewed I went to pieces. I decided I was washed up. What you and Tom have said is right, Shelly." He paused, blinking a lot. "It isn't easy to say this out loud, but I ran back to you to hide, and for some comfort. You've always been my security blanket when things didn't go well. I love you." He stared at her and she put her teeth into her bottom lip. "No way am I going to pretend that isn't true. I made a hell of a lot of mistakes, but you were the only woman I ever loved. And I love my boy. But do you remember what you always said to me?"

Shelly sniffed and wadded up a Kleenex. "I'm not sure."

"You said a place in the sun would always come first with me. You said being recognized as someone was the most important thing in my life, and I guess you were right." He flapped the letter. "This is what I never expected to come off. This is an offer from a TV station. They want me to be a sports commentator. It's national."

Tom shifted his hand to Philip's shoulder. "And that's what you want?"

"Yes. I want it so badly I can taste it. Tomorrow I fly to New York and the next day I do a screen test. But they say that's just red tape. I'm a cinch for the job."

"What else are you telling us?" Shelly asked.

"I'm telling you that this has made me look at myself. I don't like everything I see, but I accept it. I'm leaving Allenville tomorrow, and I don't know when I'll be back."

"And Philip?" Shelly said.

"He's already said what he wants. I think we should listen. You and Tom will take good care of my boy."

AFTER BEN LEFT, promising to be in touch soon, Tom had gone over to check on his mother and sister. Shelly sat quietly in a chair while Philip walked back and forth in front of the bookcases, his hands behind his back. She and Tom couldn't wait any longer to talk to him, and she prayed they could say the right things.

Tom came back, slamming the door behind him and straightening wind-tossed hair. "Okay," he said so brightly Shelly grimaced. He glanced at her and raised his brows. "Come and sit down, Philip. Your mom and I have a few things we've wanted to talk over with you."

Philip turned around. "About the two of you?"

Shelly's stomach revolved slowly. "That's right. There have been . . . um, there have been some changes."

"Yeah, I know." Philip moved his weight from foot to foot and chewed on a lip.

Tom glanced at Shelly. "You heard what your dad said, he thinks it's a good idea for your mother and me to take care of you. And you said you'd like that."

Philip puffed out his cheeks and did another weight shift.

"Anyway," Shelly said, scooting to the edge of her chair, "we know you must be wondering exactly what's going . . . I mean, you'll have some . . ." She looked helplessly at Tom who had hitched his jacket back and planted his hands on his hips.

He cleared his throat. "Your mom and I—"

"Yeah, I know," Philip interrupted, turning pink. "Kurt and I talked about it. You two have been . . . well, it's like you're going together, right?"

"Right!" Tom nodded, grinning. "Exactly."

"Only not *exactly*, right?" Philip continued.

Shelly closed her eyes.

"Philip, maybe we're spending more time on this than we have to." Tom spoke very quietly, and Shelly slowly opened her eyes. His arms were folded tightly about him and he rocked onto the toes of his boots. "Do you want to tell us what you think we wanted to discuss with you?"

Philip hunched his shoulders and frowned. "I think you were gonna tell me you've decided you've gone together long enough and you're getting married." He blushed furiously. "It's gotta be tough on you to say stuff like that out loud but it's okay with me."

# HARLEQUIN
## *American Romance*

## COMING NEXT MONTH

### #309 SAVING GRACE by Anne McAllister

Cameron McClellan wasn't sure what he expected from his month-long vacation at Gull Cottage—a break from business, carefree days with his son, maybe even a chance to recapture his own youth. But when he arrived to find a great big bed with a nubile blond woman in it, he found new meaning to the question "Who's been sleeping in my bed?" Don't miss the final book in the Gull Cottage trilogy.

### #310 CODE OF SILENCE by Linda Randall Wisdom

For three years Anne Sinclair had been running from the law, changing her name, her appearance, her address. Then she came to Dunson, Montana, where her daughter made friends and Anne tried to make a home. Her fear prevented her from trusting anyone, especially Dunson's sheriff. Yet Anne was attracted to Travis Hunter—an attraction that could be her downfall.

### #311 GLASS HOUSES by Anne Stuart

All that stood between Michael Dubrovnik and the creation of Dubrovnik Plaza was Glass House and its obstinate owner, Laura de Kelsey Winston. Laura had the colossal gall to challenge the most powerful and feared man in Manhattan. Michael thrived on challenges and welcomed a battle of wills. And this was one battle he was going to love.

### #312 ISLAND MAGIC by Laurel Pace

Vaness Dorsey's visit to Parloe Island was meant to be a temporary respite before she resumed her job hunt and got on with her life. But Great-aunt Charlotte's rambling house needed tender loving care and the South Carolina island needed someone to protect its beauty. But the most compelling reason to stay on was Dr. Taylor Bowen. For he understood Vanessa's need—to belong, to care, to love.

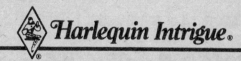

# Harlequin Intrigue®

## High adventure and romance— with three sisters on a search . . .

Linsey Deane uses clues left by their father to search the Colorado Rockies for a legendary wagonload of Confederate gold, in #120 *Treasure Hunt* by Leona Karr (August 1989).

Kate Deane picks up the trail in a mad chase to the Deep South and glitzy Las Vegas, with menace and romance at her heels, in #122 *Hide and Seek* by Cassie Miles (September 1989).

Abigail Deane matches wits with a murderer and hunts for the people behind the threat to the Deane family fortune, in #124 *Charades* by Jasmine Crasswell (October 1989).

*Don't miss Harlequin Intrigue's three-book series The Deane Trilogy. Available where Harlequin books are sold.*

DEA-G

# Harlequin American Romance.

## SUMMER.

The sun, the surf, the sand . . .

One relaxing month by the sea was all Zoe, Diana and Gracie ever expected from their four-week stays at Gull Cottage, the luxurious East Hampton mansion. They never thought they'd soon be sharing those long summer days—or hot summer nights—with a special man. They never thought that what they found at the beach would change their lives forever. But as Boris, Gull Cottage's resident mynah bird said: "Beware of summer romances. . . ."

Join Zoe, Diana and Gracie for the summer of their lives. Don't miss the GULL COTTAGE trilogy in American Romance: #301 *Charmed Circle* by Robin Francis (July 1989), #305 *Mother Knows Best* by Barbara Bretton (August 1989) and #309 *Saving Grace* by Anne McAllister (September 1989).

GULL COTTAGE—because a month can be the start of forever . . .